Submissive

Submissive

ANYA HOWARD

APHRODISIA

KENSINGTON BOOKS

http://www.kensingtonbooks.com

APHRODISIA BOOKS are published by

Kensington Publishing Corp.
119 West 40th Street
New York, NY 10018

All Kensington Titles, Imprints, and Distributed Lines are available at special quantity discounts for bulk purchases for sales promotions, premiums, fund-raising, and educational or institutional use.

Special book excerpts or customized printings can also be created to fit specific needs. For details, write or phone the office of the Kensington special sales manager: Kensington Publishing Corp., 119 West 40th Street, New York, NY 10018, attn: Special Sales Department, Phone: 1-800-221-2647.

Aphrodisia and the A logo Reg. U.S. Pat & TM Off.

ISBN-13: 978-0-7582-2880-2
ISBN-10: 0-7582-2880-5

First Kensington Trade Paperback Printing: May 2009

10 9 8 7 6 5 4 3 2 1

Printed in the United States of America

For Robert Perry, my husband, true love, and best friend.
Thank you for your everlasting encouragement and inspiration.

ACKNOWLEDGMENTS

This novel is published with great appreciation to several unforgettable people. Author & friend, Devyn Quinn, who believed in this story and my writing. My good friends and colleagues of Wild Authors—Annmarie Ortega, Devyn Quinn, Marianne LaCroix, Stephanie Kelsey, Adrienne Kama, Sara Reinke, and Tyler Blackwood. I also wish to extend my gratitude to faithful friend and proofreader, Claudia McRay.

Submissive

1

Partly out of habit, partly out of need, Bruce Wolff dug into the long pocket of his robe and pulled out a pack of cigarettes and lighter. Putting one between his lips and lighting it, he glanced over at the coffeepot. He'd not even started brewing that yet. Any other day he'd have made a pot before even lighting the first cigarette. He knew he must be depressed; his routine was never screwed up like this. And he knew already he was going to take a day of sick leave from work. Just the thought of having to go in and babysit the convicts on his block chafed. Pervs and murderers, all of them, their needs and wants taken care of by the taxpayers. He hated listening to their complaints, threats, and nonsense.

Bruce sighed and turned to look for an ashtray. There was one on the dishwasher and he picked it up and carried it to the den, where he sat down in the recliner. He knew he should probably eat, too; he'd lost his appetite last night when he'd realized Gillian wasn't going to show. But he couldn't eat or even worry about the coffee. He could think of nothing but her.

The thing was, they were worlds apart. She was an artist, supporting herself with a gig as a night waitress, a job she hated. Fair enough. Slinging hash and refilling coffee cups for truckers wasn't fun. No wonder she longed to escape into a fantasy world—and she'd given him a glimpse of it in her sketchbooks.

He'd never seen drawings like that. Not remotely based on real life, of course. She'd created an imaginary realm peopled with devotees of BDSM. But it was discipline with a magical difference. Women out of his wildest dreams, costumed for bondage, made to obey by dominants that were sometimes male, sometimes female, and sometimes not human at all.

And he'd had to go and ask her if she had a secret life on the side. She'd taken her time to answer while he was thinking up about a hundred ways to chastise her naked ass. And then she hadn't said a thing.

Scared off any chance I had, he thought bitterly.

A pang of remorse swelled in his chest. For the first time in many years Bruce felt close to tears, and pressed his thumbs to the corners of his eyes until the sensation passed.

"Jesus," he groaned. "I'm going to be alone forever."

The house seemed to echo in agreeing silence. Bruce closed his eyes and deliberately tried to think of other women he knew, fresh conquests that awaited him. The world is full of women, he told himself; appreciative women, women not so young and strange as Gillian Nordstrom.

His thoughts were interrupted by a rap on the door in the kitchen. Bruce's breath caught in his chest, and he listened to make sure it wasn't just the wind banging the screen. The rap came again, a definite knock made by someone at the door. Bruce rose to his feet and strode swiftly into the kitchen.

He drew back the little shade on the door window and was disappointed to see a guy standing on the stoop. He wore a long gray coat, unbuttoned, and a black ensemble of trousers and sweater. Not old, not young. Bruce figured he was one of those fire-and-brimstone types, the kind that made it their habit to tout their religion door to door. Easy enough to get rid of.

Opening the door, he squinted at the dude and cleared his throat. "What do you want?"

He expected the usual invitation to be saved. Too late for that. Way too late, pal, he wanted to say. But the guy smiled gently and said, "Hello, Bruce. I would like to speak to you about the women."

Bruce shook his head, uncertain he'd heard clearly. "Women?"

The stranger glanced around. "It's cold out here. May I come in?"

Bruce crossed his arms and glared at the stranger. "What did you mean, the women? Who are you? Are you selling something?"

A soft pale glow came over the stranger's features. There was something strangely calming in his soft brown eyes; something that eased a little of Bruce's wariness.

"I do not come to sell you religion," the stranger said. "Or to sell anything else. My name is Sethlucius and I come to show you a way out—"

The hair on the back of Bruce's neck stood up. "What the hell are you talking about?"

"If you'll allow me a few minutes' conversation, you will understand. I know you are dissatisfied with your work and life . . . and how very distressed you are by what has happened with Gillian Nordstrom."

That wasn't public information. Unless she'd blogged about it. Bruce grew impatient, and his voice was fierce. "Are you a friend of Gillian's?"

Sethlucius exhaled slowly, a dulcet sound in the quiet winter air. "I know of Gillian, but she's not the reason I am here. You are virile and strong-willed and have more insight about the spiritual nature of passion than you realize. Because of your qualifications, I've been sent, as I tried to say, to show you a way out of the numb existence you call reality."

Bruce felt more wary than ever. But there was something disconcertingly candid about this Sethlucius, as if the man was reading his own consciousness. For a moment Bruce thought he was dreaming. This couldn't be a real person, nor could this discussion be real. Maybe Gillian's freaky talent for fantasy had changed the way he thought. Whatever. He was spooked.

When Bruce closed his eyes and wished the vision away, he heard the lilt in the man's voice, "And who knows, maybe I can coax you to brew that coffee—if not for yourself, then as hospitality for a guest?"

Mind reader. Bruce eyed the man for several moments. He wondered if he should go get his gun or call the police. What the hell. He'd play along. Nothing better to do at the moment.

"You said qualifications," Bruce said at last. "Are you offering me a job?"

Sethlucius nodded. "Yes, as a matter of fact. I am. A job with better benefits than you'll ever find working as a correctional officer here."

The way he'd said this piqued Bruce's interest a little. "You're looking for a guard, then?"

"Yes, we are."

Bruce was still hesitant. "Take off the coat and leave it here."

Sethlucius lifted a bemused brow. But he removed his coat and folded it over the handrail. "You can pat me down if you need."

Bruce was embarrassed, but he did this, too. And once he was certain the man carried no weapons, he let him inside. The snow was falling heavier now, and the color of the sky had changed to a rich cobalt blue. This shade calmed Bruce somehow, and as he closed the door, he turned toward his strange guest.

His heart nearly stopped when he saw the room had disappeared. The two of them were enclosed by pure iridescent light. Bruce looked back at the door, saw it, too, was gone. Staring at the man, Bruce urged his rational mind to awake his sleeping consciousness and end this walking nightmare.

"It is no nightmare, I assure you," Sethlucius said. The next moment a white cup appeared in his hand, and Bruce could even smell the bitter aroma of the coffee and see the steam that rose over the rim. "Here, I made it myself."

Bruce felt his patience flee. "I don't have time for this. I choose to wake up now."

Sethlucious shrugged. "Drink, Bruce. I think it will prove just how very awake and more importantly, how alert you are now."

Bruce contemplated the cup—imaginary, surely, but he took it anyway. He raised it, and sipping, his lips were scalded. Sethlucious lifted an eyebrow.

"I should have warned you, it is hot."

Bruce gulped the beverage, almost savoring the scorching liquid. The deliberate act made him feel he might have some control over this wild vision.

"I want you gone," he muttered. "Dreams are useless inconveniences." Suddenly, the thought gave him some hope. Perhaps when he woke up he would find the last several days had all been part of this dream; that Gillian was still in his life, that he still had a chance with her.

Sethlucius's brow furrowed a bit. "That's all you really want, isn't it? But I'm sorry, Bruce, I cannot give you Gillian. You must pursue your own destiny, claim your own right to your satisfactions in life, just as Gillian must find hers."

The truth of those words tolled in Bruce's heart. Whatever this being was, he knew the situation, and Bruce was too close to cracking to care whether he was real or not. In fact, he hoped this Sethlucius was real; his offer was genuine. All Bruce hoped for was a chance to forget his past mistakes and what could have been. He wanted nothing more than to find a way to escape the despair that threatened to suffocate him altogether.

"Very well," he said, trying to stifle the desperation in his voice. "Tell me your offer. But first, explain your illusionist's act. I don't appreciate lame tricks."

Sethlucius blinked, looking startlingly innocent and younger than just a moment before. "I have no tricks, Bruce. What you see is what is."

Bruce cleared his throat, about to argue that he was no idiot, when he saw two great silhouettes rise from Sethlucius's back. These were shaped like a pair of great wings, and as he stared at them he could see they were covered with plumage, brilliantly, flawlessly white. Bruce was cold with fear, and the coffee cup fell from his hands. Where it landed he didn't know, and his attention was captured by the rosy aura around Sethlucius. The man grew to an extraordinary height. Bruce found himself trembling like a child beneath a countenance radiant with an understanding that what he sensed came not from dreams or hallucinations, or for that matter, anything akin to life as he knew it.

"This mortal delusion has held you long enough," Sethlucius said. "Come with me, Bruce, to a place where your fulfillment awaits. Where you indeed may know and luxuriate in the man you were meant to be."

The words sounded surreal to Bruce. Yet despite the voice of prudence that told him to turn his back on this angel-man, Bruce knew that he was not hallucinating.

At length Bruce nodded and gave Sethlucius his answer. "I will go with you."

The sigh of the breeze through the Smoky Mountain pines was cruelly seductive. It had often tempted Gillian to run to the mountains and disappear there into the lush and wild darkness, to abandon all for the possibility of fulfilling a fantasy she had long cherished in secret.

But she'd never wanted anything more than Bruce Wolff. How could she, however, in good conscience, allow him to get involved with her? She knew she'd never be satisfied with a man who didn't share her BDSM penchants. Bruce, as sexy as he was, was still an officer of the law. She had never been able to trust many people, and when she did she wanted them to know her for what she truly was. The thought of baring her soul to Bruce, just to lose him, was a prospect she wasn't prepared to face. Showing him her sketchbooks had been a mistake.

Tonight on her break, Gillian had escaped to the parking lot. She wanted to try again to shake off the habit of looking around for Bruce while she worked. It was silly and selfish, she knew— but she still expected him to stride through the doors at any moment, to rally her with one of his jokes and undress her with his smoldering dark eyes.

The need for a cigarette blocked out the woeful mood that the mountains so often stirred in her. She drew her lighter from the pocket of her uniform dress and a cigarette from the pack stuffed deep in the bottom. The first inhale of the cigarette was the first calm breath she had had since coming to work that afternoon. She started smoking only days after starting work as a waitress at Thomas Family Steak House. The cigarettes settled her nerves. Most students at ASU did not smoke except pot, but she found she needed something—and preferably something legal—in order to deal with the harpy who actually ran the steak house.

Leaving on a light in the restroom or accidentally ladling an ounce of gravy more than the manager's stingy rules allowed had already cost more than one job. And heaven forbid any female employee eye the manager's husband.

Not that Gillian or any other waitress was interested in that pussy-whipped personage. He was as undesirable as the usual male patrons, whether they were the tight-assed fundamentalists or one of the hippie professors who regularly showed up to satisfy their munchies at the salad bar. Once in a while a good-looking businessman came in for dinner, and sometimes other correctional officers came in while escorting prisoners back and forth between the county jail and their last trek to the state prison.

She thought of Bruce painfully as she drew on the cigarette. Several times over the last few weeks she had asked his fellow officers if they had seen him, and they replied he must have taken an unexpected vacation. She even called the prison once and asked if he was on duty, but of course they were not about to give out information about one of their officers to a non–family member. Countless times she had gone to sleep with potent images of him in her mind. The fantasy of him handcuffing her to the backseat of his vehicle and ravishing her with a bestial and remorseless passion was still with her.

Shooting a look around the lot and seeing no one, she arched her back until her breasts pressed against her uniform. She imagined Bruce's lips skimming over them, his tongue prodding her nipples, his teeth nibbling until they were rosy and sore. Hearing her breath grow rapid, Gillian sighed miserably. Twenty years old, and she had never been with anyone. She was starting to believe there was something wrong with her.

She knew what she wanted: a man who could make her entire body come alive with desire. Someone who possessed her soul completely, so that it knew no comfort without a tantalizing and persistent physical hunger. Brute strength. Sexual heat. Uncompromising masculinity.

From the parking lot Gillian looked over the edge of the stone safety wall and down on the distant sprawling campus. Not many students ventured up the steep drive to the restaurant anymore.

Gillian closed her eyes, sick of the real world. Being a student sucked. Everything sucked. Her lurid dreams seemed far more real to her than this. It had been crazy to whisper of them to Bruce, hoping to pull him into her fantasies.

She massaged the back of her neck and wound her ponytail about her fingers as she contemplated the aching lust that had gripped her for days. Standing in the shadows, Gillian peeked around, and, confident she was alone in the parking lot, let her hand stray to the hem of the orange dress. She raised it and stroked her sensitive thighs. They were slick with the moisture from the crotch of her panties. As she slipped her fingers under her panties, tracing her vulva, her clit quickened. She plunged two fingers into the wet slit, pounding it and rolling her thumb over her clit as she thought of Bruce. She imagined him massaging her breasts roughly as she bent over a chair, his cock driving in and out of her wet, straining pussy intensely. Gillian's need was animalistic, and an orgasm jolted through her. She was not satisfied, no, but relieved somewhat as she pulled her hand from her panties. Only then did she notice the cigarette had fallen from her right hand.

Her mind snapped awake, and with a pout of distaste, she stooped to retrieve the still-lit butt from the pavement. She would have to smoke it quick and go back on in because the hired help weren't allowed a moment longer than ten minutes for their breaks. Just as Gillian retrieved the butt, she heard the back door sigh open and saw a feminine silhouette slip out into the night air. Gillian was certain it was the ever-bitchy manager, and flinching, dropped the cig again.

With a sigh, she stood and crushed it out completely with the sole of her shoe, only then realizing it was not the manager who was walking toward her. The cool, finely boned face was familiar, but she was sure it was not one of the new waitresses— not in that unusual skirt and those stilettos. Squinting in the moonlight, she tried to remember the face.

"Have one to spare?" the woman asked, with a glance to the

crushed butt. Gillian recognized the husky voice. The Goth queen, she thought to herself, recalling the unkind title her coworkers had privately given this customer. This woman had become a Saturday night regular shortly after Gillian started working. Not a true Goth, for her makeup was always perfect, but in her dark designer clothes and expensive jewelry, she was as close to Goth as most of the local farm girls-turned-waitresses had ever seen. Gillian had a feeling that she came here with the hopeful expectations of meeting someone.

She pulled the cigarette pack from her apron pocket and the woman accepted one. As Gillian offered her lighter, the woman lifted her auburn hair gracefully to the side of her pale, slender neck.

"You have worked here for a while," the woman said with an uncertain smile as she exhaled.

Gillian felt suddenly uncomfortable, wondering what this woman was doing in the staff parking lot. But it was not really her concern, and besides, her laid-back demeanor was welcoming.

Before Gillian could answer, she sidled close and brushed Gillian's wrist with her fingertips. Gillian smiled awkwardly, hoping this woman would not feel her discomfort.

"Gillian," she murmured huskily, "how would you like to be done with this establishment and this provincial town?"

Gillian cleared her throat. She wondered suddenly if the woman was one of the escort-service proprietors from the nearby city. They were known for cruising out here now and then in order to size up prospective employees from the college.

"Well," Gillian said slowly, "who wouldn't? But I have another year to finish before getting my bachelor's."

"Yes, an art major," the woman said and licked her crimson lips. "But I sense your wellsource of wisdom yet calls to be dipped."

Now Gillian felt a chill. She had shared none of her life's ambitions with this woman. Why, she had been too daunted by her to ever start a conversation except to take an order.

"Excuse me, ma'am, my break is over." Gillian gave a congenial nod and started to stroll back toward the door when the woman's hand grasped her forearm, bringing Gillian to a clumsy halt. Gillian jerked about, terrified, angry, and found herself mesmerized by the sensuality in the bold gray eyes that met her. The woman's fingers clamped over Gillian's chin and she drew her mouth close to her face. Much too close.

"I am not interested in a whore," the woman said, "I want the hungering lust of your soul. Your pussy must be starved."

Gillian shrieked and pulled her arm away. She turned and lunged toward the restaurant. As she threw the door open, she saw the kitchen just as she had left it minutes before: the assembly of young men and women in their stained, ugly uniforms and net-pinned hair. The manager was too preoccupied to see her, ranting at one of the other waitresses from over the saloon doors at the front, demanding the tea be watered down before it was served. Gillian's panic turned in a new and sickening direction. Gillian backed out, and let the door swing back on its hinges. No one had seen her.

She wondered if she had gone insane as she turned and looked at the Goth queen. Why did this woman's words affect her? It was ridiculous, but she was seized with the most urgent desire to flee here altogether, say good-bye to her job and college, too.

The woman's heels clicked across the pavement as she sauntered up to Gillian and clasped her hands like a delighted little girl greeting her best friend.

But her voice was all charming crispness. "You will come with me, Gillian? Depart this place and discover your true self?"

Be careful what you wish for. It seemed she'd gotten it.

Gillian blinked and glanced at the delicious white cleavage peeping over the front of the woman's dress, the tiny hard nipples poking through the silk. How she wanted to tear the fabric away, nurse those breasts, and suckle the woman's firm, smooth mouth.

And when the next moment the woman reached for her skirt and lifted it, Gillian's clit sprang to life and her nipples hardened.

"What are you doing?" she said softly.

"Come here," the Goth queen whispered and gathered Gillian's ponytail in one hand and with it drew her close. The woman's lips brushed over Gillian's, parting them, and her tongue pressed deeply into Gillian's mouth. A shiver quaked through Gillian's breasts and her fingertips glided over the woman's lean, firm arms. She accepted the probing kiss, and when the woman's mouth grazed down over her throat, she moaned and her pussy grew even moister. Never had she known such mindless desire for another human being.

She felt the band yanked from her hair so that the breeze whipped blond tresses over her shoulders and arms. The woman unbuttoned every last button on the front of Gillian's uniform. Anyone looking from the doorway would see her standing there, half naked under the funky blue-green glow of the security lights. Though there was no one, fear only increased the heat between Gillian's thighs. The woman stooped and yanked Gillian's panties down over her hips and down her legs to her knees. Gillian moved her hips pleadingly, oblivious to everything but the red lips kissing the insides of her thighs.

She curled the ends of the woman's hair with trembling fingers. "Oh, yes," she crooned deeply, "devour me with your mouth!"

The Goth queen threw her a quick, thoughtful smile. "We have need of women like you, Gillian. If I give you the satisfaction you crave, you must join with us. Your pledge will be more binding than blood."

Gillian blinked, trying to concentrate on the strange words. "Women like me? What does that mean?"

"I am Madame Nevja, a recruiter of Disciples of Pleasure," the woman answered and her tongue flicked out to rub the hood of Gillian's clit.

Gillian echoed the reply. "Disciples of Pleasure." One or both of them had to be insane. Yet she did not care, except for the pleasure Nevja's actions promised, and she laughed wantonly. "Sure. Whatever."

"It is no joke," Nevja said.

Gillian touched the soft skin of her temple. "Sure, I'll be your recruit, you have my word. Now, please, just fuck me, fuck me now with your mouth!"

At once the woman parted Gillian's pubic hair and then her glistening wet nether lips. Her mouth smothered Gillian's pulsing clit and with her tongue she strummed it until it was swollen. Over and over again the wicked tongue waved across the pulsating organ, and then down to enter the sodden nether lips to plunge inside Gillian's drenched pussy. Again and again her stiff tongue fucked Gillian. She parted Gillian's buttocks, and with her forefinger, fucked her virgin anus. Gillian's sensitive inner walls shuddered intensely. Her clit suddenly seemed to explode, and her sex and anus were filled with an orgasm that blew away the last refrains of her unsatisfying act of masturbation.

She was panting, when through half-lidded eyes she saw that she was still holding the woman's hair around her fingers. The Goth queen was all cool poise again as she smiled and lowered Gillian's hands. Nevja drew something from one of the scalloped cups of her bra. She parted Gillian's buttocks again and plunged something long and slender into her ass. It was soft and warm, like beeswaxed ginger, and the embarrassing sensation it imparted inside Gillian was a nameless ambrosia.

"You have been recruited," Nevja said, and the heavy toll of the words drowned even Cynthia's voice coming from the restaurant door. Gillian paid no heed. She wanted to escape . . . wanted to go beyond every limit.

Drunk with satisfaction and feeling light-headed, Gillian gave no resistance as the woman pulled her panties back up and led her by the hand across the pavement to a long limo with tinted passenger windows parked at the remote end of the lot.

The woman tapped on the driver's window. The door opened and out stepped a tall youth with a sandy ponytail that hung from the back of his starched blue chauffeur's cap. This he tipped to Gillian and opened the passenger door.

Gillian felt a single twinge of reluctance and looked back. *I am a fool*, she thought desperately.

"Get in, Gillian," Nevja ordered.

Gillian gave in, distracted by the sight of the front of Nevja's dress poked by enticing nipples and then by her long, perfectly manicured indigo nails. They were intimidating, those sharp nails, and Gillian was sobered a little by the sudden instinct to flee. Before she could, however, Nevja shoved her inside the vehicle. Gillian pushed up angrily from the plush seat and turned around, hitting at Nevja's knee, which was rising to enter.

"Let me out of here!"

Nevja bowed and looked at Gillian complacently. "You have made a vow, Gillian, and there is no turning back. Now be silent and stay on that seat or I shall have Tepcha restrain you."

Gillian panicked and screamed. With hands and knees sunk firmly into the seat, she rammed her head into Nevja's belly with all her weight. The woman fell back into the driver's arms. At once Gillian bolted from the vehicle and ran toward the entry doors of the restaurant. She ignored the heaviness she felt, the sense of unconsciousness approaching; she did not care if her dress was flapping open or what her coworkers or anyone else might think when she came flying through the doors. All that mattered was returning to the comforting dullness of ordinary things.

The Goth queen hissed something and Gillian heard Tepcha's feet pounding the pavement behind her. Just before she reached the green and white striped awning of the entryway, he snatched the ends of her flying hair and yanked her back hard against his chest. He heaved Gillian up with his free arm so that her kicking feet swung above the ground and hauled her back to the limo and threw her roughly over the seat. This time the door was shut before Gillian could clamber to her hands and knees. She spun about toward it and at that instant heard the driver's door open. To her dismay, she saw there was no handle with which to open the door. An electronic lock. Hearing both passenger doors lock, she beat the dark window desperately with her fists.

"I take it back!" she screamed, angrier, more frightened than she had been in her life. "I take it back, you bitch!"

Then from above her head she heard Nevja's frosty voice. "Soon, Gillian, you shall learn the value of a pledge . . . and much more."

Gillian's vision grew darker than the tinted windows, and as she pounded on the door she heard both doors up front slam shut.

"No," she said, but her voice was only a faint murmur in her ears. Her head sank into the upholstered seat. She dimly saw an oval aluminum intercom staring down at her from the ceiling. Just before she drifted to sleep she overheard Nevja issue a cool, incomprehensible order to the driver.

Be careful what you . . . This was Gillian's last thought. *So careful . . .*

2

It was not the intercom Gillian's eyes saw when she opened them, but the full yellow moon shining down from the black velvet Appalachian sky. She was lying naked on the damp grass, her mind finally clear of the drug that had been inserted into her earlier that night. At least she supposed it was that night. She glanced around and saw no one else in this clearing somewhere in the woods. Trying to rise, she found her wrists were clamped solidly to the earth. Stretching her neck left, then right, she saw that each wrist had been bound with wide metal staples. Arching her legs beneath her, she struggled to push the staples free of the earth, but they had been driven far too deep; her arms were secure.

"Oh, God," she whispered, her heart pumping with terror. Again she arched and with a growl, pressed with all her might against the staples. They did not budge.

Hot tears came to her eyes. She tossed her head, desperate to forget the rising panic that threatened to sweep away her reasoning altogether.

Then she felt it: an encroachment in the crisp mountain air, something drawing closer to her vulnerable, bound body. Her eyes darted this way and that, but for a moment she saw nothing except the shrubs against the bordering woods. Still, she heard what seemed like drawn breath. A second later something loomed forward out of the shadows from all directions about her. She saw silhouettes gathering over the untamed grass, figures that strode toward her.

She gasped and watched as one by one the circle of figures began to glow in their forming solidity, developing features and taking on proportion, depth, character. Men, women, donned in garments of whispery hues, they were smiling, some of them, with the most ethereal quality. They whispered among themselves, the soft sound striking a hammer of terror upon Gillian's heart. As they drew in on moonbeam-sandaled feet, Gillian felt the last reserve of calm abandon her. She screamed and closed her eyes and pressed against the staples until she felt the metal cut into her flesh.

At once the hush silenced, and she felt something descend over her. It was weighty, real, and smelled of a raw musk so thick and drugging that it suppressed her terror and replaced it with a mad, ripening lust.

She opened her eyes and looked into the masculine face of the being that had stooped and unveiled itself over her. He was fearsome, unearthly in his dimensions and the sienna eyes that glowed in the darkness. Even his skin glowed faintly green over lean muscles as smooth as a woman's, dappled with sweat, replete with the musk that played with her rationality.

The ends of his long hair tickled her face. Determined not to be seduced again, she tossed her head angrily. "Go away! Go away!"

The being looked to the other watchers, and his eyes narrowed at one in particular. "Is this not what you wish, Gillian—to know the ecstasy of perpetual desire?"

Gillian shivered at the voicing of her most private and dearest of fantasies. She followed his eyes and saw the figure of Madame Nevja among the encircling host—glowing and ethereal like the rest of them now, her face bright with assurance.

"Speak up, Gillian," Nevja bade.

The being looked down at her, its great eyes thoughtful as he smoothed her damp cheek with his fingertips. "Is this as you wish, Gillian? Heed not any vow you may have made in haste. Open your heart to me, and know you shall come to no harm by the truth."

Gillian trembled under his looming face, yet for all her fear, she imagined his large succulent mouth grazing over her sex.

"I—I—" Her voice faltered as for the first time she felt his naked cock crush against the V of her clenched thighs. It was proportional to the rest of his dimensions, and she wondered, without wanting to, just how well he could use it.

The musk thickened in her nostrils, and she saw a soft gleam of lust in his eyes.

His lips caressed her ear and he said softly, "You would have me pry your legs open and fuck you until dawn?"

Gillian's first thought was to dispute it, to tell this creature, whatever he was, that she would rather die than to allow herself to be used again. But as he moved up over her so that she could see his naked torso better, she knew it was self-deceit. They had frightened her, Nevja and her servant, by abducting her the way they had, forcing her to awaken stapled to the earth, naked and bound in the woods. She knew these beings were nothing close to human, and yet, if it had only been explained to her before— yes, she would have come willingly, if just for the unlikely but precious chance she would know a little moment of liberty from her mundane, predictable life.

"Yes—" she said thickly.

"Yes?"

As she looked into his eyes his features shifted . . . she saw not this beautiful, heavenly being, but Bruce Wolff. Sensual, formidable—and so powerfully human—Bruce Wolff. The image only remained a moment, but her body softened and quivered with passion. She nodded and glanced shyly at the others still watching.

"Yes," Gillian whispered. "But must I be tethered to the ground?"

An answering smile graced his lips and he kissed her then, pressing her mouth open with his penetrating tongue. Her mouth quickened and her body flamed. He cupped her head to the side of his face and said, "Had Nevja been mistaken, we would never again have had this opportunity to see you so pleasingly laid out. And even though your opposition would free you, we are not ashamed to come away with at least an image of what we desire."

Gillian was beginning to understand that she was safe for the moment, in a bizarre way, to be sure. She replied with a nervous titter, "But that is wicked."

"No. That you do not believe," he murmured. He kissed her again, this time his huge tongue plowing into her mouth, and with one hand he scooped her breasts together, heaving the nipples together, his fingers pressing into them delightfully, painfully. With his thumb he then massaged both nipples until they were stone-hard. Gillian moaned, further excited. With his other hand he forced her thighs apart and pressed her vulva open. His fingers ran up and down her pussy lips and he gently squeezed the clit. She felt her fluids pour over him and when his attention swayed to the cleft of her thighs, her clit throbbed again for attention. As if knowing this, he sat up suddenly, leaving her mouth craving his drilling tongue. He lifted her legs so that her bottom rose from the ground, and dividing her legs a little, draped his mouth over her vagina. His tongue invaded her there, parting the labia and crushing her clit. He suckled it roughly, then tenderly, lolling it back and forth under his tongue until Gillian knew an orgasm was close to bursting through her. But the next moment, he threw her legs open and set them about his waist. She saw his cock then, purplish and erect, inflexible as marble, and the size of it filled her with a delicious dread.

He entered her slowly, stretching her pussy with his cock, engorging the orifice. Watching an intense look sweep over her face and breasts, he began to thrust hard and quick, pounding her so thoroughly she feared her pussy would burst. She clenched her legs about his waist willingly, loving the savage fucking. At last, she exploded with such merciless rapture her shrill shriek pierced the air. His sweaty loins continued to grind upon her throbbing sex, but soon he stiffened and his seed exploded deep inside her.

Several moments later, he withdrew and lowered her legs back down to earth. Straddling her waist so that his softening cock lay against her lips, he said, "Cleanse me, Gillian."

Eagerly, she sucked the dewy cum from the head of his organ, and the taste of it left a brilliant tang in her mouth.

He lowered himself down over her and kissed her lips. Gillian's thighs were hot and sore. Yet, she craved him again already, or, if not him, one of his companions, and the realization almost overwhelmed her.

"You are ordained," he whispered and his tongue penetrated her mouth a moment. Then he rolled her over onto her left side so that her tethered right arm twanged with the stretch. She made a discomfited sound and tried to roll back over. He responded by giving a hard slap to her upturned buttock.

"Oww!" she cried, and wished she could rub the smarting throb.

"You will sleep now, Gillian," he said and she felt him spread her buttocks. Again, a long slender waxen object was inserted inside her anus and, confused, she whimpered.

"No," he said. He kissed her throat and suckled the flesh

there. "It is not for the same reason as before, but rather to protect your sanity. Your soul will solace your body when the two are escorted into Nemi."

Gillian frowned, uncertain of anything now except the electricity his mouth sent down her throat.

"Escorted," she whispered and saw one of the other beings beaming down upon them, his or her face registering the same self-restrained lust Nevja had worn earlier. Pinned so helplessly in her nakedness, Gillian's face burned with a sweet shame. But she was feeling heavy-headed again, more rapidly now than earlier in the parking lot. She wanted to ask what or where Nemi was, but the next moment the question was lost, along with her consciousness.

The perfume of jasmine and pear blossoms wafted heavy through the air, waking Gillian to eye-smarting sunlight that shimmered through fruit-laden branches sprawling above her face.

The memory of her lusty ravisher flooded back even smarter. Sitting up, she was aware that her vagina was wetter than the dewy grass beneath her. She rubbed her eyes and looked around, seeing that she was in a lawn of thick, verdant grass. Everywhere budding fruit trees and flowers grew. Hearing gurgling water to her left, she looked and saw a fountain of stone. Water rained into it from the carved basket that rested on the shoulder of the nymph statue standing in the middle of the pool. Through the trees to the right, Gillian glimpsed the posts of an wrought iron fence. It was about the posts of this seemingly limitless fence the yellow blooms of jasmine grew.

Gillian wondered where he was, and only as she stood to look for him did she realize she was still naked. Her chest and breasts were still flushed with passion and his cum leaked down her aching thighs.

"Where are you?" she whispered. No response came, and

she walked about on the velvety grass and searched the beautiful place.

Past the fountain she trod, and through a thick grove of fruit trees, until she reached a moss-strewn brick path hewn between two great avenues of monumental, sweeping-branched oaks. She thought she glimpsed the solid outline of a building up ahead, when suddenly two figures ran out before her: two young women as naked as herself but for gem-encrusted rings clamped to their nipples and leather cords lavished with jingling bells at their ankles. They giggled breathlessly behind their hands, but at seeing Gillian, their eyes widened and it seemed all they could do to keep their composure. The taller of the two, with disheveled, shining red ringlets bouncing over her shoulders, approached Gillian, leading the other, a brunette with pronounced dimples in her cheeks.

The redhead bit her bottom lip as if to stop the next burst of laughter. "What is your name?"

Gillian cleared her throat and eyed again the structure beyond.

"I-I am Gillian. Have you seen—" she stopped herself, at a loss for the name of the being who had recruited her. "I am looking for someone. A large man."

The brunette giggled again behind her fingers. "It is pleasant to be tightly packed!"

The redhead studied Gillian thoughtfully. "I think she is a new arrival, Lara, and expecting to be met by Xaqriel."

Lara's eyes sobered a little and she wiped away an amused tear. "Oh."

The redhead said amicably. "I am Alexandra, this is Lara. You are a new arrival, Gillian? Brought here by a very large man with the most delicious smell?"

Gillian nodded and Alexandra's eyes scanned the boughs of the trees. "He brought me also. And he is here, though just where, none of us may know. I am surprised, however." She frowned a little and mused, "Madam usually welcomes the new ones. But then again, she has probably had to meet with the guards concerning the fate of the escaped prisoners who were recaptured this morning."

Lara grabbed her friend's arm and whispered into her ear, something that brought a gleam to Alexandra's blue eyes.

Nodding, Alexandra said, "Gillian, why don't you come with us? We can take you to Madam."

Gillian was sure she was having one whopper of a hallucination brought on by whatever drug had been slipped into her anus. This place was unearthly, too beautiful to be real. But the being—that exquisite man—he had been real, of that she had no doubt.

"No," she stammered, "I only want to find him." She closed her eyes and took several slow, deliberate breaths. But when her eyes opened again, she was still standing on the avenue with its lush, pagan scenery.

Lara sighed indolently and took her arm. "But we only see our recruiters when they choose for us to see them! You cannot expect special consideration."

Gillian tried to brush her away, but Alexandra suddenly clutched her other arm. Her hold was at once gentle and fervent.

"Come, Gillian, we can play a time!" Casting a heady smile to Lara, the two of them threw their arms about Gillian and lavished her face and shoulders with kisses.

Lara whispered, "It is not easy to steal away. Who knows when we may have this chance again?"

Alexandra turned Gillian's face with her long fingers and kissed her. Her hungry lips were tart honey, but Gillian's body responded curiously, and she sucked the tongue that pressed into her mouth. Lara bent and gathered Gillian's breasts and fed on them until both nipples were erect. Gillian's sex swelled again, and reaching with timid hands, she touched the pelted triangle of a slit that pressed into her thigh. She did not care which girl it belonged to, and combed the soft hair and unfolded the drenching-wet nether lips.

Alexandra moaned softly and shuddered. "Come with us," she whispered.

Each girl took one of Gillian's hands and led her between two of the trees bordering the path. Through the warm shadows they led her, to a clearing nestled deep in the woods.

"The guards have more important things to attend to for a while," Alexandra remarked and pulled Gillian down to the carpet of grass and forget-me-nots so that they faced one another on their knees. Lara bent over them and tilted Gillian's face upward, covering her mouth with her own, while Alexandra cupped Gillian's breasts and sucked them hungrily.

A hallucination, Gillian told herself. Not that she cared, ripe with desire for these vision-women. She faced Lara and spread the ruby folds of her pussy, delving two fingers in. The girl grinned and, moaning softly, began to ride up and down over her fingers. Alexandra sank to the ground behind Gillian and, parting Gillian's thighs, buried her face in her crotch. Her tongue roved over Gillian's clit so that it swelled and her pussy muscles throbbed. As she worked Gillian into a lathering heat, Gillian licked Lara's wide areolas with her tongue, relishing the honeydew taste as she continued to pump her hungry vagina and tease her clit with encouraging kisses. Lara rode Gillian's fingers methodically, as if every stroke was the last, while Gillian's hips undulated wildly under Alexandra's ministrations. At last, Lara's nether muscles clenched hard and she squealed in orgasm.

Lara pulled herself from Gillian's slick hand and shivered, once, twice. Then seeing Alexandra feeding on her delta, Lara pulled Gillian onto her back over the soft grass. Alexandra smiled to them once and spread Gillian's legs farther apart, devouring her pussy as if it were a long-awaited meal. Lara skipped over behind Alexandra and fell to her knees. Parting the redhead's vertical lips, she began to taste at the flesh within.

Alexandra licked Gillian's sex with lascivious talent, lifting the pounding clit with the tip of her tongue, fucking her anus with her forefinger. Gillian grasped her bouncing breasts as her hips rocked over the ground, licking at her own nipples and moaning with every mounting sensation Alexandra's mouth produced. At last, she climaxed and Alexandra's tongue plunged into her vagina and whipped the orgasm far into her contracting orifice.

Then Gillian heard Alexandra gasp and felt her hands fall away. Sitting up, Gillian watched as the girl's forearms sank to the ground and her hips waved shamelessly under Lara's devouring mouth. Gillian smiled softly and kneeled with her face to Alexandra's. She kissed her deeply, stifling the girl's breathless moans. She clamped Alexandra's breasts and tweaked the be-ringed nipples, teasing them this way and that as her tongue explored the inside of Alexandra's mouth.

At length, she felt Alexandra's spine quake. Gillian sat up on her heels and saw the girl's cheeks tint with crimson.

The next moment she heard a loud rustling of the flora behind Lara. Her eyes lifted and she saw a flash of yellow come through the brambles. It was a woman, with brown hair caught back from her brow by a golden mesh circlet. She held a wooden paddle in her high-raised hand. Before Gillian could speak, the paddle swooped down on Lara's backside. At the strike, Lara shrieked. She spun around and, with a loud sob, crumpled to her knees before the saffron loin skirt hanging between the woman's legs. Alexandra rolled to one side and, seeing the woman, covered her face with her hands. The woman's eyes flashed at Gillian, but only for a second, before grasping Lara by one hand. She yanked Lara to her feet and spanked her with the paddle.

With Lara punished and wailing, the woman next pulled Alexandra up, and wielded the paddle across her buttocks with the same unforgiving fury. When the chastisement was over, both girls were weeping and rubbing their reddened backsides with their palms. A man came up through the brambles then, dressed in a white loose-sleeved shirt tucked into the waistline of his beige pants and leather boots that rose to his knees. In one hand he held a spear. Although he looked fierce as he regarded the chastened girls, he did not lift the weapon.

"How dare you sneak off from your duties," the woman scolded. Her angry brown eyes moved from Lara and Alexandra and then to Gillian, and back again to the other two girls. "To take advantage of a potential crisis just to evade your household duties! A single chore in two days and you had to find a way out of it!" She caught hold of Alexandra's ear and waved the paddle in front of her eyes.

Gillian glanced nervously at the man, but she could not restrain herself any longer, "Leave her alone!"

The woman's face snapped toward her and the implacable set of her features made Gillian almost feel the threatening paddle weighing over her own backside.

"You must be Gillian, our latest recruit."

Gillian's inner voice told her to run away through the trees, to hide until she could find the being who had brought her here.

"I . . . I," she stuttered, but the denial that came to mind was impossible to utter. "Yes . . ."

"You shall be silent, young lady, while I address these brazen Disciples."

Between the woman's uncompromising tone and the man's watchful eyes, Gillian knew flight was futile, probably even unwise.

The woman regarded Alexandra and Lara darkly and made an indignant sound. "So you two enticed her to join your little act of rebellion, knowing full well she has no experience with the rules!"

Alexandra's red-stained face looked horrified. "We meant no wrong to her, Madam! We had no design to bring her trouble, honestly!"

Madam was quiet a moment before answering, "I believe you, Alexandra. But you have given her an improper message upon this, her first day. For that shall the two of you embrace the Rapture Pillars—after I have given you over to some of your roommates that they may ensure you resume your forsaken chores. By whatever motivation they might fancy," she added.

Lara sighed woefully at this announcement and Madam grabbed her by the arm again and spanked her even harder than the first time. The girl sobbed loudly, hanging her head. Madam said to the man, "Take them back now, Sir Thomas, to resume their duties, and make sure and send for two or three of their roommates."

The man answered by nodding and, with a forbidding look at the girls, said, "Head to the house!"

Pouting, the girls scurried before the man toward the path where they had met Gillian. Moments later, a loud smack rang through the air, followed by a second, and she could hear their soft whimpers trail up the distance in the direction of the building she had glimpsed before. She watched as Madam smoothed the wide surface of the paddle with her fingertips. Gillian looked at the golden breastplate the other woman wore: a delicately cast, decorative thing, it lent an exotic, almost Egyptian cast to her looks. Pressing her lips to the paddle, the woman tucked it into the waist of her skirt and turned her eyes to Gillian.

"I am Madam," she said, "keeper and proprietress of this place. By the look in your face, I can tell you believe me quite the monster, Gillian."

Gillian was uncertain what to make of this woman who had so rudely interrupted the exquisite moments enjoyed with Lara and Alexandra.

"Why did you do that—spank them, that is?" Gillian felt herself blush, and wanting to avoid thinking why it was she did, continued, "Who are you to order about Disciples? That is why we are here, I know—to experience pleasure. I also know that I was not brought here by you, nor did I expect to find myself in some . . . some rose-tapestried jail!" Gillian bit her bottom lip, angry with herself now for ever agreeing to the offer of that seductive being, or giving in to Nevja in the first place. She inhaled deeply and stood with her feet planted firmly on the ground.

"I vowed to be a Disciple of Pleasure, not a prisoner!"

Madam took a step toward her so that her breath tumbled like perfume over Gillian's collarbone. "You dare question the choices of those girls, or any of our submissives? When you know as well as any of the hypocrisy of your world's inhibitions? There is no shame in choosing submissiveness if it is a practice one is drawn to. To imply such a choice is a weakness is to mouth words that you do not believe."

Gillian's skin tingled. "And how do you know all this?"

Madam smiled tenderly. "I know, as does he who brought you here. We learned much about you from his in-depth observation, as well as Nevja's reports. For example, that you are a true adventurer, Gillian. More so than you ever knew.

"You were recruited to help us redeem those imprisoned here. Too many humans are just ordinary citizens in their respective societies, with extraordinary capacities for destructive attitudes toward sex. The cowardly abusers, the insecure gender-haters, the self-important chaste, the pampered knaves, they are all here, and here they shall remain to be taught to accept and embrace pleasure, to set aside their respective intolerances and injustices to others."

The inside of Gillian's head felt raw. Every tangible thing in this place was so much more vivid, defined, real, as if all she had ever set eyes on in the world she had left behind had been nothing more than faded, tattered illustrations. She tried to dismiss it, to think in rational terms.

"If this is so," she asked, "why am I here?"

Madam looked at her for a long moment. "There are a few things you ought to fear, Gillian—disobedience to me or my guards, primarily. Secondly, however, there are certain creatures that venture here occasionally, the Dhjinn-E'noch, and these you must take care to avoid, as they are beings of obsessive passion, known to abscond with our prisoners and Disciples if their passions are drawn to that certain individual. Of course, our skies are patrolled by our own guardians, so these creatures do not often seize the opportunity to trespass. The third thing you must remember—do not cross the fence. To do so would cast you into uncertain and often fluctuating ethers. These spaces are inhabited by things you do not wish to encounter."

The ghost of a chill passed over Gillian and she crossed her arms so Madam would not suspect. "And what is this place," she demanded, "and who was that being—that man, whatever—who brought me here?"

Madam looked at the ground thoughtfully. "We call our land, in your language, Nemi. As you may have noticed, we all speak the same tongue. That is because all here share one speech, the speech of ultimate reality, of which Nemi is an outstation."

Gillian blinked. She had not noticed a change to her speech or that her thoughts sounded any different to her mind's ear. Her common sense struggled to believe what she was hearing and, more than this, that this lovely landscape was anything more than a dream.

"Ultimate reality?"

"True reality, as opposed to the counterreality that most of mankind perceives. And the one who brought you here is called Xaqriel. He is of the race called the Ur'theriems or, if it is easier for you to understand, beings composed of all elements—earth, water, fire, air, and spirit. Archangels, some of your people call them."

"I see," Gillian said and moved the toes of her left foot across the grass as she evaluated this explanation.

As if in confirmation of her unspoken distrust, Madam said gently, "I know, as you wish more than anything to believe, Gillian, that one cannot embrace pleasure by feeling guilt in the act, or by casting judgment on how others find pleasure."

Gillian shuddered with a terror at once tantalizing and over-powering. Madam was smiling coolly now. She drew the paddle from her sash and raised it in the air, moving to stand behind Gillian.

Gillian turned on her and said with harsh panic, "Put that down!"

Madam seized her arm, and turning Gillian about again suddenly, brought the paddle down across her bare buttocks with a loud smack. Gillian jumped, and yowling, immediately wrenched free of the woman's hold and began to back away into the thickets.

"Stay away!"

"You will make this difficult," Madam commented patiently. "I can make it more difficult, Gillian! My guards patrol these woods."

Gillian spun around, looking here and there, stopping suddenly when she spied a man pacing through the branches not more than twenty yards away. She felt Madam's hand on her arm and gasped back the frustrated tears that came to her eyes.

"Now, why don't you stop this display, Gillian, and come home?"

"Home," Gillian repeated. The echo of the word seemed to resonate through a dark and dreadful cavity she had too long pretended did not exist within her.

Madam's company was its sweet contrast. She slid the paddle back under her sash, laced an arm about Gillian's shoulders, and led Gillian back to the path between the avenues of great oak trees. Gillian brushed back the stinging tears, taking comfort in the warmth of Madam's close flesh. The path closed upon the lawn of a great house that was shaded by more oaks encircling it. The design was a mélange, with tin-shingled gables and verandas on the upper floors and a wide front porch with nine white, graceful columns. On the front door there was a round plate of glass, stained with what appeared to be the image of a lilac blossom. As they ascended the porch steps, Gillian studied the two freestanding pillars flanking this door. About seven feet high each, they had been fashioned each of a single trunk of cedar, carved and polished, so that they looked like two huge spindles.

The door was opened by a man, dressed like the one who had taken the other girls away. Gillian hardly saw him, for she was awestruck by the sumptuous foyer. A burgundy carpet sprawled over the dark pine-board floor, and the paneling was wallpapered with floriated hunter's green velvet. On the walls hung antique-looking black-and-white photographs set in golden frames. They were mostly portraits of young, naked women, though there were a few stirring images of men either cropping women or spanking them open-handed. There were also a few paintings. Sensual, dynamically hued images they were: satyrs chasing after nymphs, mermaids luring lusty youths, a decadent woodland orgy. As Gillian proceeded with Madam, they passed a door to their left standing ajar so that Gillian glimpsed a long tiered table in the room, laden with flowers and ferns in shimmering silver and glass vessels. To the far left corner of the foyer was a great staircase draped with carpet of hunter's green. At the very rear stood a high double door of heavy wood. Another guard stood at these doors, holding a glass of what appeared to be water in one hand, as he contemplated the young, brown-haired woman kneeling on all fours at his feet. She wore a white togalike dress, though the front of it was pulled down so that her naked, heavy breasts swayed over the carpet. A leather strap had been placed about her face, holding in her mouth a huge bit. The end of the bit was shaped like a man's balls. Gillian surmised that the inner part was molded into a phallus. The girl's only show of emotion was the frustrated knit of her eyebrows. Other than this, she remained perfectly still in her humbled position.

Madam glanced down at this girl while addressing the guard, "And how is our Maggie behaving in your company, Sir Roger?"

Sir Roger eyed Madam with a slight smile. "She is well suited to my pleasures," he replied, "and I suspect by the end of the week she will be ready to bridle her tongue toward the prisoners. Going inside, Madam?"

She nodded and the guard grasped the girl by the hair to lift her. He led her away so that she stood with her face against the wall. He returned and opened the doors for Madam to proceed and Gillian followed slowly, surprised to be walking on cool floorboards now. Her eyes strained a moment as they adjusted to the duskier light of the room they had entered. As Roger shut the door behind them, she felt a strange, almost dejà-vu sensation pass over her.

It was a spacious room, rich with rosewood paneling and gleaming silver chandeliers. More paintings decorated the walls here, and there were several baroque love seats and divans set about. Against the walls were strange apparatuses, objects Gillian suspected were used for restraint. Among these items were two treading machines with wrought-iron frames and handrails. A young woman was using one of these, her back turned to them as she marched steadily upon the moving treadmill. With each lift of a knee the girl's lavender tunic flounced up her backside, so that Gillian caught a quick but clear view of her well-reddened behind.

In the center of the room stood an enormous aquarium fashioned in the shape of a great goldfish bowl and rimmed with gold. Three young women were swimming in it, their hips and legs sheathed in mermaidlike tails that partially revealed their bottoms. Shells covered their nipples but all the rest of their flesh was bare. One of them splashed out of the water as Gillian walked by with Madam. As the girl pulled herself halfway over the rim, she threw her wet hair over one shoulder and cast Gillian a curious smile.

Past the aquarium Madam trod, over a large oriental rug on which four overstuffed leather chairs and a couple of sofas covered over with crimson velvet set, arranged to make a semicircle of furniture forming a sitting area. Two guards sat talking on one of the sofas, but at seeing Madam, they got to their feet.

"Madam," greeted one of them. Gillian was intrigued by this one's stiffly combed blond hair and handlebar mustache. He could have stepped out of an Old West portrait.

Except for the Byronic outfit, of course. And more fascinating than even his appearance was the antique-looking leather holster at his belt and the ivory handle of the pistol she could see sheathed in it.

"This is Gillian, gentlemen, our newest recruit," Madam said. "Gillian, this is Sir Peter."

The blond man smiled at Gillian warmly and taking her hand, kissed it. Gillian felt a giggle rise to her lips. The scene was unreal, but pleasant.

Madam gestured to the other guard. "And Sir Vincent. As with all the guards, you are to address them as Sir."

Long of jaw, with ferocious blue eyes, this very tall and olive-skinned man seemed intimidating and dour. Even his sensual mouth looked dangerous. Through his unbuttoned vest thick black hair curled out over the collar of his white shirt. Unlike the blond man, he carried no pistol, only a coiled whip on the hip of his belt. It was enormous, not a plaything of pleasure, and it frightened her even more than the other's pistol.

Vincent must have noticed her staring, for he said suddenly, "I assure you, it is used for the control of the prisoners only." A smile—faint, genuine, and frightening—passed over his lips. "We have other instruments of correction for unruly Disciples."

These words rang so loudly in Gillian's ears that she hardly heard Madam's next words.

"I must go check on the situation with the recovered prisoners and register Gillian formally. I would appreciate the two of you evaluating her and indoctrinating her on the seemly conduct expected by our Disciples. I shan't be too long."

"It will be our pleasure, Madam," answered Sir Peter.

Gillian was shocked. How could Madam just leave her here with them—and with nothing to wear?

3

"I will return, Gillian," was all Madam said. "For now I leave you to listen to the instructions these men will give you."

Madam squeezed her shoulder affectionately and turned about. But at seeing her head back toward the door, Gillian refused to hold her dismay any longer. She ran after her, catching her by one arm. The emotion drained from Madam's face as she regarded her.

"You're not going to just leave me here," Gillian demanded, "naked, are you?" She heard giggles from the swimmers and threw them a baleful glance.

"You are bold in your panic, my Gillian." A touch of warmth briefly glinted in Madam's eyes, but she lowered Gillian's grasping hand away. "As I said before, your primary worry should be disobeying me and those who represent my authority. I will be lenient one last time. But from now on, you shall obey or know the severest correction. Now, control your panic and do as these men instruct."

Gillian shivered in anger and crossed her arms. "Yes, I suppose—"

"You suppose?"

Gillian blinked impatiently. "Yes, I understand. But I want something to wear!"

Madam laughed, but the composed sound of it sent a blade of terror through Gillian's stomach. "I will have you tied to one of the pillars you saw on the porch, with the dunce's cap to wear, if you make such demands of me again!"

Gillian felt a protest come to her lips, but somehow she held it back.

"As Peter and Vincent would have instructed you shortly, you are to address me as Madam. And never, ever speak to me again without being given liberty to do so."

Gillian watched her turn sharply and walk back to the door, and as she left, Gillian saw the disapproving look in the face of the door guard. When he closed the door again, the panic Gillian had known moments before swelled into a mindless terror.

She turned on the other two men and glared at them.

"Come here, Gillian," said Sir Peter tenderly. He took a step toward her and she backed away, scanning the entire room for another door.

"Stay back," she panted. She saw an outline between two of the room panels and bolted toward it. Yes, it was a doorway. When she spied the ceramic handle, she seized it.

But her hands were snatched back suddenly. The next thing she comprehended was being spun about and heaved into the air. A shriek of fury let loose from her throat and she kicked the air with her feet and beat her fists against the guard's chest. When she saw it was not Vincent who held her, but the blond Peter with his radiant, calming smile, the surprise she felt weakened her struggle.

"Now, now, is this any way for a civilized young lady to behave?"

When she shook her head, he set her down again. A wave of

unspoken emotions poured over Gillian. *How can I be angry at this man?*

The next moment he embraced her fiercely, sending a bolt of warmth through her thighs. As his lips crushed her mouth, all desire to flee melted against the clean, manly smell of his fair skin. It was a fragrance more intoxicating than the finest wine. He lifted her arms over her head, and holding her wrists together with one hand, kissed her throat. Her neck and spine tingled luxuriantly and all rational thought ebbed under a wave of desire. With his free hand he lifted her left breast and rolled his tongue over the nipple until it hardened in his nursing lips. The other breast he sought next, stimulating it until Gillian began to moan. His hand descended to her thighs and parted them. He stroked the folds of her pussy until they were inflamed and soaking, and massaged her clit until it felt like a hot ember about to explode.

Still binding her hands together over her head, he guided her back over to the sitting area. Vincent had pulled off all his clothes from the waist down and was now sitting on the sofa. His cock was so engorged it was scarlet. He grasped her hips and kissed her belly, and drew his tongue down to her vulva. But his intimidating regard frightened Gillian. She bucked her hips defiantly and searched Sir Peter's face for help.

"You," she begged, "you, please!"

"Shhh . . ." He threw her hair over one shoulder so he could kiss her throat again. Her body ached for him, but his hold slipped under her arms. Vincent lifted her legs, and spreading them straight out from her hips, pulled her forward. He lowered his mouth over her drenched sex, and with his tongue, prodded through her heated folds. He massaged her clit with hard little circles until it beat against his lips. Even as she strained to resist him, his skilled tongue continued to stroke and strum her clit until her hips were thrashing in the air. When at last she climaxed, the driving tongue did not relent. Gillian was panting as his tongue thrust into her vagina. Peter kissed her neck again with a kittenish lightness that made her spine tingle even as her pelvis rocked in shameless rhythm to the fucking tongue.

"Sweeter than nectar," Peter sighed. "Kiss me, Gillian!"

Her face tilted back to meet his kiss, and when at last she came again, he inhaled the moan that escaped her lips.

Gillian's skin was beaded with perspiration as Vincent stood up and pulled her from Peter's arms. Her fear of him was replaced by an emotion nameless and overpowering. She kissed his mouth and licked his bottom lip, enjoying the solid taste of it. He smiled and laid her down on the sofa. Through her heavy eyes, she gazed up at his cock towering above the thick patch of raven curls and her vagina quickened with renewed passion.

"Fuck me," she cooed, touching the iron-hard shaft, "fuck me with that!"

With a soft laugh, Vincent grasped her legs and wrenched them apart. He worked the first two fingers of his right hand into her pussy. She could feel her still-contracting muscles clamp him.

"Still hungry with passion, beautiful Disciple?"

She began to pitch herself against his penetration and nodded, hoping her pleading eyes would entice him. But just as suddenly he released her.

"On your belly!"

She whimpered in disappointment, yet she obeyed. Again her thighs were spread, but this time it was her anus he probed with a slick finger. Gillian felt indescribably humbled. He maneuvered himself onto the sofa so that he sat behind her with her legs draped over his lap while he boldly prodded her rear. Each stroke went a little deeper, creating a surge of sensation at once painful and arousing. She could hardly keep her hips from writhing, and when she saw Sir Peter peering down at her, a deep blush reddened her face.

"No, stop it," she exclaimed. She reached back and tried to pull Sir Vincent's probing hand away. To her shock, he smacked her hand. Protesting, she twisted and tried to rise to her knees. Immediately his hand rose and he spanked her soundly.

The blows stung and she began to sob, though in truth she did not know if her tears came more for the humiliation or the encompassing sense of both discomfort and pleasure washing through her. After a time, the discomfort of her being anally probed subsided into an embarrassing passion. The continued invasion prompted sensation in her vagina, too, making it feel all the more desirous for the attention of his huge member. So wicked was this sensation that she was sure he knew it. But on and on he worked his finger, until her backside undulated lasciviously to meet his thrusts. It seemed an eternity he fucked her this way, but after a time, he lightly touched her clit with the fingers of his other hand. The little organ climaxed immodestly.

She was breathless as Vincent raised her again and stood her up on her feet. He sat back down so that his erect penis reared between her legs. He dabbed a finger at the musky juices on her thighs and, with a sensual smile, turned her by the hips so that her back was to him.

"Bend over slightly," he said softly.

At her compliance he lowered Gillian's hips a bit. As the head of his cock entered her pussy, he lifted her legs and set them down over his thighs so that the organ stuffed her completely.

She moaned as he pinned her arms against him, kissing her neck as he began to bounce her upon the impaling cock. Sir Peter came and kneeled before her. He tweaked her bobbing breasts, the slight pain intensifying her sense of helplessness. And then lowering to his knees, he unfolded her inflamed pussy lips and suckled the pulsating clit. Gillian's entire body felt like one ravenous orifice. Sir Vincent's cum shot into her, igniting another climax that exploded fully throughout her sex.

She went limp in Sir Vincent's strong arms. His hot lips grazed her throat and Sir Peter gathered her breasts in his hands and sucked them gingerly.

Sir Vincent was merciful now, lowering his legs and holding her firmly by the hips and steadying her on her feet. As he rose, too, he patted her ass and nodded to Peter. Putting his pants back on, Sir Vincent walked off from the sitting area, leaving Gillian to blush self-consciously under Peter's smiling gaze.

He kissed her cheek. "You are doing well," he assured. "Just remember not to question the instructions, and all will go smoothly."

"It is not finished?"

Before he could answer, Sir Vincent returned. Over one shoulder he carried the girl she had seen on the treadmill. As he lowered her to her feet, Gillian caught the girl's lips purse. But the expression vanished almost instantly, and bowing her head, she drew her hands submissively behind her back.

Sir Vincent gestured to the sofa and addressed Gillian. "Sit down."

She obeyed, and was surprised when he ordered the girl over her lap. The girl draped herself over Gillian's thighs with a low purr, one so soft Gillian knew the men didn't catch it. As the girl spread her hands over the floor, Gillian looked questioningly up at Sir Peter. But he said nothing now.

"Charlotte was found bullying one of the better behaved Disciples for a piece of chocolate the girl had earned," explained Vincent. "The finale of Charlotte's correction will serve, also, as a demonstration of what may befall you for indecorous behavior."

Gillian understood what he wanted, but she could not bring herself to do anything but stare at him.

"Hold her hair that she may not move or fall," he bade in a

tone too stern to ignore. "Spank her, Gillian—spank her with vigor until I tell you to stop."

Taking a deep breath, she nodded and clenched a handful of the girl's hair in her left hand. She looked at the girl's down-turned face, seeing the tenseness of her features, the quiver of her lips. Gillian's right hand rose over the flushed bottom, but her will froze.

"I can't!" she whispered.

"Now, or it shall be her turn with you!"

Gillian's heart jumped and without another thought, her palm bore down over the girl's tender buttocks. Over and over again she spanked her, bringing a refreshed blush to the skin. The girl's hips strained right and left in the effort to dodge Gillian's punishing hand. She whimpered loudly as the minutes drew on, and Gillian's palm grew warmer with each new delivery.

At last, Sir Vincent laid a hand on Gillian's shoulder and said it was enough. With the chastisement over Charlotte panted and sobbed, though, Gillian suspected, more in anger than re-pentance. Vincent's cock was swollen again already under the fabric of his pants. He smiled lustily and caught the girl up, throwing her back over his shoulder. He carried her away, but Gillian was too numb with her own shock to see where it was he took Charlotte. She could not even raise her eyes to the gentle Sir Peter.

"You found that distasteful," he said.

"Yes," she whispered, "... or at least ... not ... not ..."

"Not arousing?"

"Yes."

"Yet you obeyed. That is excellent." His praise was like sweet cream to a cat.

"Not without being told more than once."

Gillian trembled to hear Sir Vincent's voice. But she was dismayed, too, wondering how there could be so little warmth from him after their intimacy.

"But I did all you told me!"

He sighed and pulled her hair back over her shoulders. "You should never hesitate or question our bidding, Gillian. There shall be no more of these incidents without consequences. Also, it is not permitted for a Disciple to speak to a superior before given accord to do so. And in the future, refer to all guards as sir."

She shivered and found it difficult to meet his eyes. She backed toward Sir Peter, hoping he would tell Sir Vincent to be quiet, or that this was just some game. She had to accept Madam's authority; that had already been demonstrated out in the woods. But surely no one actually expected her to kowtow to all these men. It was subservience, pure and simple.

And yet the thought of its actuality made her clit quicken . . .

She looked to Sir Peter desperately.

"It is proper, respectful," he said.

"Now, kneel on the floor," Vincent instructed her.

With an impatient sigh, Gillian did so. He asked her many questions regarding the information about Nemi that she had been given so far. She answered, as respectfully as she could manage.

"Madam has told you all the necessities," he replied when she was finished. "However, there are a few other vital things to remember. In contact with the prisoners, you may not speak with or associate with them unless instructed otherwise. And although you probably will be assigned tasks here in the household, remember that certain prisoners are assigned regular tasks of maintaining and cleaning the premises. With this in mind, just as when you are outing at the prison, be wary to avoid unprivileged speech with these trustees.

"Also, arguments and quarrels, acts of jealousy and pettiness are not allowed between Disciples. If and when you are given over to one of the Madam's apprentices—the Leather Wives— you must show them the same respect as any guard. At all times you are expected to be sweet-spoken and tidy in your person and take care of all those items given to you for personal use.

"Let me remind you again that you are expected to be obedient to all guards. We were recruited specifically for qualities of firmness and for our aptitude at restraining our tempers. Therefore, you have nothing to fear about being mistreated. This, however, does not preclude us from dealing fit punishment as we see needed, nor from enjoying those special talents that qualified you. Now, have you any questions about anything, Gillian?"

Gillian stared at his hands on his hips. She was absolutely secure in the knowledge this man would yield his life to protect her and any of the Disciples. She was equally sure that despite even their recent intimacy, this man would yield no mercy in punishing her for any transgression she might make.

Her earlier stupefied reaction to Nemi's startlingly vital ambiance was gradually absorbing into her consciousness, as if her soul had recognized that which her physical form had not foreseen: that she had been destined to endure the pleasurable but mortifying trials of Nemi.

She bowed her head and answered humbly, "Yes, sir."

Madam returned at last and told Gillian it was time to settle her in upstairs.

On the second floor, voices and giggles sounded behind every closed door. Gillian had no way of knowing if these issued from the prisoners or the Disciples. As Madam's tone had been brusque since taking her from Sir Peter and Sir Vincent, Gillian thought it best not to ask. So she admired the hardwood floor and velvet wallpaper as they made their way through the upstairs halls. A light breeze passed through the raised windows. They did not meet anyone else, although when passing a pair of glass doors, Gillian saw several figures on the veranda beyond. Several women, all clad in leather lingerie and boots, clamored about a naked male sitting on his ass in their midst. Gillian did not see his face, as it was bowed between his knees.

Madam's voice drew her curious eyes away at once, "This will be your room."

Madam opened the door, and at her gesture, Gillian walked through. It was a long, narrow room of cedar-paneled walls. Four slender beds were headboarded against the upper wall, all covered with white spreads and canopied in white lace. On the wall down a ways from the farthest bed, was set a wide, deep-paned window. To the other side of this window stood an antique vanity, complete with a white-cushioned stool. A little table stood near the door they entered, and upon it were an opaque glass lantern and a cloisonné matchbox.

An enormous painting hung on the wall down from the table: a scene of winged men disrobing and ravishing a group of women. With its majestic size and sensual, bright hues, the artwork dominated the room. There was an engraved plaque of gold set beneath the frame and Gillian tried to read it, but her eyes were drawn back to the picture. The men were especially fascinating, with their deliciously taut muscles, aroused, ruddy penises, and great dusky wings, somewhat translucent. At first glance one might have thought it was only shadowy auras outlining the men's backs.

Madam touched a foot post of one of the beds. "This one will be yours. There is a dress for you in the bathing room yonder, and all the necessities to bathe and relax."

Gillian looked to the door at the end of the room that Madam motioned to, and noticed, too, the peevish look on her face.

"I had intended to have you dine with me this evening, and take you to the Temple of Purity afterward. But other matters necessitate my presence elsewhere."

The mention of a temple whetted Gillian's curiosity, but before she could ask for permission to speak, Madam continued,

"It will wait till tomorrow. Take a bath and rest awhile. This evening you will be accompanying your roommates to the prisoners' pavilion for dinner. You are not to leave these rooms until your chaperone comes to escort the four of you there. However, if an emergency does arise, there is a bell."

Gillian followed her eyes to the silken cord hanging through a copper circlet on the wall near the bathing room door.

When Madam was gone, Gillian felt weighed down by the sudden solitude. She could hear nothing from any of the other rooms, only a cricket or two through the window. She was glad to enter the bathing room and found there a porcelain sink, commode, and a deep claw-foot tub—all with plumbing. The tub was set upon a tiled dais with a small, plush rug to step out onto after bathing. A full-length oval mirror was anchored to the wall just beside the sink. A stack of towels had been set on a little table nearby, along with a brass tin full of brushes and ribbons. On the shelf beneath the small window were dozens of jars. As she read the hand-printed labels on the bottoms of the containers, Gillian realized Madam had not exaggerated. There were shampoos, bath gels, salts, and oils of all sorts for the bath. For after bathing, there were perfumes, powders, moisturizers, and lotions. There were cosmetics much more refined than anything Gillian had ever seen, as well as feather and rabbit-tail puffs, even applicators devised of leather-tipped quills. And laid out on the stool beside the tub was the dress Madam had promised.

Gillian examined it, finding to her dismay that it was not really a dress—it was too short for that. At least there were panties she could wear underneath it. As Gillian pressed the dress to her and looked in the mirror, she knew she would have to be careful when bending over if she did not want to reveal the underwear.

"At least the window is shut tightly," she sighed.

She drew the tub full and poured in some tuberose bubble bath. Her muscles ached as she luxuriated in the hot water, and her pussy was tender. But soon the pains diminished, and by the time she was ready to drain the tub and rinse off, she was more than ready for a nap. She yawned while she combed her hair and dressed.

Right now she could hardly hold her eyes open, and walking out of the bathroom, she crawled into the bed Madam had assigned her. The sheets were almost sinfully welcoming. Within moments she was asleep.

Later, consciousness returned when someone rocked her shoulder and whispered her name. She opened her eyes to find another girl sitting at the edge of the bed, and other feminine voices sounded from the bathing room.

"Hi," said the one beside her. "I'm Pearl. Madam asked me to make sure you were awake and ready, and tell you to wear these."

Gillian sat up and the girl laid a pair of shoes on her lap: white patent-leather slippers. A pair of silver bells had been sewn to each.

"Oh, and these,too." Pearl handed her a pair of white socks.

"To keep me warm," Gillian said.

"No." Pearl smiled brightly. "They will look pretty on you." As she stood up, Gillian saw what the girl was wearing: a short-hemmed salmon silk toga, with nothing else but belled anklets.

"Is that what you always wear?"

Pearl glanced toward the bathroom. "If I'm allowed," she said. "You had best get dressed. Sir Douglas, our chaperone, will be here shortly to take us to the pavilion."

While the girl darted off to the bathing room, Gillian enjoyed her relative solitude again. The voices in the bathing room stilled at Pearl's entrance, and Gillian could hear them whispering. Probably curious about her, of course, but that was only to be expected. At least they were allowed to dress.

She thought about Lara and Alexandra, naked but for the belled anklets and nipple clamps, and she felt a little guilty. She could also envision herself running off with them to the woods again. She knew her own heart would beat wildly at the fear of being caught by a guard but, strangely, sensed that the fear would prove as sweet as the taste of their succulent pussies and greedy, honeyed mouths.

The fantasy made her thighs flush. She tried to think of other things, before one of the roommates suspected the fantasy by the look on her face.

Gillian felt guilty again when the other two roommates emerged from the bathing room. Candice wore only cords of bells about her ankles, and Mary-Jo the same, along with a collar of blue feathers at her throat. Mary-Jo must have been in some trouble this day, obviously, for her backside was still glowing red with someone's handprint. But the three of them all seemed happy, and they welcomed her kindly enough. Candice even showed Gillian the engagement ring on her finger.

Gillian's eyes widened as she looked at the exquisitely old-fashioned setting. "It's lovely. But . . . you're a Disciple and you're going to be married?"

"Yes," Candice answered with a dreamy sigh. "To Sir Golden. Madam has already had the prisoners begin work on a little house for us over in the residents' village."

Gillian smiled. "It is lovely," she said at last, still mystified.

The chaperon arrived shortly. He was slight of bone and short—not even as tall as Gillian—and the crop he carried was the only fear-inspiring thing about the man. He ordered Gillian and her roommates out of the room and escorted them downstairs. The twilight sky outside the staircase window turned deeper blue as Gillian followed her roommates. The guard with the leashed girl was sitting on the bench in the foyer as they passed through. Gillian surmised he must be on his break, as an emptied tray sat on the bench beside him. The girl sat in his lap, moaning behind her gag as he played with her breasts and nuzzled her throat. Gillian did not realize she had slowed to look at them until Sir Douglas almost walked right into her.

"What are you gaping at, girl?" he snapped. "Make haste!"

She jumped and paced briskly to catch up with her roommates, who were already waiting attentively on the porch.

As the chaperone followed her out the door, a motion to Gillian's right caught her eye. She looked and saw it was from the spindlelike pillar there—a girl bound, her arms and widespread legs pulled back against the wood. Her wrists and her ankles, too, were bound at the backside of the pillar by the loose ends of heavy silk cords secured into the wood by wide metal-teethed clamps. The girl's mouth was stuffed with the same kind of phallic bit as had been on the guard's girl.

Only as her eyes moved Gillian's way did she notice the familiar bejeweled clamps on her nipples.

Alexandra!

Alexandra's expression was one of contrite resignation. Gillian looked quickly to the pillar to the left, and indeed, there was Lara, bound just like Alexandra, her mouth silenced by a dildo muzzle. Lara's face was turned away, but Gillian saw tears rolling down her chin and over her throat and breasts. As Sir Douglas came through the doorway, he gave Lara a disgruntled look.

"It could just as easily be one of you up there, young ladies," he said and granted Candice a confidential half-smile. "Even you."

He then led them from the porch, and the girls followed him to the right of the lawn and through a little gate Gillian had not noticed before. The pebbled path on the other side took them through a close avenue of hazel trees that opened on to a grassy meadow. Just ahead stood a high torch-post and a wide encompassing fence of barbed wire. Sir Douglas opened the gate and entered the meadow. A great canvas pavilion stood in the center of it, and far beyond this there was yet another gate that led, it seemed to Gillian, to another enclosed yard. A little station looked to be situated just behind this other gate, and in the far distance Gillian could make out what appeared to be a dismal redbrick structure.

The prison.

As they walked across the meadow, the smell of cooked food and the lilt of softly played music drifted out from the pavilion. Two guards were posted at the entrance and one of these drew the entry flap aside for them. Sir Douglas clapped his hands and ushered the girls inside ahead of him. As Gillian was about to follow the others, Sir Douglas held her back.

"I heard how you panicked this afternoon," he whispered. "Just remember, we shan't allow any harm to come to you. Sir Leonard will accompany you inside."

She looked at the man who came up beside her. He was tall and muscled and carried a spear. Beside him, Sir Douglas looked like a child playing some masterly role.

Why, he couldn't even lift me, she thought, how could he ever hope to protect me?

"Thank you, sir," she said. "If you don't mind explaining to me, what exactly am I supposed to do at this meal?"

"You do eat, don't you?" he said lightly. "Aside from that, hold yourself proudly so these men will have no choice but to take notice of the natural attractions of your form and sex. You see, Gillian, these prisoners, well, all the prisoners of Nemi, have over the years selectively denied the natural appreciation of sex. To them lust and the pursuit of carnal pleasures are the greatest of downfalls. Some are terrified of divine judgment for their personal penchants. Others simply hate the gentler sex for various, degenerate reasons. All have spent their adult lives perpetuating untruths and stereotypes that accommodate their fears and cowardice. It is your mission to help exorcise these flaws.

"Never be ashamed of yourself, your passion, nor your body. Should one of these prisoners show an interest in being intimate with you, know that by doing so, you are fulfilling the purpose for which you were recruited. Sir Vincent has shared the results of your evaluation with the guards inside, so all know you are a submissive, by both nature and psyche. You are expected to behave accordingly: sweet, deferential, obedient, and graceful of conduct; and never shall you be expected to do anything that goes against this, your natural disposition."

When he had finished speaking, Gillian thought about his words. It sounded easy enough. And taking a long breath, she bowed her head and followed Sir Leonard inside.

The pavilion was illuminated inside by the soft glow of colorful glass lanterns affixed to the crossbeams of the supporting poles. A long, low table stood in the center, decked with plates of fine china, glassware, and dishes and bowls filled with food. There were forks and spoons laid out at every plate, but strikingly, no knives. On cushioned benches at either side of the table sat men of all ages and bearing, dressed in uniforms of light cotton. Gillian guessed these men to be the prisoners, as other guards passed through the sidelines.

These guards were more heavily armed than the men at Madam's house; some carried spears and others carried sabers sheathed in scabbards. They watched vigilantly as her roommates approached and took seats between some of the prisoners. There were several other Disciples present as well at the table, and two more, dressed in belly-dancer ensembles. A band of musicians sat on wide wood stools positioned beyond the table. They were not prisoners, Gillian thought, for they wore colorful shirts and fine suede pants. The music they played accompanied the dancers' sensual undulations with a rich, Arabic melody.

Gillian had no idea what she was supposed to do, and Sir

Leonard did not offer a suggestion. When another guard passed through the entryway, she saw Sir Douglas standing just outside, getting a light for his cigarette from another guard. It was not until that moment that she realized she had not once craved a cigarette in all the hours spent in Nemi. Not that magical moment of the first draw; not the soothing feel of the slender form between her first two fingers. Oddly, she knew no envy in watching Sir Douglas enjoy his—instead, she saw a fleeting vision of herself kneeling between his bare legs and inhaling his hard cock into her mouth.

She gasped at herself.

"What's wrong with me?" she said aloud, not even knowing she had uttered the words until Sir Leonard spoke brusquely.

"Indeed. Why are you gazing outside? Go take a place at the table!"

Gillian flinched. Before she could even hope to ask where it was he wanted her, his palm swooped down smartly across her backside. It was not a hard enough spank to hurt, but it sent her scurrying to the table. She looked about timidly, not even able to guess what was expected, when the bearded prisoner sitting to her right looked up. The baleful disgust in his black eyes washed like icy tar over her skin.

"A new whore," he muttered and turned his face rigidly straight ahead.

"Gillian."

The gentler voice brought her grateful attention to the man across the table. Unlike the hateful one, he had a generous smile, and his large dark eyes were sparkling, fascinated by the scene.

"You are Gillian? I am Clive. Pearl said Madam would send me a treat tonight."

She looked down the table uncertainly and saw Pearl walking behind some of the other men at the other side. She draped her arms about two of them and kissed their cheeks. One of them tossed his head impatiently; the other simply stared ahead and mumbled. She went on and greeted the next two the same way, oblivious that Gillian hoped for her notice.

The prisoner who had spoken rose to his feet. "Come around and sit with me. I have waited so long for this meeting."

Gillian could feel eyes upon her from a number of the prisoners, stares so malevolent that her instinct urged her to back away and flee out the doorway. But then another guard from the other side of the room stepped to the table. The uncompromising look he gave her subdued her impulses. She bowed her head and walked about the closest end of the table and came to stand before the waiting prisoner.

His smile was almost bashful as he gestured to the bench. Gillian sat down, catching the grunt made by the prisoner to her other side.

The one who had insulted her before now sneered at her admirer.

"You are a whore," he hissed. "I shall eat nothing contaminated by your presence!"

Clive did not seem to have heard a word of it. Instead, he shared the food from his plate with Gillian. He even offered the wineglass to her lips. She felt the rude one across the table growing more and more heated. After a time, Clive took a piece of sugar-powdered cake from a platter and told her to eat it, too. As she nibbled on it, he lifted her hair aside and shyly kissed her cheek. Suddenly, the rude one slammed a fist on the table, jarring it and bringing the attention of everyone.

He leaped to his feet and shook a pudgy finger at Clive. "This is hell, my friend—hell! And here you disgrace our people by feeding a concubine!"

Several guards rushed out of the shadows and encircled him, gouging his waist with the heads of their spears.

"Come along, Stephen," one of them ordered, "your meal is finished!"

Fear flashed in Stephen's eyes. He raised his hands amiably.

"Have mercy on me, I have been ill," he said. When after a second order he still had not moved away from the table, one of the guards turned his spear and jabbed his shoulder hard with the butt. He ordered Stephen outside, and the prisoner's legs started to move, but in the next moment Stephen jerked his head to one side and spat at Gillian. The spittle only struck the table, but it was enough to bring the handle of one guard's spear crashing over the back of his neck. He staggered forward and was caught by another guard before falling. Several spearheads gouged roughly into him now, making him move at last to the entryway.

Clive sighed and whispered in Gillian's ear, "I am no longer as he."

He had the eager, nervous look of an adolescent boy on his first date. She managed to smile at him, but her discomfort at being in the midst of so many resentful men did not ease. In general they seemed bent on ignoring the Disciples with the most unnatural coldness, turning their faces from the lips speaking in their ears and averting their eyes at every peep of flesh in their line of vision. Far down the table, however, Gillian saw one man had taken a Disciple onto his lap. He was obviously mesmerized by the girl, tracing her flesh gingerly with his fingertips and listening as she spoke—as if the fate of the world hung on her words. In the shadows past the musicians, she saw Pearl again.

It was not a prisoner on whose lap Pearl bounced, but a guard. He was a stout man with short curly brown hair, and he fucked Gillian's roommate with the ardor of a tomcat losing his virginity. Pearl's face was thrown back. Gillian could see the wide parting of her lips. The reflection of the lantern lights shimmered on her sweat-dewed breasts and the tinkling bells at her ankles.

The musicians stopped their playing. She peered to where they sat. They laughed among themselves, and all took long swigs from the stone jug they passed around before taking up their instruments again. It was a faster tune now, and a few of the Disciples jumped up and started to dance with one another. Some of the prisoners groaned, but Gillian saw more than one pair of eyes watch the girls with something besides antipathy. Soon the dancers' flesh was flushed and their lips ruddy with glee.

As the night went on, some more of the prisoners began talking to the Disciples. A few of them seemed actually interested in the girls; Gillian caught a genuine lusty smile here and there. But the other conversations were nothing more than blatant attempts to tell a Disciple to be "good." She was glad to see the Disciples could and did react with the same indifference these exemplars of righteousness had shown them earlier: turning their faces from them completely, and if the man pressed further, simply walking away.

One of the men, however, could not endure being ignored. The prisoner's eyes glowered when his girl walked away and his face grew livid. He picked up his plate and threw it at her, messing her back and hair with food, and bringing the musician's tune to an abrupt halt. The prisoner jumped up from the bench and raised his hands and started to babble, beginning to sway on his feet with his eyes turned back in their sockets when the guards accosted him.

He came to his senses only after he kicked at those who held his arms until he was taken outside. Not everyone could be redeemed, Gillian thought. So be it. An uncomfortable hush fell over the table, and the musicians set their instruments down and passed around their jug again.

Despite the preparations Gillian had received, and Clive's kindness notwithstanding, the presence of most of the prisoners was almost suffocating. All she could think of was finding some way to get outside and fill her lungs with the fresh night air, to forget the bloodless men like Stephen and the babbling crazy.

Clive spoke her name again and she had to make herself meet his eyes. Even with his obvious interest and manners, she suspected it had not been too long since he had looked upon Disciples with the same enmity as the others.

He surprised her pleasantly, when next he asked, "Would you care to take a walk, Gillian?"

"But that's not allowed, is it?"

He grinned and waved a guard to the table. The guard's reply to his request astonished her.

"The others will keep a discreet watch, Clive, but yes, you may take this girl for a walk."

The guard escorted them as far as the entryway, and informed the guards there that Clive was taking her outside.

Her heart fluttered. She was not sure it was wise, and almost hoped they would object. Instead, they directed Clive toward a beaten path between the pavilion and the prison grounds, and to a grove beyond the path. Clive's hand felt secure as he clasped her own, and she almost smiled as he led her away.

"Come."

He walked her on down the path, to the shadowy edge of the grove. She glimpsed the barbed wire not too far within the trees. As for the prison, she tried to avoid looking at it. She inhaled the air and found it just as fresh as she had hoped. Trills of songbirds sounded from the tree branches, and somewhere behind them she thought she heard booted feet surveying the territory beyond the barbed wire.

Clive laughed softly and pulled her by the hand into his lap. As his arms laced about her, she shuddered, though she liked the fragrance of him. It was so different than the sourness that rose from most of the other prisoners in the pavilion.

"Gillian," he whispered. "Would you have me spread your legs and take you right here in the open field?"

She suffered his kiss and found it pleasant enough. He bunched her breasts up so that her cleavage popped over the

neckline of the short dress, and with his tongue, traced the areolas of her nipples. Her entire bosom swelled with fire, and the
pang of desire that pulsated through her pussy made her forget
the guards altogether. His eyes were sweet and tender.

A pang of grief came over her. His eyes were dark and piercing like Bruce's, she thought. And for a moment all she could
think of was the terrible desire to see Bruce again. She wished
she could, even now, confess to him the desire and fondness she
felt for him.

But Gillian remembered what was expected of her.

She smiled and linked her hands about Clive's neck and heaved
her breasts to his lips. "Why don't I take you, Clive—strip you
down and fuck you in this open field?"

He gave her a tentative smile and combed his fingers through
the length of her hair. "You are a naughty girl to speak this way,
Gillian."

He kissed her again, and this time she let herself truly enjoy
it. His hands about her waist seemed as hot as the insides of her
thighs. Without another word, she pressed her right fingers gingerly over the crotch of his pants. She got a single moment's feel
of its hardening bulge before he cupped her shoulders roughly.

"What are you doing?" His displeasure was unquestionable,
but she kissed his mouth lightly, sure her desire would overcome his hesitance.

"What I want to do."

"I do not care for your words, young lady."

His disapproval made her want him all the more. "Are you a
virgin? I can make you forget you ever were."

Clive frowned and caught her hands behind her back. "No.
Do not speak like this."

Gillian was more confused than ever. "But I thought you
wanted this."

"I want this—I want you, yes." He smiled a little again and

let go of her hands and traced her lips with his fingers. "But no more talk like this."

"All right."

"I long to see you writhe," he spoke huskily, "and beg for more, but at my discretion."

She laughed and was glad when he kissed her and rolled her down on the grass. He lifted the hem of the short dress, pulled the panties down to her knees, and stroked her thighs.

"Soft, pretty legs," he murmured and touched the moist nether lips beneath her pubic hair. "Properly passionate, Gillian!"

He stroked her vagina with his right hand. Her clit swelled under his touch, and it seemed to her that he was particularly fascinated with this small organ. He lay over her open legs, and licked and stroked it some more, until she was sure she would burst in his hand.

Clive made a deep, satisfied sound. He sat back up, pulled her panties off, and spread her legs wide. Then he removed his pants and threw them aside. Kneeling, he pressed the head of his hard cock against her pussy. He was slick with desire, and the heat of it coaxed her juices. He plunged in gracefully and, spreading her legs now as far as they would go, fucked her deeply. But his thrusts were slow and the emotion on his face as he savored each stroke was almost painful. Gillian's pussy swelled desperately for a full-force screwing. Her hips rose to meet each leisurely thrust, and she began to writhe on the grass, moaning so plaintively she was sure everyone in the pavilion could hear her.

"Faster!"

He paused and eyed her again with displeasure. "You have much to learn, little Disciple. I am a prisoner, yet at least I know my place. Still, I will have my freedom through training you at every possible opportunity."

She wailed as he started the slow fucking again, clawing the grass as her pelvis rocked in rhythmic desperation. And just as she neared climax, he said, "You will now finish this with your sweet mouth."

Clive withdrew and watched as she got on all fours and whirled toward him and took his organ into her mouth. She only had to suck a moment or so before he came, firing with such force she hardly felt it shoot down her throat.

He pulled her by the arms to her knees and kissed her forehead, and wiped her mouth clean with his hand.

"You have not disappointed, sweet Gillian."

She watched as he stood and reached for his pants. Her pussy throbbed so sorely for gratification that she had to hold her hands behind her back in order not to touch herself. When he was dressed again, he told her to rise and hand him her panties.

"Why," she asked, trying to hide her frustration with a smile, "I will need them, you know."

He shook his head and, bending over, snatched them up. He caressed them against his cheek and said, "They are mine for now. You might get them back when you come to visit."

"Visit?"

His eyes shifted to the direction of the prison. "There."

Gillian felt a shiver of repulsion. That awful place? Never.

Clive straightened her dress. He cupped her face between his hands and kissed her long and adoringly. When their lips parted, he took her by the hand and escorted her back the way they had come. On their way, Gillian spied a guard making his rounds outside the borders of the prison grounds. She could not make out any features, but he paused as she and Clive passed his line of vision. There was something familiar about his silhouette and she thought for a moment it was perhaps the guard she had seen in the woods with Madam that day.

No, she thought, that man had been thin. This one was huskier, more solid.

But she forgot him when a glint of light caught her attention. Clive's footfalls slowed as her eyes moved to the path ahead. Three men accosted them.

No ordinary men. She would have guessed each stood easily seven foot tall. It was not their size that made goose bumps rise to her skin, however, but that she could see straight through their naked, iridescent forms. As Clive's protective arm went about her shoulders, she made out the fine outlines of wings arching out from either side of their backs. They all possessed three pairs of silvery wings, layering vertically down their backs and extending to the heels of their feet. Still, she could tell that the span of these wings were as great as or more than the dimensions of the respective men.

Clive whispered urgently, "Turn your eyes, Gillian."

But she could not seem to look away, and suddenly, one of the winged men turned and cast his magnificent eyes toward them. At once, Gillian felt crushed by an unexpected, overwhelming lust. Her knees weakened and her pussy ached with a tormented passion. She was only dimly aware of Clive lifting her into his arms and carrying her away.

"Who were they?" she asked as he neared the entranceway of the pavilion.

"You will find out in time, sweet."

Two guards came up beside Clive as he set her down near the doorway. "Go within," he said. "I will join you shortly."

She sighed thoughtfully and glanced at the amused faces of the guards. "You will tell them what we just saw—"

He touched her face affectionately. "The Angels pose us no danger, Gillian. But I must speak with your chaperon."

Angels! The word echoed in her mind. *I thought angels were celibate, asexual beings...*

One of the guards took her hand. "Come along, Disciple." She looked back at Clive as the guard escorted her inside, and her heart raced when she heard Clive ask to speak with Sir Douglas.

Her reaction to the unnerving encounter with the glowing men faded away under the nagging question as to what it was exactly Clive planned to discuss with her chaperon.

4

Gillian was not to see Clive again that night. Sir Douglas gathered his wards only minutes later and ushered them back to Madam's house.

As they stepped onto the porch, Gillian saw at once that Alexandra and Lara had been taken down from the Rapture Pillars. The intimate whispers and soft moans from the shadows told Gillian the two were probably nearby, with whomever had released them. The household itself was alive with talk. Past the right wall of the foyer, a door was now standing open. In the room beyond were Disciples sitting on their knees with their naked backsides toward the door. A woman dressed in black leather pants and a burgundy blouse paced the floor and was scolding the young women. Gillian did not catch what the scolding was about, for Sir Douglas was following on her heels. She felt the agitation of his breath all the way up the stairs.

They returned to their room, where the lantern on the table had been lit and the flame shining through the opaque glass filled the room with soft illumination. Gillian was sleepier than she had expected and was glad when Sir Douglas ordered them to prepare for bed.

She started toward the bathing room with the others when he called her to stop and turn around.

He gestured to her bed, his voice firm again, "Stand over there, Gillian."

As she obeyed, he patted the handle of the crop that hung through a loop at his belt.

"The prisoner Clive is very taken with you, Gillian. He has waited some time for a Disciple who shared the penchant his rehabilitation has allowed him to cultivate. His is pleased with you enough to request that you serve as his love-attendant in the prison when it is determined he is eligible. This may be some time, I have heard, but I will make the recommendation you be put in his service when the time does arrives."

The memory of the prison loomed before Gillian's eyes. The image filled her with fear, and she started to plead that he keep her from the dreadful place, "Sir Douglas—"

He lifted an eyebrow. "I am not finished. Aside from his favorable report of your talents, however, he also informed me that you addressed him in a manner unbefitting a submissive. Is this true?"

Gillian was shocked. "All I tried to do, sir, was please him; let him know I found him . . . hot."

"Hot," Sir Douglas repeated, and his mouth tightened as if suppressing a smile. "Do you not realize by now that it is not up to a submissive to voice an opinion on whether the prisoner whom she serves is hot or otherwise?"

Gillian nodded. "Yes, Sir Douglas," she replied, but was shocked again when he lifted the crop from its loop.

"Good, Gillian. Now, bend over the bed and hold on to the mattress."

Her heart thundered, and she was seized with earthly indignity.

"No!"

For the first time, his tone was genuinely stern, "Now!"

From the door of the bathing room, her roommates watched silently.

"I pleased him," she protested, "and no, I won't bend over this bed!"

His eyes flashed angrily and when he reached for her, she brought her forearm up sharply and knocked his wrist away. She turned before he could snatch her hand and bolted out the door. Down the corridor she fled, hearing him run after her.

As she took off down the stairs, he shouted for aid. The guard downstairs came fast to block her way. He might have captured her at the bottom, but she ducked just in time and flew under his reach, and ran on through the front door and out onto the porch.

"Stop her!"

Heavy feet pounded from the shadows of the porch as she fled down the steps to the lawn. From a nearby bush, another masculine shadow darted toward her. Reeling sharply, she ran toward the great oaks flanking the path. She could hear the men close behind, and had no idea where to go or how to avoid them for long. She thought of nothing but resisting that untried passion her spirit intuitively knew would be kindled were any man to correct her as Sir Douglas intended to.

She dashed behind one of the oaks just as two of the guards passed by, and, suspecting the others were scouting the outer edges, she crept about slowly, watching for signs of their shadows. When she saw one of them emerge from under a branch, she sprinted to the great trunk on the opposite side of the avenue.

A violet-green mist suddenly rained down over her. She was swallowed into a vortex of heat and scents so embracing that her terrified scream could not be released.

But she heard one of the guards shout, "Here!"

The next moment, the vortex released her and as she gasped for air, saw the guards running toward her from all directions. The first who reached her coiled his arms about her waist and hoisted her high into the air. She stomped her feet against the air itself, in fury at the terrible, invisible thing that had thwarted her escape. As she struggled in the guard's arms, the others trotted up. One of these was Sir Douglas, and his eyes were incensed.

But he turned and raised his eyes to something above them all, and said breathlessly, "Thank you, good Patron."

Gillian turned her head and looked, seeing, high in a branch above them, one of the glowing Ur'theriems. His wings were folded behind him and the front piece of a glimmering gold loincloth fell between his gigantic legs. He regarded her thoughtfully, and suddenly Gillian recognized his face.

Xaqriel!

He addressed Sir Douglas. "This Disciple has forgotten the dangers that lurk about, as well as her station. Carelessness is as dangerous to her well-being as the fear of self-fulfillment. Make certain she is corrected for both."

"Yes, certainly," Sir Douglas answered. He bowed his head to Xaqriel and then told the guard holding Gillian to carry her to the roots of the tree she had headed for.

The guard delivered her to the spot he had indicated, and set her on her feet as the other men came over. Sir Douglas drew out his crop again and snatched Gillian about the waist. He was stronger than she thought, and although she struggled to wrest herself from his hold, he sat down in the grass and pulled her over his lap. She tried to crawl off his thighs, but one of the others knelt and pinned her hands in front of her, while another held to her ankles. The crop struck her bare behind, scoring her flesh with stinging heat. She had hardly gasped when it came down again. He whipped her again and again, so that her buttocks soon felt swollen by the smarting pain. The implacable look on the face of the guard holding her wrists only added to her humiliation, and she begged Sir Douglas to stop.

The crop paused, and Sir Douglas's tone was hard with emotion. "You would speak unbidden? Gillian, your attitude needs much correction! I see now there is no alternative but to ensure you are treated with only the firmest hand. I will take full enjoyment in correcting your every single flaw, no matter how long it takes!"

He tossed the crop to the grass and spanked her already sore buttocks with a strong hand. Gillian squirmed over his lap and her wails ascended into the night air. Though she wept, the guard holding her arms did not take his eyes from her, as if his spectatorship was part of the chastisement.

At last, Sir Douglas stayed his hand. Gillian's buttocks surged with fire as he nodded to the guards. They let go of her limbs now, but Gillian was terrified to move without Sir Douglas's command.

He lifted the crop again and with the end, spread her thighs. With his fingers he patted her pussy lips, and to her chagrin, her vulva swelled with life. His forefinger delved into her sex, rousing her desire full force. And when the crop struck her backside again, her clit throbbed.

"Crawl onto the grass and remain on your hands and knees," he ordered.

Gillian did not question. She did just as he instructed, lowering her face before the trunk of the tree. She heard him rise and hoped he was going to take her back to the household now, away from the eyes of the others.

Instead, he lifted the length of her hair and pulled her about to face him. His pants were unbuttoned, and now he lowered them. With his free hand, he massaged the head of his cock.

Two guards came over, and even though she could not see their faces well, she felt the lust in their eyes.

"Fuck me with your mouth," Sir Douglas commanded, releasing her hair, "but do not lift your hands."

She crawled before him and took his cock into her mouth. As she began to pleasure it, she felt hands upon her backside and whimpered as her nether lips were spread and fingers pinched the head of her clit. It pulsed wildly and a few moments later, a cock, narrow but long, entered her pussy.

The guard screwed her madly as she sucked Sir Douglas, and when her own pleasure began to build, her chaperon warned her to keep her thoughts on her work. She sucked to the root of his cock, not dallying in her efforts until his semen filled her mouth. When Sir Douglas had composed himself, he stepped aside and another guard took his place. This man's shaft was velvet iron, his passion so eager that he rocked her face as she sucked. Soon his cum also burst down her throat.

As he withdrew, she felt the climax of the one screwing her, and the jolt of it whipped her hungry passion into a frenzy. When he stepped away, the last one thrilled her pussy anew, fucking her so hard her breasts slapped against one another.

Xaqriel's light hovered down from the trees. He knelt before her and pulled aside the golden cloth of his loincloth. Tilting her chin up, he parted her lips with his thumbs. His huge cock swelled in her mouth. Deeply he fucked her mouth while the guard continued to fuck her needy pussy. The guard strummed her clit as he worked, soon bringing her to a tormented orgasm. After his own climax, he slapped her sore backside and withdrew from her drenched orifice.

She was still shuddering with ecstasy as Xaqriel's cock plummeted into her mouth and a rush of fluid, like honey and spice, jetted down her throat. Sir Douglas came about to her backside again. With his hand he spanked her, but now her cries were silenced by the great organ still pumping into her mouth.

When at length Xaqriel pulled out, he grabbed her beneath the arms and pulled her to her feet. Using his right arm, he inclined her back, and with the fingers of his left hand he pinched her clit. It pounded between the mighty fingers and Gillian hardly knew she was moaning until one of the guards stooped and kissed her mouth.

Xaqriel rearoused her passion until she was at the threshold of another orgasm. Then he drew his touch away, leaving her draped in his arm and undulating wantonly. She heard him speak something to Sir Douglas, and then he stood her up straight again. He turned her about by the waist and placed her palms against the tree trunk.

The crop struck her buttocks again. She whimpered, not understanding how they could punish her again so soon after enjoying her. Xaqriel came to stand at her side, gazing into her face. Gently, he wiped the fresh tear that rolled down her chin.

Gillian wailed under the strikes of the merciless crop, and Xaqriel, smiling, spread her legs wide and began to massage her dripping sex.

When finally the crop stopped, he spoke into her ear, "Domination and pleasure—these are your soul's calling, Gillian. Hopefully, this demonstration will help you to see things clearly now, and it will help right the damage wrought by the ordinary world that nurtured your fear of these needs."

She was crying so hard she could see nothing but her hands pressed against the bark. But she wanted to melt in the heat of his illumination, to hide a little longer from the truths he spoke. But it was not to be, and she knew it, for she had hid all her life and that time was gone.

His wings raised and she heard a muffled flood upon the air. When she dared to turn her face the only thing she could see of him was a dusky delineation flitting over the canopies of the oaks.

"It's late. Time this one was to bed," Sir Douglas said. He took her hand and led her back to the house, and when she had not the will to obey his command and stop her crying, the stinging crop compelled otherwise.

5

The first rays of daylight appeared over the horizon as Bruce made the walk back from the pavilion grounds to the guards' compound behind the prison. All the night men were making their way to their homes, laughing and talking as they walked by. He was in need of a cigarette, if just to forget something he had seen that night—or thought he had seen. A Disciple, in the company of a prisoner; she'd looked so much like Gillian that he'd gawked at them for some time. Probably nothing more than an illusion caused by the starlight. Yet it had haunted him the rest of his shift and he looked forward to sleeping off the memory.

William shuffled by and offered a cigarette. Bruce readily accepted, as he was on his last pack. But he wasn't worried; Madam had assured the guards that the next shipment for the commodities store would be arriving the next morning. The Saphorians, angels of light and sound, who recruited Earthling guards, were always reliable in their deliveries. Besides, whenever he was in dire need of anything—or at least really wanted anything—fate in Nemi had a strange knack for making the items show up, literally at his door, before he ever got bent out of shape over it. Like the television and the DVD player with all his favorites that had arrived days before. He did not even care that the television had no cord or there was no outlet for it or anything else in his residence. Heck, it was enough that he could tune in to his favorite shows and movies any time he wanted. He was not one to question gifts.

Everything Bruce purchased with his credits in Nemi just simply worked: his razor, the little fridge, the reading lamp by his bed. He knew that not every guard had these things; at least not those who had come to Nemi before electricity had been invented on Earth. Those men did not seem to need those things. Their chalets were furnished with the comforts and luxuries to which they had been accustomed before arriving.

"Someone's waiting for you," William commented. Bruce followed his eyes to the front of his chalet. It was Gina and Rose, and they waved gleefully when they saw him. A quick smile came to his mouth, and William did not seem to notice the brittleness of it.

He clapped Bruce's shoulder, and telling him to have fun, went on his way.

Bruce grunted wearily. Gina and Rose were the last living souls he wanted to see at this moment.

What the hell do they want at this hour?

He had first met the two Leather Wives on the prison grounds one day shortly after he had come to Nemi. They had arrived to deliver a number of Disciples for their work duties and afterward just hung around. They showed a great interest in the conversation Bruce struck up. Not that talking was what he really wanted to be doing with them at that time. They were cute— well, Rose was cute, with her freckles and her big knockers. Gina was outright gorgeous. Wide lips, fine Italian features, a lingerie model's figure. Before meeting them, he had intended to pursue one of the delicious Disciples at the first chance available. But all his adult life he had been attracted to Italians, and Gina just simply turned every right knob.

Just talking to her that day had given him a boner. He had rambled, trying to engage them as long as possible, unable to think of anything but her pouting lips and the long, shapely leg that peeped through the slit of her black skirt.

In the course of the conversation, the two women had unexpectedly confirmed his deepest hope. "We do everything together!"

So he'd invited them to his chalet that night. They had arrived with a bottle of wine and a case of fine cigars. He knew Leather Wives were not supposed to have access to the commodities store without Madam's express permission. But he would not tell. How they gushed over the furnishings of his room, which was filled with appliances and gadgets they had never seen before or imagined. It was the first time either had even tasted a cold bottle of beer. The young women had coaxed him into telling them everything about his culture. And so, over dinner he indoctrinated them in the computerized, technical twenty-first century.

But they'd been particularly fascinated by credit cards, malls, and the rights of women in the society he had left behind.

Bruce had finally made some strides in other directions when he offered to read their palms. They giggled as he'd sat between them on the sofa, stroking their palms in turn and telling the name of each line. As he revealed what he saw in their respective palms, he had leaned in close to the women, and held their fascinated gaze while he spoke. Neither of them flinched or backed away, and soon enough he swiped a kiss from each. A little while later, they'd asked to use his bathroom and returned in their birthday suits.

It had been a very satisfying night. The two returned from time to time over the following weeks, always providing sex easily. Gina, he was always anxious to see. He told himself that it was better to have a Leather Wife than a Disciple, as these women did not sleep with guards except out of pure choice. His chest ballooned every morning that he could tell the other guards that Gina had come knocking on his door the night before.

But as he became familiar with the girls, he grew to feel used at times for more than sex or company. Gina did not hesitate to ask for this or that from his belongings, and in time she ended up carrying away so much from his place that the compound commander warned him that Madam was beginning to take notice of the growing hoard of gifts collecting in Gina's room at the household. Not seemly, the proprietress claimed, for a Leather Wife to accumulate so many knickknacks and baubles without officially courting a man.

Gina had revealed to him that she was growing discontented in Madam's household and with her life in general. She'd said the other Leather Wives were jealous of her control over certain Disciples, and the trustees showed their disrespect at every turn. She was often angry with Rose, too, though on this subject she was vague. But she was angrier with Madam, for questioning her disciplinary actions, and the guards, whom she complained spoke too familiarly.

The more often Gina visited, the more quickly she demonstrated her anger and the more violently. As she recalled the latest details of her life, she often took her wrath out on Bruce's furniture, throwing cushions, overturning chairs, once even throwing a glass against the wall. She was also turning into a slob. During her last visit, Bruce asked her to put a candy wrapper she tossed on the floor into the trash. Instead, she retorted coldly that he must be looking for a Disciple instead of an equal.

He had apologized and later, when they had sex, he'd attempted to be more tender than ever. He'd asked her about her own experiences and life while on Earth, and showed his interest in everything she revealed. But there, too, she seemed more concerned in gossip or venting. When she left, she'd asked for a pack of cigarettes and the silver candleholder he had recently obtained at the store. He gave her both and received not a word of thanks in exchange.

Rose had showed up the following dawn, just as he was about to go to bed. She'd been furious, accusing him of coming between her and her friendship with Gina. When he told her he had no idea what she was talking about, she threw herself at him, demanding he make love to her like a male Disciple. He'd kissed the crown of her head and laughed. He had not really been laughing at her, but at the presumption that he could ever pretend to be submissive. Rose shook with rage and threw off his comforting arms. Before leaving, she'd claimed that Gina had said his was the sorriest cock she had ever had.

Now, days after that incident, the two of them were smiling like innocent kittens as Bruce stepped under the overhang of the chalet.

"Hello, Bruce," purred Rose.

"Are you well?" Gina asked.

He was still entranced by her symmetrical beauty, those full lips that seemed incomplete without something to fill them. And Rose was dressed in simple leather pants and a white spaghetti-strap shirt, cut low so her massive cleavage almost swelled out. With the curls of her auburn hair bouncing on her shoulders and her blue eyes flashing, he thought she had never looked prettier.

He unlocked the door hesitantly. "I'm pretty tired, ladies. Why don't you come back later today?"

They made unhappy sounds. "Oh, but we came to apologize," Rose said. "Let us come in and make up for the rude way we treated you before."

He regarded her eyes thoughtfully. "Well . . ."

"Please," Gina said huskily and stroked his arm. She gazed at him innocuously, her dark, sensuous eyes flashing. "I have missed you and our talks."

Talks. Well, that was an odd way to put it. She had talked and he had listened. At least Rose had found his jokes funny and listened when he revealed personal information about himself. Gina had only stared off into space.

"Can't you even offer us a beer?" Rose asked.

"Oh, okay." He ogled her heaving cleavage and sighed. "But I want some sleep soon."

"You've never thrown us out before," Gina crooned and settled the weight of her perfect breasts into his arm.

He smiled, and the sense of being used seemed only a trifling thing, given her tempting pout.

"Who said I was going to throw you out?"

The pout turned into a leisurely smile. He unlocked the door and followed them inside.

Two beers and a steak later, Bruce joined the girls in his bedroom. They had been whispering in there for some time, chomping on a box of fine chocolates and listening to the radio by his bed. Alternative rock was playing. As he entered, they sat up and asked who the group was.

He undressed to his boxer shorts and considered just letting them have the bed to themselves while he took the sofa. He still was not completely convinced of their regret; they seemed to have forgotten an apology as soon as they had walked into the chalet. Besides, he was used to crashing on his couch back on Earth. Then again, on Earth there had never been two women waiting for him in the bedroom.

They were both fully undressed, and he saw their clothes had been tossed haphazardly throughout the room. Even though they were messy, he could not help but be aroused as they looked at him, their tits bouncing, their hair falling untamed over their shoulders. Bruce sighed. He wanted sleep even more than their bodies right now. If they slept in his bed, he might never be able to reclaim it without creating bad feelings between the three of them. Yet, he suspected that if he complained, they might never be back.

He was still trying to decide on the sleeping arrangements when Gina crossed her legs. He forgot everything then except getting between those long, silken curves. As he stepped toward the bed, he realized he was rubbing his cock in his hand. Both girls' eyes widened and Rose raised her breasts with her hands and licked her huge areolas. He sunk on his knees to the mattress and crawled up between them.

He kissed Gina and then Rose, and grappling her huge tits in his palms, nibbled the voluminous flesh. Gina lay on her side and watched as he lowered Rose down into the mattress and drew her legs apart. She was soaking wet to his fingertips and as his cock entered her pussy, he sucked first on one jiggling breast, then the other. He pounded into her, savoring her moans as much as the jostling flesh before his eyes. She climaxed with a wail and a shudder, and pulling out, he moved over to Gina.

She smiled and touched his face, kissed the dark stubble on his face.

"You know what she said wasn't true, don't you?"

"You mean that comment about my sorry dick?"

"Uh-huh," Gina whispered and let him suckle her hardened nipples. "You know how to work that tool better than most."

Gina's hips swayed beneath his caressing hand and her thighs parted easily. Her sex singed his hand, her juices flowed. He looked over to Rose, blew her a kiss, and, lowering himself over Gina, kissed her mouth.

"Let me suck you off," she whispered.

"All right." He straddled her chest carefully and lowered his cock to her dusky lips. She brought her hands between his legs and grabbed it, clenching the base, and took the head into her mouth.

It was almost heaven to him, this tight, tight sensation. She sucked him eagerly and his pelvis moved back and forth to meet her mouth.

But as he looked upon Gina's half-closed eyes, he saw suddenly a face chiseled of coldest marble. She wanted him now for this and for whatever else in the future, he could only guess. The sensation of her drawing mouth dwindled until it was just a mild stimulus. He was hard, but not as he had been. And though she worked to get him off, he knew then he would never again come in her mouth.

"Let me at that pussy again," he murmured and slipped down again between her legs. He rubbed his cock until it was hard as stone again, and then drove into her. Draping himself over her, he fucked her more roughly than he ever had. His thoughts, however, were different this time; he did not see her shapely legs and perfect face. He had no thought but of fucking the orifice presented. Gone was that pride he had known when telling other men that he had screwed the loveliest Leather Wife in Nemi. Only this mindless physical sensation of pounding in her slit.

Just before he came, he withdrew and spewed his cum over her pubic hair and stomach. When the shudder of his orgasm passed, he saw the disappointment creased on her face.

"Indeed, you must be very tired," she said and pried her pussy lips apart and massaged her clit between two fingers. "Want to watch me get off?"

The vision of her yawning crimson sex faded, and all Bruce could see was that which had disturbed him earlier. The face glancing at him from the meadow—a Disciple, reminiscent of Gillian. God, how often he had fantasized of ravishing her innocent mouth and ripping off her ugly waitress uniform. She had been the first female he had met who had actually seemed interested in knowing him for who he was. How urgently he'd wanted to claim her, to hold onto her as he'd held no other woman.

The offer from the Saphorian, Sethlucius, had whacked his head. During the ensuing weeks, he convinced himself it had been all for the best, that the naive blonde Gillian could never have compared to the stunning Gina.

Gina looked up at him now through sleepy lids, bunched her breasts together, and pinched the nipples seductively. But he was not interested, did not know if he ever would be again. He got off the bed and started to dress.

Her voice was husky—another time it would have entranced him, lured him back to her side, "Where are you going?"

He did not answer. He left them to the bed and lay down on the sofa, with the celestial transmission of a cop drama turned up loud enough to drown out any sound from the bedroom.

Bruce awoke late the next morning to find Rose nibbling on his ear.

He groaned as his eyes opened to the sight of her straddling his waist. Her breasts descended to his lips. He had never been one to wake up cheerful, especially if he did not get at least five or six solid hours of sleep. But the primal urge of his loins was stronger this morning than the customary surliness.

He grasped the fleshy orbs and sucked on them until the nipples were small gems in his mouth. Rose maneuvered her hips down so she could scoop his stiff cock out from his boxers, guided it into her pussy and started to ride.

He savored his pleasure until she climaxed, then held to her hips and worked her hard up and down. He came fast, a mechanical, bodily response. But when he was thinking clearly again, he was glad it had been her who had awakened him this way instead of Gina.

"Nice," he yawned, stretching his arms and legs while she bobbed idly over his dwindling hard-on.

"Good morning," she smiled brightly. "Was it really nice?"

"Of course."

"Nice enough that you would let Madam know?"

He frowned. "Well, yes. But why would you want me to?" He smiled decadently. "Turns you on to know you've been bragged about? That's cute."

She shook her head and he caught the shadow of a purse at her lips. "She wants to send me home—Gina, too."

A nameless and unpleasant wariness crept over Bruce's skin. "Why?"

Rose shrugged and this time her lips pursed truly, bitterly. "Madam doesn't think we are good enough." She sighed and added, "She said we are lazy, selfish. Can you believe that? Told me I have forgotten what I'm here for—as if anyone could forever care about those nasty prisoners. Then she got all worked up one day because Gina hit a girl, a Disciple. But the girl deserved it. She wouldn't hand something over that Gina asked for. Those Disciples are not supposed to hoard, you know."

"Well, what did the girl hoard? A guy?"

"No. Some stupid trinket box she had asked the Ur'theriems to bring from her home on Earth. Claimed she'd had it since she was a little girl. But she has no need of such things. Gina liked it, and asked for it when the girl was under her keep. The girl refused and Gina slapped her. But the selfish sub deserved it!"

Bruce shook his head, appalled. "No. I would say, how dare Gina. She is supposed to be a disciplinarian, not an extortionist."

Rose looked shocked. "That is very unfair to say, Bruce."

Bruce rubbed her thigh. "Get up." She did so, but with the most devastated of looks. As he stood up, she sighed irritably.

"Well, can't you speak up for us? Madam's made arrangements to have the Ur'theriems take us back to our respective times in two days."

He threw Rose an exasperated glance as she went on, "Not

even for me? Why should I go back, and to where they found me—to when they found me?"

Bruce shrugged, tired of the conversation. "You need to ask yourself if there's some truth in what Madam says. Why does she claim you're selfish? Fix whatever problems that made her come to that conclusion, and maybe she'll change her mind."

Rose crossed her arms in a sulky way. "She says a lot. Mainly, I think, she knows I hate those Disciples, have for a long time. Clingy, needy females, you know. I prefer the company of strong women and mindless males." She said the last with a crooked smile, but Bruce knew she was not altogether joking.

"And you're not needy with Gina? And she doesn't cling to everything she can grasp?"

She regarded him quietly. "That's a stupid thing to say."

"Mindless male, you remember."

Rose threw her hands down. "Oh, come on! You've had some fun with us, haven't you? You don't really want to see us sent away, do you?"

He rubbed his hands through his short, dark hair. "Hey. You prefer to associate with what you call strong women? Then be one. You don't need a man's aid, then, if you are. And Gina, too. Why do you have to use me like this? Because you really do think of me as weak? Guess a strong man would just turn you over his knee and teach you to get your act together."

Rose shivered then, in anger so potent her face turned livid. "Oh, shut up!"

She looked across the room then and her eyes softened a little. Turning, Bruce saw Gina standing in the doorway to the bedroom. She was already dressed and holding Rose's clothing.

"We were wrong, Rose. Bruce has been around these other men too long. He's starting to think all women should be subservient, half-naked Disciples."

She walked in and handed Rose her garments. As Rose dressed,

Bruce took his last pack of cigs from the coffee table and packed it across his palm. He noticed Gina must have found his comb, for her hair was brushed out, glossy dark locks tumbling down over her shoulder blades. Her lively complexion had paled, though, and her eyes sparkled with cold indignity.

"You would believe all these fabrications on Madam's part, Bruce?"

"Fabrications? I hardly think Madam would lie."

"So, you believe them. And yet, you had sex with us."

"Why not? Evidently, I mean nothing to either of you but what I can offer. A tumble in the sheets, a little departure from routine, gifts, and free meals—an ear to listen while you bitch about the duties you resent, the proprietress who expects you to act with some manners, some civility. You slept with me, Gina, but I was just a cock to you, nothing more."

"You just can't appreciate a woman with self-will and intelligence!"

"Oh, I know you are intelligent," he said, opening the pack and lighting up. He regarded the cool smile, the lack of warmth on her face. "You certainly have the self-will. But you want and want and never think to give back. The Disciples have the inner strength to yield to their carnal needs. They give back, too, and that's what you resent."

Her mouth hardened, and despite her incomparable beauty, he never wanted to kiss her again.

"Come on," she said to Rose. "Don't expect us back, Bruce."

Rose pulled on her boots and walked with Gina out the door. They did not look back as they left and slammed the door so hard it jarred. He did not care anymore and hummed as he tore the sheets off his bed. He threw them into the hamper of dirty clothes and then flopped down on the mattress.

He drifted quickly off, into the best sleep he'd enjoyed since meeting Gina. Hot, erotic visions of the Disciple he'd seen earlier filled his dreams. Her face and body was poignantly reminiscent of Gillian; and she was his disciple—naked except for a collar that declared his ownership. But she adored him and took pleasure in his masterly commands of her own pure and passionate accord.

6

Gillian awoke late in the morning and guessed it was close to noon by the position of the sun outside the window. Her roommates were gone, but she found a fresh dress on a stool next to her bed. It was pink and just as short as the first one. Her slippers were sitting under the stool, with a pair of innocent white anklets. A pair of white cotton panties lay across these.

She bathed quickly and returned to dress. She had just slipped on her shoes when the door opened.

It was Madam, dressed in a long, rose-dyed tunic that was pinned over one shoulder with a cameo brooch. She looked radiant, her hair piled in ringlets. What little makeup she wore looked very natural. But there was a hard air to her this morning, and Gillian wondered if Sir Douglas had informed her of what had happened during the night.

Madam stood by Gillian's bed silently as she put on the shoes. But once she was finished, said, "Bring me a brush from the bathroom, Gillian, and hairbands and ribbons."

Gillian obeyed and when she returned Madam instructed

her to sit on the corner of the bed. She brushed Gillian's hair, swiftly and efficiently. Parting her hair, she banded the two lengths at either side of her head and decorated them with the ribbons.

"You will be eating breakfast outside this morning," Madam announced. "This is not our usual custom, Gillian, but I have been informed of your behavior last night. I know Sir Douglas has already dealt with your unseemly flight, but I want to be sure you remember that the lack of decorum you displayed while serving the prisoners will not be condoned."

Gillian's mouth flew open and a single sound of protest froze. Perhaps Madam only intended to segregate her from the others for a while. That she could handle easily enough.

She looked at Gillian thoughtfully before sending her out of the room. The downstairs was alive with activity this morning; prisoners were coming back and forth, apparently endeavoring to clean the household. Some of these were actually working; others were simply dictating jobs to Disciples. The guard she had seen the day before with his gagged Disciple opened the front door for them. Alexandra was scrubbing one end of the porch when they stepped out, while a prisoner supervised her progress from the swing. A slender switch lay across his lap. She did not look up as Gillian and Madam passed by, and Gillian wondered if her stay on the Rapture Pillar had worked to subdue her willfulness.

Two guards paced the grass as Gillian followed Madam down the steps into the yard. One of these was Sir Peter, and his bold gaze sent a stab of humiliated desire through Gillian's thighs. She flinched and blushed as Madam snatched her hand and led her on to the western side of the house.

A box-tiered garden hugged the siding here, and one prisoner worked to weed the flowers, while a second polished the wood plank of a swing hanging from the nearest oak. Madam said nothing to these men. Instead she led Gillian to a heavy metal pole, about three and a half feet tall, which stood between the tree and the garden. A woman waited here, and Gillian knew at once she must be one of the Leather Wives. Her age seemed indeterminate to Gillian, though she dressed much like a college girl in lowslung jeans and a white peasant blouse, a pair of ankle-length high-heeled boots, and a small ruby piercing her left nostril. Her makeup was moderately Goth. Only the tight rolled braid of her brown hair atop her head and the crop tied by a cord about her thigh lent her a more mature look. She smiled at Madam as they approached. Gillian saw she held a glass container, capped at the short-necked mouth with a large rubber nipple that had been molded into the shape of a phallus.

Atop the pole an upright U had been bolted. A rubber-encased bolt was inserted low on the inside of both arms. The end of a wide leather strap had been buttonholed over one of these, and there was another button slit cut into the loose-hanging end. Madam wedged the bottle between the bolts so that the nipple was aimed at Gillian.

Madam nodded as she regarded first the pole, and next, Gillian.

"Looks like they brought it down to the proper height, Camille."

"Sir Peter is talented at estimating height," the Leather Wife replied.

"Gillian, kneel," ordered Madam. Before Gillian could think, Madam pressed her down by the shoulders in front of the pole and lifted her chin. "This is your breakfast, with royal jelly and other nutrients. You will drink every last drop, if you do not wish to find yourself kneeling here again for your next meal."

Gillian was horrified. "But Madam, please let me—"

"No. You may not speak. Now take that nipple into your mouth."

Gillian swallowed and hesitantly complied. The nipple was as big as a real cock and stuffed her mouth entirely. The Leather

Wife drew the strap about the back of her head and buttoned it around the free bolt. Gillian's face flushed in humiliation.

Madam eyed her sternly. "Nurse it, Gillian!"

She did so and discovered at once how very tiny the opening for the liquid to pass was. She had to struggle just to get the first drop out. Although the drink did not taste bad, it did not taste good, either: a thick milky concoction with a flat flavor. As Gillian worked for the next drops, Madam pulled the hem of Gillian's dress up and peeled down her panties to her knees so that her bottom was exposed. Gillian closed her eyes and flinched in anticipation of a spanking.

"You will hold this hem up while you are here," Madam said, "and if you are caught with it down, you will be whipped until you are scarlet."

Gillian made a penitent sound. Already her lips were tired from the effort to nurse the phallus. From the corner of her eye, she watched as the two women walked over to the shadow of the oak. They spoke quietly to one another, and Gillian was close to tears, wondering desperately if she could ever live down this present embarrassment. It had not been willfulness that had led her to disobey Sir Douglas, so much as fear.

What will they do if I ever deliberately defy them?

The prisoner at the swing rose to his feet and stretched. When he turned in her direction Gillian closed her eyes.

She heard someone advance quickly, and before her next breath was drawn, a paddle swooped down across her backside.

Gillian heard Madam warn, "Keep your eyes open! Don't you think for a moment you are allowed modesty!"

Gillian's eyes opened and Madam spanked her several more times. It took all her effort to keep the hem up as Madam walked away, and to her added chagrin, the prisoner at the swing threw her a wink.

Although the women stepped out of her line of vision, she

could hear their conversation and listened, if only to take her mind somewhat from her humiliating punishment.

"Sir Peter came to me with a request from the Warden's office," she heard the Leather Wife say. "Prisoner Clive has put in a request for this girl."

"He's not ready," Madam said. "The guards gave me a full report. Apparently, he shied from using a firm hand at all with her."

"Ah. At least, he has demonstrated much improvement."

"Yes. I believe it won't be long before he throws off his inhibitions completely. It's easier to coax manly behavior when the prisoner is young."

"And to this end he won't be given custodian privileges for awhile?"

"Oh, no. A reprieve now would only negate the improvements. To be lenient would end up making him incorrigible."

Gillian was intrigued by this talk, wondering what flaw or flaws Clive had that needed rehabilitating. She hoped they would talk longer and answer her curiosity, but Madam said she had other things to attend to. When she was gone, the Leather Wife strolled by Gillian and rapped the surface of the bottle with her fingernails.

"Drink!"

Gillian cringed but worked harder to suckle, and when the Leather Wife was satisfied with her effort she joined the prisoner who had been working on the swing.

"Very good, Prisoner Mitchell. Now, I want you to bring me a divan and a flask of that oil we keep for sunbathing."

"Yes, Domme Camille." He ran off quickly. When he returned, he was carrying a divan of lightweight wood and a dark, corked bottle. He set the divan in the full sunlight as she directed, then started picking up the tools and cloth and jar of wax from the ground. Domme Camille told him to return everything to the house and find Sir Hugh for instructions.

Gillian paused in nursing a moment to relieve her tired mouth, and as she did, Domme Camille removed her crop and set this on the ground. She next stripped out of her clothes, down to a blue bikini beneath. Lying down in the divan, she called to the other prisoner.

"Prisoner Jay!"

He turned at once, his mahogany brow beaded with sweat. But as she raised the bottle, Gillian noted the concealed smile as he came and knelt beside her. Domme Camille turned over and unhooked the back of her bikini top.

"Do a better job today, Jay."

"Yes, Mistress."

He poured some oil from the flask into his palms. This he massaged into her back and arms and then down thoroughly over her midriff and legs.

"Better, yes," she murmured. "I'll call you when you're needed again."

"Yes, Mistress," he said pliantly. But he was staring at the length of her, tense, as if it was all he could do to summon the will to turn away. When at last he returned to his work, his efforts were more industrious than even before.

While Domme Camille sunbathed, she peered up from time to time to observe them.

Except for the sounds of Jay's gardening and the birds fluttering in the trees, all was very quiet. Gillian grew drowsy from the sun that beat down over her skin and had to catch herself from slowing down on the nipple.

After a time, however, she heard Domme Camille jump up from the divan. Taking up her crop, she stepped over to Gillian and whipped her soundly. Gillian's ass throbbed and she whimpered miserably behind the nipple. She was close to tears again as Domme Camille lay down on her back and instructed Prisoner Jay to oil up her front side.

A little while later, a shout from behind the great oak broke the quiet. Gillian could see from the right of her vision three prisoners emerge, shackled by their ankles one to the other. Two guards pressed them forward from behind. One of these pointed his spear toward the prisoners and ordered them to kneel on the grass.

"Domme Camille," he reported, "your well diggers were arguing."

She sat up at once, her mouth hardening. She glared at the three kneeling men, who were all now bowing their heads humbly.

"How dare you," she seethed, rising to her feet. "I trusted each of you!" She stepped about them slowly, her anger growing with each breath. "Would you prefer I just send you back to dwell with the selectively dominant males?"

They shook their heads as one. The middle prisoner wrung his hands and looked at her pleadingly.

"Mistress, please, not that! It was a foolish mistake!"

She slapped him so hard Gillian flinched.

"You will not address me without permission, Henry! If you three keep acting as if you are entitled to choose your behavior, then you shall be returned to the fold of the alpha males."

The prisoners nodded their heads silently.

"Ah, then, I shall give you one more chance. But never again will you act like dominant men, is this understood?"

They nodded a second time, with more enthusiasm, and she said, "Now stand and pull those pants down to your ankles."

As the men set to obey, Domme Camille gave Jay a hard look that made him turn his attention back to his work. She glanced at Gillian and said to one of the guards, "Make sure that one is finishing her meal, Sir Victor."

The guard who had addressed Domme Camille walked to Gillian's side. Terrified, she slurped so hard now on the nipple that her swallows produced a very undignified sound. He inspected the bottle and patted her head, and stepping behind her, stroked her between the legs, exploring the heat of her vagina.

He parted her thighs gently and touched her clit, arousing it with his fingertip. He smacked her quivering cheeks as she held up the hem of her dress, then walked away, leaving her frustrated.

"She's almost finished."

"Good," Domme Camille answered. But her attention was leveled on the prisoners, who now stood naked below the waist. Gillian blushed to see their endowments. The one at the end of the line nearest her had a slight erection and the faces of all three were scarlet.

The Leather Wife took her crop again and walked behind them. "Bend over and grasp your ankles!"

To Gillian's amazement, the three prisoners complied quickly. Domme Camille strode up close to the first one in line and raised her crop. She brought it down smartly and continued to whip his buttocks until he was clenching his lips together to suppress his cries. When she finished, the man's backside was glowing with reddish stripes. He remained bowed humbly as Camille moved on to the next in line. She wielded the crop with the same merciless hand. And when this one broke his silence with a grunt, her blows reined down furiously.

She paused and spoke to him coolly, "I will not tolerate rudeness, Craig. You shall sleep cuffed on the floor tonight."

"Yes, Mistress!" Gillian saw that his cock was fully aroused. Domme Camille grinned and stroked his balls lightly so that his pelvis braced.

"Good, Craig, very good. Now stand and demonstrate your willingness by stroking your cock until you come."

His eyes widened. "But Domme Camille!"

Again she flailed him harshly and he let out a muffled shriek.

"Remain bowed, then, and bring yourself to climax."

The guards were looking at the ground and Gillian could see they were uncomfortable with the situation. Nevertheless, they did not move away.

Craig was breathing rapidly as he cinched his cock and began to masturbate. Domme Camille thrashed his backside while he stroked, only stopping when his cum splattered over the ground. He was panting, his face as abashed as his backside. The Leather Wife said nothing more to him and proceeded to the last prisoner. This one showed the willing compliance of the first. When his buttocks were well tanned, she reached around him and tugged on his cock until he had a lofty erection. By the contortions of his face, Gillian feared he would lose his jism, but Domme Camille removed her hand before it happened.

She turned to the guards and said, "Take them back, and if they show any further insolence, have them bound where all may observe."

"Now stand up," she barked at the prisoners. They did so, their backsides all branded red by her crop, and with their heads hanging, followed the guards back the way they had come.

Camille sighed heavily when they were gone and lay back down on the divan. "Jay, come here."

The prisoner came and sat down on the grass beside her. She stroked his hair as she spoke with him, so softly Gillian could not understand a word exchanged. Not that she was interested in prying on an intimate conversation. It was evident that Prisoner Jay truly cared about Domme Camille, and after a time, he kissed her cheek.

At last Gillian heard her say brightly, "Have my lemonade when I return?"

"Of course, my Domme," he answered. Camille patted his cheek, smiling, and rose from the divan.

She regarded Gillian's feeding bottle and declared, "Well, you are finished. Good girl." With a loud, final smack on Gillian's bare bottom, she unhooked the strap from her head.

"You may release the nipple now."

Gillian's dignity had never known such solace as when she let loose of the rubber phallus. But she remained on her knees with her dress pulled up while Camille dressed again and tied the cord for her crop about one thigh.

"Jay," she said, "you may rest a time."

He came and bowed at her feet and kissed the tops of her boots, whispering something Gillian did not catch. Whatever it was brought a fleeting smile to the Leather Wife's lips.

"Let go of the hem, Gillian, and pull up your panties," she said at last. "Madam has instructed that now you are to be taken to dedicate yourself to God Real."

7

Domme Camille led Gillian down a long path cut at the back side of Madam's property. There was a clearing in the lush woodland here. Willows curtained the edges of the place and tiny wildflowers freckled the deep blue-green grass. There was a circle imprinted in the center of the clearing, where the grass folded over itself and created a spiral. At each of the four quadrants of this circle stood an immense statue. They appeared to be angels, fashioned of a rock Gillian did not recognize. A long altar of gleaming solid gold was set in the middle of the circle.

"This is the Temple of Purity," Domme Camille explained as they walked in. "There is no holier place in all of Nemi. All of us—the Leather Wives, the Disciples, the guards—are welcome to use this sanctuary for prayer and meditation. You have been chosen by a recruiting Ur'theriem and approved by Madam and her advisors. As long as your heart is dedicated to the doctrine of pleasure, you are one of us. Nothing can disgrace your rank but your own repudiation."

Gillian heard footsteps cross the grass behind them. Turning, she saw a figure approaching, garbed in a pink, hooded robe, and at the figure's side were two women who wore nothing but silver headbands with sheer ivory veils shielding their faces. One of the women carried a scourge across her breast, the other a silver platter upon which was laid a loaf of honeycomb. The robed figure came to stand before the altar, and as the platter was set upon it, she took the scourge from the other woman. Gillian watched as the robed one raised her arms heavenward.

"Kneel, Gillian," said Domme Camille.

As she did so, the robed one turned toward her. She slid the hood down the back of her neck and contemplated Gillian. She was like no woman Gillian had ever seen before. Facets of amber glinted in her hazel eyes and her wide, thin lips were hued of palest green. In the bathing sunlight, Gillian could see that her skin consisted of iridescent, milky scales. Gillian blinked and then saw that her hands were scaled as well. Her long fingernails were thicker than a mortal woman's and naturally prismatic.

Gillian shivered and the robed one said, "I am Anev' ja Lis, Priestess of Pleasure, and daughter of the heavenly concubine, Sophia."

Gillian was speechless, appalled by her own ill-mannered staring, and searched the ground for something to look at as the woman spoke.

The voice caressed her with compassion, "And yes, as your feelings suspect, I am not human, nor mortal. My sire was my mother's captor, one of the races of the Dhjinn-E'noch. But there is nothing to fear, Gillian, I will not harm you."

As Gillian lifted her eyes as the priestess's lips turned up at the corners in what seemed a gentle smile. "You may always speak freely within this circle, Gillian. Tell me, are you ready to dedicate yourself? To pledge yourself entirely to the cause of pleasure and its twinned components—self-contentment and love?"

"Yes."

"Then speak your affirmation."

The priestess gestured with a hand toward the altar. The veiled attendants were standing at either side of it now, looking almost like statues for their unflinching poise and fair skin. Gillian glanced at Domme Camille, and taking a long breath, crawled to the altar. She blinked uncertainly.

"What . . . what should I say?"

Anev' ja Lis bent and kissed the crown of her head. "Whatever your heart speaks, my dear. And it does not have to be aloud."

Gillian turned to look at her for confirmation it was all right to keep her pledge silent, when she saw Xaqriel standing before the statue at the eastern quadrant. He was clothed in only a wide belt of deep brown with wide, gauzy strips of fabric made of the sheerest smoke, which hung between the fronts of his legs, so that his titanic endowments were visible. The wings he had used the night before were but dusky gossamer outlines.

It might as well have been a delusion for all I can see now.

His amber eyes seemed to penetrate her suddenly, to caress the bare flesh beneath her dress. Her cheeks smarted and she looked back to the altar and felt the priestess's hands on the nape of her neck. They were cool and dry and the touch pulled her thoughts back to the ritual.

"When you are ready, Gillian, clear your mind of everything but the desire of your heart."

Gillian nodded and closed her eyes. She breathed deeply for a few minutes, until all cares vanished but for the duty she had pledged herself. She saw it first as a spoken word: pleasure. The word repeated itself over and over in her mind until she heard herself voice it. As she continued to speak, the word evolved into a melody without beginning or end, a song without language. A horizon of rich colors flowed before her eyes. Something snatched her up and with her ascended its summits, then whisked her to green and soaring mountains and carried her over meadows of sylvan pinks. Into an ocean of browns she plummeted, and in turn she was uplifted by tender blues. Over a canvas of black did she spirit, and in the next moment, indigo stars birthed before her. Into them, she was absorbed.

Her breath quailed, and she looked up into the face of a great figure of radiant whites, shades of which she had never imagined. Its formless limbs twisted and bled, showering her in a deluge of fresh, fertile reds. These buoyed her soul so fast that her lungs opened again. She tingled from head to toe with delicious sensations and her entire body glowed in all the loving hues and shades of eternal love and endless passion.

She was blinded to mortality and she cared not. Out of the sensuous lights hovering nearby she heard a lush and symphonic voice say that she was ready . . .

"I dedicate myself to pleasure."

She was not sure she had spoken the words or simply embraced them. But beyond the engulfing sensations, she knew the priestess had thrice struck her shoulders with the scourge.

Something pitched within the ethereal womb. It expanded and grew before her spiritual eyes, fashioning itself from out of the primordial colors to form a towering phallus. Her sensations quickened, and she was drawn into it. She went happily, yearningly, eagerly, draping her soul over the head of the phallic shaft. She plunged over it, and its thunderous heartbeat pulsated through her.

A voice steeped in virility chased away all other considerations: "It is well then, my Gillian."

All suffused into shades of gold, and from this splendid sea, a man emerged. For a moment, she considered that it was Xaqriel, but no, this one was too perfectly human. His dark, seductive eyes bore into hers as he advanced.

"We are one flesh, you and I—one mind, one spirit, one bright and luminous ray of heaven."

His words rocked her with a surrendering, poignant ecstasy. She flew to him and felt her arms sweep about his neck. His solid fragrance was distinct, reminding her of a scene from a dream she had somehow forgotten. His hands went to her buttocks and he scooped her up. Her eager legs wrapped around his waist. The head of his cock pounded against the opening of her vagina and his mouth feasted on her throat. With a guttural moan, he seized her hips and brought her down, impaling her with exquisite pain. He bounced her heartily upon himself, grinding his pelvis to meet her bobbing hips. Up and down his hard, thick cock she rode, the head of it a blazing hammer against her wanton core. When she climaxed, the fire exploded through her and sent her soul soaring, and then sucked her back like oxygen, so that she was in his arms again.

She looked into his face, with her real eyes this time, and almost swooned for recognition of the familiar, provocative features.

From beyond the web of souls, she felt something touch her mouth. A voice beckoned. She did not want to respond, but then something defined of virility and dusky gossamer swooped down and tore her away.

"Home for now, Gillian."

She opened her eyes to find the priestess offering a bit of the honeycomb to her lips.

Her arms and sex still tingled from the man. Bereft, she wept.

"Oh, God, where is he?"

Anev' ja Lis kissed the tears away and announced, "Sister Gillian, eat now and be a part of everlasting consciousness and immortal femininity."

And as Gillian fed upon the sweet bee nectar, her soul was grounded again.

With the ritual finished, the women left Gillian alone in the circle so she might meditate. Xaqriel departed, too, not speaking a word before vanishing. It was a peaceful aloneness they had left her to. In the sweet fresh air, without fear of anyone of the household bursting upon her repose, it was the first time she truly had to relax since coming to Nemi. She sat cross-legged before the altar and gazed into her own thoughts for a long time, thinking over everything she had experienced since coming to Nemi.

For the first time, I am needed and wanted entirely just as I am.

It was a strange feeling to know this. Even after she had disobeyed the rules, they wanted her. Many of the prisoners made her uncomfortable, yet she was sure she would get used to their disapproval. She was beginning to admire the reliably stern Madam. The guards made her feel safe. Her roommates were all sweet girls. She saw that, together, Leather Wives and Disciples were the balancing forces of Nemi. She continued to wonder about the elusive Ur'theriems, mainly why they cared so much about Earth and the fate of its inhabitants. But there were other questions as well.

What exactly were Ur'theriems? That handsome Xaqriel, was he one of them? Were they truly angels, or incubi, or something else altogether?

"Demons of spirit."

The unexpected words startled her. She spun on the grass toward the speaker and saw a figure standing in the shadowed clearing between the spiral and the woods. Naked and as towering as Xaqriel, his entire body was covered by skin of stone-gray scales. His eyes had the look of a human's except that his irises were yellow. A mane of pewter-colored hair fell wildly about his shoulders. His mouth was at once cruel and exotic, and when he stepped to the very edge of the circle, every hair on Gillian's body stood on end.

Somehow she managed to rise and speak. "Who are you?"

"Come out here where the shade is kinder, so that I may see you clearly," he answered.

Gillian could not have moved if she had wanted to. He

paced the boundary of the spiral, his features revealing a myriad of emotions she could not decipher. When he looked up again, his eyes had changed to a soft shade of olive. Almost seductive they were now, and with them, he canvassed her from head to toe. His right hand touched his great manhood. It was russet-colored and had a fat spade-shaped head. He stroked it slowly, from the heavy balls to the head and down to the root again, compelling it into an upward-arching snake in his palm.

Gillian looked all over for signs of the others, but there was none. She tried to tell herself there was nothing to be afraid of; this was surely only one of Xaqriel's brother angels.

His lips formed a circle and he blew toward her. A blast of heat wafted through the boundaries and licked her flesh. Her senses were drugged with an overpowering lust.

"Come to me, little one!"

Light, feminine voices sounded from the woods, snapping her hypnotized mind back to consciousness. She watched as he cocked his head toward the sound and narrowed his eyes. As the voices drew closer, his scales altered to a mottled tint of indigo, and then into an ill orange hue. The air grew hotter until suddenly his legs and torso burst into flame. All of him above the waist diminished to a swirling semblance of flesh. As Gillian faltered back, gasping, she watched his face spin and blacken, and before the next inhalation of her breath, the creature of flame diminished into an indigo spark no bigger than her fist and rocketed into the cloud-wisped sky.

Gillian was relieved to see Domme Camille and one of the priestess's attendants walking toward the circle. She ran to them and told them what had happened.

Domme Camille's brow furrowed and she and the attendant both searched the sky.

The attendant murmured a single word: "Dhjinn-E'noch."

The Leather Wife smiled wryly at Gillian. "You were wise to stay in the circle, for his kind cannot pass through it. But you must take care now to never venture alone out-of-doors. Now that he has laid eyes upon you this close, he may come looking for you. We must report this to Madam."

Gillian sighed. She felt as if she should miss the enlightening privacy the moments alone had allowed. And yet, such moments were not to be had often, she realized, and her instincts sensed the day still offered ripe and exciting prospects.

"Now, be silent again, dear Gillian," Camille told her firmly, "for your probation is over and 'tis time for real work."

8

For extra security, Prisoner Jay accompanied them to the pavilion. On the way, Domme Camille told Gillian that she would be working that afternoon for one of the prisoners given limited trustee privileges.

"Although not ready to be trusted outside the immediate scrutiny of the guards," she explained, "these men have been evaluated as ready for supervised governing of the Disciples. And though there will be guards about, you must remember to show this man obedience. Always be compliant, submissive, eager. So for the afternoon you must think of him as your master, and seek to please him as you would me or any other Leather Wife."

Upon entering the meadow grounds, Gillian looked at the pavilion. Sunlight poured through the canvas and the breeze played with the ribbons that were tied at the tops of the poles. In the distance two guards stood at the section of fence near some shade trees. A single prisoner paced near the pavilion's entranceway. He pulled aside the entrance flap for a Disciple who emerged with a chamber pot. It was not the pavilion to which Camille headed but toward the far grounds at their left. Passing two guards talking among themselves, Gillian then spotted what she had not seen during the night: a small stream on the other side of a knoll beside this part of the fence. It flowed from the surrounding woodland and cut gently through to meander toward the prison outskirts.

She followed Domme Camille down the knoll, where six or seven baskets of dirty laundry had been assembled. Nearby was a clothesline that hung between two high wood braces. Two Disciples knelt on the bank and washed clothes, piling the wet, clean items into the baskets that must have previously contained the dirty heap now turned out over the grass nearby. A prisoner overlooked them from the knoll. Upon seeing Domme Camille, he trotted over and inclined his head.

"Domme Camille," he said. Despite his pleasant tone, Gillian perceived a hint of mockery in his voice.

"Prisoner Thomas W., our new Disciple, Gillian, will be under your supervision for a time. When you are finished with her, the guards will oversee her until my return. Oh, and I shall have enough lunch sent for all the girls."

The prisoner shrugged. "There's really no need. The prison maids always send more than enough."

Camille nodded and gave Gillian a parting cautionary look. "I'll be back in time to take you for dinner in the household tonight, Gillian. Do behave."

Gillian watched her start away with Prisoner Jay and turned with a silent sigh to Prisoner Thomas W. He was an unimposing man with sandy hair, but the smirk on his face betrayed his inflated ego. Still, he spoke congenially enough.

"You will carry the loads of washed laundry to the clothesline to hang."

She nodded and waited as the other two girls washed what was left of their load. When the basket was full, she picked it up and toted it away, finding a cloth caddy filled with clothespins on the line. While she worked, a shrill squeal arose from across the meadow. Gillian looked up to see the prisoner she had seen earlier at the pavilion entranceway now chasing a Disciple through the grass. The guards watched, too, as he caught the Disciple by the wrist and heaved her up over one shoulder. She fussed as he carried her into the pavilion and moments later, Gillian heard the rapt sound of a fleshly chastisement echo from inside. The Disciple wailed out in despairing apology, and the guards exchanged grins and went back to their conversation.

When Gillian turned back, Thomas W. was regarding her hard. As she lowered the basket, he walked up on her.

"No one told you to stop working, did they?"

She shook her head, and she saw how he was trying to mimic the self-possession that came so easily for the guards. He amused her in this, but she knew better than to let him see it.

"No, sir."

"Well, don't do it again."

During the next hour, Gillian secretly caught sight of the prisoner at the Pavilion as he and the Disciples came out again. He held a double chain in his hand. It was locked to the wrist cuffs that had been put on the girl she had seen before. He turned her over to the guards and started toward the prison gate. Gillian did not watch further, remembering the recent warning. Her arms were starting to grow tired from the continual lifting of the wet clothes. To her relief, a guard arrived soon with a tray of sandwiches and grapes and a small-lipped stone jug. These he handed to Thomas W. With the guard gone, Thomas W. called the girls to come eat with him on the grass.

As they all left their tasks, he sat down and patted the ground to his right. "Here, Deidre." And gesturing to his left, "You here, Patsy."

Gillian saw them obey immediately, each reclining daintily on one hip. Thomas W. looked up at Gillian and said, "You may sit across from me, just like they do."

She complied, though she found it distasteful to have to face him. As Thomas W. divided the lunch among them all, she wondered why she disliked him so much. Her feelings toward Clive had been so different.

When they were all finished eating, he made an announcement that startled her.

"You may now show me your appreciation, girls."

Gillian watched as Deidre and Patsy bowed and kissed his bare feet. As their lips pressed his feet, he shoved up the hem of Patsy's violet dress and pulled her panties down. Then, pulling down those under the hem of Deidre's gold jumper, his hands roamed over their upturned pussies.

He eyed Gillian expectantly. "Well?"

She flushed, but made herself crawl around the tray and kissed the same foot that Deidre's lips pressed.

"Very good, girls," he murmured and lay down on his back. "Patsy, take off those bloomers and come here."

Patsy hopped up and removed her panties. She went to Thomas W.'s outspread arms and mounted his chest. His hands plowed up her dress so that he could grope her breasts. Over her lascivious moan, he told Deidre to unbutton his pants.

His cock was hardly the biggest Gillian had ever seen, but it was erect and pointed straight to the sky.

"Deidre, you take care of that," he said, "and Gillian, you eat her pussy while she does."

Gillian lifted her head as Deidre crawled to his side and drew his cock into her pursed lips. Thomas W. pulled Patsy's hips up so that her pussy hovered over his face and parted her pubic hair. As Deidre concentrated on sucking his organ, he drilled Patsy's damp sex with his tongue.

"Are you just a voyeur, Gillian?" He watched as she crawled behind Deidre. His eyes were still upon her as she grasped Deidre's hips and began to work her tongue over the exposed, glistening mound of Deidre's pussy.

A few moments later, he drew Patsy down completely over his mouth. Gillian concentrated on her own task, prodding Deidre's ever wetter slit with her tongue. After a while, she paused and masturbated Deidre's clit with two fingers, watching as the girl's head bobbed up and down over the prisoner's cock. The sight of her firm, tanned buttocks whetted Gillian's own desire; the rising moans from Patsy made the desire almost painful. She plunged the forefinger of her other hand into Deidre's pussy and felt the girl climax.

Deidre moaned deeply and paused in her sucking as the orgasm passed through her quivering limbs.

"Oooh," she cried out. Swaying her butt back and forth, she begged, "Deeper now, fill me!"

Thomas W. stopped eating Patsy's cunt and said, darkly, "You mind your own work, Deidre."

She whimpered but obeyed. Gillian licked her pussy and thighs, careful not to stir her too much lest it break the girl's focus. Soon Patsy wailed and fell forward, shuddering fiercely. Deidre reacted by sucking Thomas W. faster and did not stop until he went limp with his own orgasm. She swallowed his cum without spilling a drop, but as Patsy dismounted, Gillian saw the grimace on his brow.

He ordered Gillian to pull up his pants and button them. She did so, looking hungrily at his dwindling cock. She didn't really want him in particular, but all she could think about was riding some man. Thomas was content just to order them back to work now that his appetite was sated. He didn't even offer Patsy or Deidre a kiss.

Now Gillian understood her dislike for him. For whatever progress he made in his attitude toward women, he sorely lacked any sense of cherishing those with whom he was intimate. She was not surprised that his privileges were limited. At least Clive's only drawback seemed to be a hesitance in taking command.

For an hour or more, Gillian and the other two Disciples

worked. When the last shirt was hung on the clothesline, the guard who delivered the tray returned. As he took it up, he spoke to Thomas W.

"You can escort them inside now," he said, his gaze sweeping over the three young women. "The girls who usually take fresh linens to the solitary ward are elsewhere today."

Thomas W. seemed to take great delight in ordering his charges to walk before him to the prison grounds. There were two guards to welcome them at the gate, but Gillian noticed their tone toward Thomas W. was far from cordial.

One of these said to Thomas W., "So, how did you enjoy an afternoon impersonating a man?"

At the guard's gesture, the three girls walked in, followed by the now angrily flushed prisoner. Gillian heard Thomas W. reply to the guard, "I've brought them back to serve in distributing lines in solitary, Sir George."

Sir George inclined his head toward the looming red brick prison. "You go on then, Weems. I'll escort them to the storage keeper."

Thomas W.'s mouth hardened and his eyes were almost contrite as he looked at the Disciples.

"See you later, girls."

He walked off then, through the heavy double doors of the prison. As the Disciples fell in step after Sir George, Gillian again was struck by the atmosphere of the place. Smoke billowed out of one of the three chimneys and voices could be heard through the barred windows. Its sober, no-nonsense design reminded her of a photograph of a Victorian workhouse she had come across once in an encyclopedia, and the rusty red bricking only added to the dismal ambiance.

Sir George opened the doors and she followed Patsy and Deidre inside. To her surprise, they stepped onto a courtyard of red stone tiles, where the full light of the sun filtered in through a plate-glass roof. As they walked through, Gillian looked up to her right and saw the bars of the cells on the second floor. The left side of the building was a walled annex. A sign that hung over the only door leading into it read: GUARDS AND SUPERVISED WOMEN ONLY. The courtyard was well maintained, with hanging plants and flowers in wooden bins set about. A shallow pool with lily pads vining over the water's surface had been constructed in the center of the stones. A prisoner sat on a bench beside it, gazing at the golden carps that swam about.

At the end of the courtyard stood a statue of what Gillian assumed was a carved effigy of an Ur'theriem with its great wings and severe countenance. Its left arm stretched gracefully up, while its right held a thunderbolt tightly in its palm. But it was the spot between its thighs that drew Gillian's surprise. A naked Disciple had been mounted right on the statue's penis, her wrists encased by manacles bolted into the stone just below the concave navel. The girl's hips strained gently but fretfully against the intrusive phallus. By the way she pouted Gillian knew she was tormented by frustrated passion as well as humiliation.

As Sir George led the trio past the statue, he playfully smacked the thigh of the bound Disciple. She whimpered, eliciting a smile from the guard. He continued past, to a door at the wall they came to. It must have been over seven feet high, and he had to unlock it before even attempting to open it.

"On in, sweeties," he said as he held the door open. The girls scurried through, entering a passageway of smooth, bright sandstone. There were doors everywhere, and as they proceeded, Gillian glanced through one that was opened somewhat. It looked like a canteen of sorts. She could see Disciples running back and forth bringing pitchers and mugs to the guards sitting at the tables. Through another door, she saw great stone ovens and hanging baskets filled with onions and other vegetables, but it was empty for the time being.

Sir George stopped at one door and ordered the Disciples to wait while he went in. He came back out soon, carrying two armloads of sheets, which the girls took and divided among themselves.

They followed him to the end of the passageway. Here they ascended a wrought iron staircase. Sir George led the girls up, bringing them through the arched entranceway of a high-vaulted circular room. The common floor was solid red brick and there were no windows except for a thick oval glass positioned in the center of the dome. Dozens of doors circled the length of the mortar wall, and candles burned in sconces between each one. A sliding panel was set high at each door; narrow wood panels, about the length of a man's forearm, all latched with chained iron pegs, dropped through iron loops that were screwed into the wood of the doors.

"I'll be waiting for you on the second floor," said Sir George. Turning, he left the Disciples and returned down the staircase.

The echo of his voice eventually died away, but the cool dankness of the place seemed to creep into Gillian's bones. She shivered and Patsy rubbed her arm briskly.

"It's not so much the temperature as the place itself," she said kindly. "But we all get used to it."

Deidre wrinkled her nose. "And sometimes this atmosphere gives the impression the air reeks, but in truth, the guards keep the cells very clean."

Gillian looked around and said curiously, "I saw cells above that courtyard. Is that not where the prisoners are kept?"

"This is the solitary hold," explained Patsy, "where the most stubborn prisoners are kept. They are confined here either because of their incorrigible attitudes, or are in wait for the verdict of the Ur'theriem council."

Gillian frowned. "Verdict?"

"Yes. If they have served a long while and it's found they are simply beyond rehabilitating, the Ur'theriems hold a hearing to determine their future."

Deidre nodded darkly. "If their crimes were not violent before coming, they are sometimes allowed to be taken back to the time when they were apprehended. If they were violent, however . . ." Her words drifted off for a moment or two and she sighed. "Well, the Ur'theriems feel it is their responsibility to eradicate them so they cannot return to harm others. It is a serious consideration, to take the chance in altering the world's destiny by the death of a mortal. But as they oblige themselves in the moment they remove a prisoner from his earthly time, they feel duty-bound in assuming responsibility for him and all those he has affected, or may affect, during the natural course of his mortal life."

Gillian was piqued again. "So, when prisoners are returned, it is to the precise moment from when they were taken?"

Both girls nodded and Patsy said, "Not like us. We were offered an enhancement to our lives, a blessed reward to transcend whatever aspects and situations of the future we might have affected had we remained on Earth. The prisoners were taken to be retrained for the good of all society."

The silence that fell between them was almost too heavy to bear. Gillian was glad when Deidre confided brightly, "I used to serve here regularly, and as much as I hate this place, at least we don't have to listen to Thomas W.'s barking voice any more today!"

This made Gillian and Patsy both titter, and they followed Deidre toward the first cell door on their route. As they took turns opening the panels and stuffing the linens through, Deidre related the histories of the prisoners she knew and why they had been taken for rehabilitation. They represented a diverse assortment of backgrounds and cultures from lowlife criminals to upper-class businessmen. All men, Deidre explained, whose willful obsessions with destructive ideals had, in the end, proved beyond redemption. Gillian peeped in several of the windows while Deidre talked.

She could not wait to get out. The prisoners' anger and resentment penetrated their cell doors to permeate the air of the entire vault with a dark, weighty bitterness. Deidre was wrong; even the company of Thomas W. was better than this gloomy place.

"We can go find Sir George now," she suggested.

Deidre made a concurring sound, and they all walked out and returned downstairs. Gillian felt the uneasiness imparted by the solitary ward slacken rapidly. She and Patsy followed Deidre as she peered into the various doors in the search of Sir George. But a deep masculine voice within one of the rooms paused Deidre's hunt.

"Well, little Disciple, I was hoping to see you again!"

Gillian flipped Patsy an inquiring look, but the girl only shrugged.

"Come here, Deidre," said the male beyond the door.

As Deidre eyed her companions, Gillian saw there was a conflicted look on her face.

"A guard?" Patsy whispered and when Deidre nodded, Patsy pushed her lightly over the threshold. Moments later heavy footfalls padded toward the door and the guard who had summoned Deidre gave them a smitten grin.

"Stay right there. Deidre will be out soon."

He closed the door and Gillian heard Deidre make a shrill, excited sound behind it. Patsy was smiling to herself and they both moved down the hall a ways. There they waited for some time, listening to the ever-growing sounds Deidre's guard elicited from her.

"It must be Sir Nathan," Patsy commented. "She mentioned she thought he was rather taken with her. He has been stationed for a time in the residents' village. Obviously, he did not forget her."

Gillian smiled. She had heard from Candice about the residents' village and was about to ask who the residents were exactly when she heard someone walking their way. She looked up and was surprised to see Clive. He had the look of one who was very confused or lost as his eyes darted here and there timidly. On seeing Gillian, though, he stopped in his tracks and beamed.

"Gillian!"

His back straightened with pride and his long legs strode toward her. He clasped her hands and covered her face with tender kisses. She was delighted by his joy and stammered for something to say when she noticed Patsy frowning and shaking her head cautiously. But Clive was talking enough for all three of them.

"Fairest angel! They said the Warden wanted me to bring something from the kitchen. He must have approved my request already! I would have thought it to take much longer!"

He turned her hands over and kissed her palms. The moist heat of his lips made her nipples harden and tingle. Yet, she hesitated to speak a word at all, lest her words betrayed her arousal again and spoil his delight.

"Ah, my precious one!"

He kissed her again, deeply this time. Gillian's limbs weakened in his tender embrace. His lips parted at last and he clasped her face between his hands.

"Come." He began to lead her down the shadows near the staircase. She glanced once back at Patsy, saw her furrowed brow and the worried shake of her head. Gillian decided she was overreacting. Why should she not enjoy Clive's kisses and let him stoke her passions with his intoxicating, flattering attention? Deidre was evidently enjoying her pleasures.

In the dim light beneath the stairs, he lavished her throat with kisses and rubbed her aching breasts through her dress. She raised her left leg and balanced it on his hip. His fingers wandered the flesh of her thigh and explored her vulva through her panties. With a laugh, he pulled them down and helped her step out of them. Her pussy swelled wetly. Clive's left hand explored the cleft between her thighs, and he licked her moisture from his fingertips. His shaft pressed hard against his pants, a stiff fruit against her groping palm. She smiled and pressed her sex against it and moved her hips pleadingly.

She could not contain her desire any longer and whispered with all the humility she could muster, "I want you!"

He murmured something sweet as he unbuttoned his pants. The head of his cock was a scarlet orb as it thrust forward. Lifting her by the waist, he leaned her against the latticed ironwork. She wrapped her legs around him and his organ penetrated her fully. Gillian's eyes closed and she began to ride his thrusts.

"Put the girl down!"

Gillian's heart vaulted. Clive turned suddenly cold as ice. In the light beyond his shoulders, she saw not only Sir George but also two other guards.

It was one of these who spoke in the thunderous voice, "I said, put the girl down!"

Clive lowered her gently and graced her brow with a trembling kiss. Her vagina ached for him, but much more alarming for her was the terror in his eyes.

A long, muscled arm reached past Clive and took hold of her. Out of the clandestine darkness she was pulled straight under a looming shadow. The man to whom it belonged was tall and lean, with a tail of steel-gray hair that swept between his shoulder blades. His face was graced with a long, finely groomed mustache and a Vandyke beard; his eyes were the same hard steel-gray as his hair. She heard Sir George demand to know what she was doing with the prisoner, but in her fright she could not move her eyes from the tall one.

He offered a raised brow and asked, "Did this man take you by force, young lady?" His deep, soothing southern drawl addled her wits. Only after he asked her a second time could she respond.

"N-no, sir."

Sir George rolled his eyes. "Then, this liaison is forbidden, as I have no doubt you already knew."

Gillian's lingering passion was tormenting. She made an unhappy little sound before thinking, which brought a flood of angry ruddiness to Sir George's face.

"I told you three to come find me when you were finished distributing the sheets!" He looked at the tall man and said, "Hand her over to me to punish, Warden."

Warden! Gillian wished she could crawl straight through the latticework to hide.

Clive spun about, his pants still unbuttoned. "No. It is my fault."

A contemplative sneer turned up one corner of the Warden's mouth. "Yes, I know that. I'm glad to know you are learning to at least take some responsibility. She has broken the rules and shall be punished accordingly. But you incited her, Prisoner Clive, and I trust you are man enough to accept due reckoning."

Clive slipped a rueful look at Gillian that wounded her deeply.

She hissed at the guards, "Leave him alone!"

The soft laugh this brought from the Warden provoked her hotly. She stomped her foot and flailed her arms in the effort to shake his grasp. He laughed louder and pulled her to him, so her back was pressed firmly against him. He crossed her arms down over one another and pinned her wrists firmly so she could not move them at all. She thought of drawing her heel back to kick him, but realized she did not want to hurt anyone, let alone exacerbate the trouble she and Clive were already in.

Patsy was still clinging to the wall when Deidre and her eager suitor came out into the passageway.

"What is going on?" the suitor asked.

The Warden gestured to Clive and told him and the other guard to seize his arms. "He can while away his time recollecting our rules created to protect the Disciples. Inform the sergeant of his ward that his cell is to be draped for the next three days and that the Disciples coming to work are not to be allowed near it."

As they forced Clive out into the passageway, the Warden observed in his even, husky voice, "I have a sense you meant no harm to this girl, Prisoner. But 'tis best you remember you are no guard with privileges. Besides, after the report I received about your reluctance to discipline this submissive lady, I hardly think you are fit to act the masterful lover yet."

Clive's face blanched and as they led him off, he could not look at Gillian at all. She hurt for him and yet as she felt the Warden's eyes smiling down at her, she knew he was right. And to her further agitation, the man provoked in her a mutual intimidation and wild lust. Clive had never been able to touch her like this.

His steady eyes swept from Gillian to Deidre and then Patsy. Even as his voice remained steady, it was evident he was perturbed with Sir George.

"You said these girls were under your charge, Sir George. But where did I meet you just before we came upon this . . . rendezvous?"

The faintest blush tinged the guard's face. "In the courtyard, sir."

The Warden regarded him for several silent moments. At last he turned to Deidre's suitor and said, "You know this one?"

The guard looked down at Deidre. "Yes. I did not know these other two were left unattended. My apologies, sir."

The Warden released Gillian's wrists. "No need. This is the first visit for this Disciple. It's apparent her chaperon here had more pressing concerns out in the courtyard." He smiled and took Gillian by the hand. His engulfed hers completely, making her feel all the more helpless.

"Take Patsy back to the handmaidens' quarters, Sir George. Deidre, may remain. I will, however, wish to speak to you later of this incident."

Sir George inhaled quickly and nodded. Without another word, the Warden took Gillian by the arm and escorted her toward the door leading into the courtyard.

The Warden's office was stationed on the second floor, beyond the marked annex door she had seen earlier. Paneled of rich cedar timber and crowded with furnishings—heavy bookcases and a desk, a leather sofa, and an oriental carpet spread over the center of the hardwood floor—it reminded Gillian of a hunting cabin. He released her to bolt the door, and she stepped nervously to the room's single window. She could see the stream rambling down past the enclosing fence. Between the fence and this part of the prison, there was a maze of hedges with stone benches and strange structures fashioned of wood. In one portion of the maze she looked down upon, there was a prisoner at work trimming a hedge while a spear-wielding guard paced the path.

"Close those shutters, young lady."

She reacted instinctively and drew them together, but her legs were frozen stiff in place as he padded up behind her.

"Turn around," he said and again she obeyed. He said nothing for several moments, and she bowed her head and tried not to fidget, but it was difficult.

At last he said, "Would you have me assume that Madam neglected to tell you it is forbidden for Disciples to speak freely with prisoners?"

His question brought back images of the guards, Vincent and Peter. She half-closed her eyes and the memory of Sir Vincent impaling her upon his enormous cock rushed back.

"Well?"

Gillian blinked, terrified he had somehow unveiled the honeyed memory. "I was told, sir."

He smiled patiently. "I suppose a pretty boy's pretty words are seductive. But it's not what you really want, is it?"

His hands drifted down her shoulder to her arms. Snatching her about the waist suddenly, he kissed her, unfolding her trembling lips with his eager tongue. Her heart pounded like that of a frightened rabbit, and yet her passion responded to his desire. Clive's sweet declarations melted from her thoughts.

He lifted her dress and stroked her through her panties, probing fingers teasing her pussy lips. Then, lifting her in his arms, he carried her to the sofa and set her down.

"On your pretty knees and face the back."

As she clasped the sofa's leather back, he grabbed her hips and pulled them toward himself. He tossed the hem of her dress over her back and whisked down her panties, sending a bolt of fire through her thighs. He slapped her buttocks playfully until her hips began to undulate. Kissing the nape of her neck, he touched her wet sex and gave a little smack to her clit. She whimpered and turned her face to look at him, but he scolded her to keep her arms laced over the sofa and her face straight ahead.

She did as told, seeing nothing but the mist of her own constrained, anguished desire as he stroked her clit between his fingers. After a time, he weighted the head of his cock against the folds of her pussy. Her back arched imploringly. With a low growl, he grasped her hips and plunged in. His pelvis and thighs pounded against her, so that the room resounded with each slapping thrust. Her sex vised with the thrusts, and when she climaxed, it was with a deep torrent of sensation. He continued to fuck her roughly, until at last his cum shot into her.

Gillian was quivering as he lifted her face and grazed the side of her throat with his moistened lips. As he sat down on the sofa, he pulled her on top of his lap. He twisted the ends of her hair around his fingers, and she dared to tease his softening cock, swatting it ever so lightly and stroking the fluid-drenched shaft. He laughed and hugged her tightly, and she loved how the downy hair of his chest tickled her face.

At length, he murmured, "Tomorrow you will be back."

She raised an eyebrow, not convinced he had the authority to command that, but she was flattered nevertheless.

"You will be a proper Disciple, one way or the other."

His arrogance was exhilarating. She dared to kiss him. To her delight he did not resist or reprimand, but explored her body with all the tenderness she doubted he knew was in his possession.

9

The conversation between the distraught Leather Wife and the Warden turned out to be one which Gillian was not privileged to hear. Domme Camille had ordered her to stand outside the Warden's door and wait with Prisoner Jay, and when at last she emerged, it was apparent she knew everything about Gillian's thwarted rendezvous with Clive. The anxiety that had been clear on the Domme's face when she came had disappeared. Her fierce glare sent Gillian cringing against the wall. As the Domme pinched her earlobe and pulled her away from the sheltering wall, Gillian saw the Warden watching from the doorway. His face was unreadable as the Domme smacked Gillian's bottom.

"I fully expect to see that girl here tomorrow," he said flatly.

Domme Camille did not answer. Still holding to Gillian's ear, she led her and Jay out of the prison.

The trek back to Madam's house was silent. Domme Camille dismissed Prisoner Jay on the porch, and once inside, released her hold on Gillian and gave her over to another Leather Wife, who was speaking with a guard in the foyer.

"Have this girl change her undergarments before dinner, Hilda. I would see to it myself, but Madam has been waiting long enough for me in her room."

Tall, buxom Hilda tossed her blond-tendrilled head and took Gillian's hand almost idly. "Yes, I heard about Gina and Rose. What a pity."

The guard grunted and Domme Camille said wearily, "More than that. To forswear themselves is one thing. To slight Madam—that is unforgivable."

She turned and walked to the door through which Gillian had seen all the potted plants the day before. Gillian frowned, wondering what the slight to Madam was. As intimidated as she was by Madam, the idea of anyone wronging the lady disturbed her greatly. She had not long to think of it, though, for Domme Hilda snapped the order for her to head upstairs.

Gillian ate in the dining room that night with the other Disciples who were not occupied either at the prison or preparing for the pavilion. The dining room was on the other side of the house. She was surprised to see that prisoners, dressed in starched white uniforms and caps, carried the food and beverages in from the kitchen door.

What did not surprise her was that Disciples were relegated to benches at four plain board tables and forbidden to speak above a whisper, while their eight Leather Wife chaperones sat in comfortable chairs at their own table. These Dommes chatted and laughed during their meal. Except for their leather boots, they had changed out of the daunting dominatrix gear for the evening and into dark dresses and distinctive accessories. Above their table hung a colorful tapestry of a girl bound by the wrists and thrown across a log in the woods, sucking the cock of the nude man kneeled in front of her, while another switched her ass.

Pearl invited Gillian to sit beside her during the meal. Her roommate was dressed in a white velvet gown this evening, with a ribbon-laced bodice and low boots. As they ate, Gillian commented that she had not realized the Disciples were allowed into this part of the house. Pearl laughed and told her all about the other rooms Gillian had not yet seen: the quarters for the trustees who lived at the household; the rooms upstairs where the Leather Wives slept; the music room, which was just down the hall. There were lesson rooms, too, Pearl explained, where the Disciples with certain attitude problems were taught proper social skills.

"What kind of verbal and attitude problems are addressed in these lessons, Pearl?"

"Madam holds special classes there every few weeks for those Disciples deemed in need of them. Etiquette lessons actually, for newcomers who have difficulty shedding bad habits learned on Earth, or those of us who have simply taken up bad habits."

Gillian grinned and said, "Have you had to take lessons, Pearl?"

The girl blushed. "Only once or twice." Her eyes darted down the table and she said confidentially, "You know Alexandra, don't you?"

Gillian followed her eyes and saw Alexandra sitting far down the bench on the other side of their table. She was one of the few Disciples stripped of her clothing, and Gillian wondered what she had done to still require such exposure.

"Yes, I know her," she replied as the sensual memory of the afternoon in the woods made her tingle all over.

"She's on the list for the next semester. Thoughtless in her passions, that's her problem, always has been. But she got carried away once too often. Now she will be sorry."

Gillian did not care for Pearl's righteous tone and was sorry to hear Alexandra was in trouble. She wondered, too, if she had anything to do with Alexandra being scheduled for lessons. It was unlikely; she had only just arrived when Alexandra and Lara seduced her into the deep woods.

The recollection of that time with them was still sweet. Just as sweet was the recollection of seeing the two bound to the Rapture Pillars; their lovely, helpless flesh exposed for any and all to appreciate, to touch, to stimulate.

No, if she failed to learn from that lesson, she was in sore need of special attention.

But then Gillian felt a wave of apprehension, for she had sneaked away with Clive just as surely as Alexandra had sneaked away with Lara. Her mouth parched, for she could not forget the Warden's prediction: as a Disciple she would be punished accordingly for breaking the rules.

Pearl whispered distantly, and the anxiety in her voice drew Gillian out of her own concerns. "Looks like they are ready to announce the tally."

Gillian saw that she was staring across the room to the Dommes' table. They were poring over sheets of parchment and marking something down on a separate sheet laid out on the table, talking quietly among themselves for the first time since dinner had commenced.

"What do you mean?"

"Oh," Pearl said, fidgeting with the ribbon cinched at her cleavage, "I don't know if you noticed today, but the Leather Wives observe us during the day; a particular Domme for a number of girls. Of course, we can only guess sometimes which one of them is watching us. After dinner, they take out the notes they have made on our behavior, comparing all acts of misconduct. The five Disciples who are then deemed to have committed the most or worst acts are given special penalties in order to set an example that the rest of us won't easily forget. See those by the wall? They are reserved for this."

Gillian looked at the stools she had hardly noticed lined up against one wall and a large, plain box nearby.

"The ones selected will be humbled in view of us all. Afterward, they will be given over to the kitchen prisoners for the rest of the night. These trustees are chosen from those on the redemption list, awaiting return to Earth, rehabilitated. They enjoy privileges the other prisoners do not."

Gillian nodded soberly. Several moments passed and one of the Leather Wives rose to her feet and called for the Disciples to fall silent. Gillian's stomach twisted when the woman's intense blue eyes flashed her way.

"For those who are not yet acquainted with our *le dessert des disciples*, we will now announce the names of those who have shown the least inclination to behave today. Those named will come forward to receive a fitting reward for it. As Domme Camille could not attend dinner tonight, she has given me her accounts, so be assured her notations have been tallied along with the rest."

The door to the kitchen opened and five prisoners walked in and lined up against the wall. The first four carried trays laden with servings of what looked like strawberry torte. The fifth stood with his arms folded casually over his chest as the Leather Wife read out the names from the sheet in her hand.

"Melody, Sharon, Alice." The Domme glanced at the list quickly and added with a wicked ghost of a smile, "Alexandra—hmm, why am I not surprised? And oh, yes, Pearl."

Relief washed Gillian's dread away. After Pearl's judgmental words about Alexandra, however, she was tickled to see her crestfallen face and wondered what act of misconduct Pearl had committed to merit this punishment. The other girls were no happier, and their respective belled ankle bracelets or shoes jingled softly as they went to meet their punishment. But Pearl looked to be glued to the bench.

The Leather Wife strode to the table. "On your feet, Pearl!"

When she still did not move, the woman grabbed Pearl's arm and pulled her up. Pearl let out a protesting whimper and covered her face with her hands as she was led away. The other three were removing their panties when Alexandra threw a contemptuous look at the prisoners. But then, as the other Disciples, she bent over a stool with her face to the wall.

The Leather Wife removed Pearl's panties and forced her down over the stool.

"Continue to feel sorry for yourself, Pearl, and you will find yourself spending the night bound to a Rapture Pillar. But perhaps that is where a Disciple who cannot resist fondling herself belongs. That pussy belongs not to you, young lady, but to Nemi, and you have been reminded of that on more than one occasion."

Pearl pursed her lips sullenly as the Leather Wife gestured the empty-handed prisoner over. He drew from the red-tissued box what looked like a candy tin and handed this to the Leather Wife. She opened the lid back on its small hinges, and the prisoner lifted out a slender phallus-shaped wand. At the Leather Wife's nod, he grinned and smacked Pearl's ass with his free hand. Pearl suppressed the cry that flew to her lips, and Gillian saw her shudder when he spread her legs and parted her buttocks.

He inserted the wand into her anus, stopping at the red bobble that stayed outside to draw all eyes to her shame. Returning to the box, he took out a tall, white cone hat. This he set on Pearl's head. It seemed all the girl could do to keep her composure, and Gillian heard her groan softly as the prisoner moved down the line of Disciples, dispensing the same chastisement.

When the last Disciple was crowned with her humbling hat, the Leather Wife waved her finger at them all.

"One word, one whimper, one cry, and I'll turn my paddle over to one of the kitchen help!"

The five did not answer, did not move. The Leather Wife returned to her table and the prisoner to the kitchen. The other four moved to the Disciples' table and began serving the tortes. A few moments later, another prisoner came out and offered little glasses of liqueur with slivers of ice to those girls who had been spared *le dessert des disciples.*

Gillian tried to concentrate on the sweet concoctions, but she knew how lucky she was to have avoided Pearl's humiliating display. Yet Pearl had been right about something: it was indeed one example she would not easily forget.

As she finished the torte and listened to the hushed conversations of those about her, Gillian's thoughts drifted to other things. She smiled to think of Clive's sweet nothings and her pussy warmed a little to recall the time spent with the very masculine Warden.

The memory of the overcompensating Thomas W. made her grimace, and she knew some regret over the disgrace she had caused poor Sir George. Then there was the chastising breakfast outside that morning. That memory brought a painful blush to her face.

But the humbling memory eased away as she thought of the ritual in the Temple of Purity. Despite all she had been through that day, the impact of that ritual had helped silence the voice that had protested so loudly before against the exacting Nemian customs. She understood now that the voice had echoed earthly customs she had never embraced, ethics that her heart, if not her mind, had known were impractical and senseless even as she went through the mundane motions of earthly existence.

The recognition of this truth was making it easier to understand the purpose of her new life. If she had one lasting remorse, it was that she had not accepted herself while still on Earth. She smiled sadly now, thinking of Bruce, the man she had fantasized about so often but did not have the nerve to approach, at least not as the submissive she was. What would have happened, she wondered, if she had allowed him a glimpse into her real nature and let him know he was the one she dreamt of releasing her from the constraints of taboo?

Even if he'd been interested, his own restraining demons would have probably turned him away.

She noticed the Leather Wife had risen again and moved to the door of the kitchen. She said something to someone inside. A few moments later, a prisoner came out carrying a towel. With this he grasped each red bobble and removed the anal wands in full view of all. The faces of the punished Disciples were just as red with shame.

The Domme clapped her hands. "Now, go and serve the prisoners tonight," she instructed them.

They removed their dunce's hats, gave them over to the Leather Wife, and with their faces downcast, followed the man who had cleaned them into the kitchen.

"Gillian."

Gillian looked up and saw it was Domme Camille who had addressed her. The woman's smile was as thin and hard as the ice in the shots of liqueur.

"You will come with me now."

Gillian followed her to the door of the very room the Leather Wife had entered earlier. Domme Camille knocked gently and after several moments, Madam opened the door. She was dressed in a long, flowing black silk gown with bell sleeves and a red ribboned bodice. Her brown hair had been combed so that it fell in cascades over her shoulders.

"Come in, ladies," she welcomed and closed the door behind them.

The room was spacious, perfumed with the countless flowers and flaming, scented candles set throughout. The reflections of these candles illuminated the polished, dark grain of the floorboards. Through the large windows, Gillian saw the garden area where she had been forced to nurse the feeding bottle. She looked away bashfully, to the great bed, canopied with black veils and its posts garlanded with crimson roses that had been planted in niches cradled on the outside of the bed's wide spindle legs. Beside the bed was a table covered with gold cloth. Items of discipline and pleasure were set here: bottles of oils, feathers and dildos, masks and gags of all sizes. Several crops lay there, too, and the paddle Madam usually carried, as well as a lengthy switch.

She trembled as Domme Camille pressed her shoulders and spoke low, "Always on your knees when you enter here, Disciple."

Gillian descended quickly, having to stifle the moan that rose to her throat. Madam looked down at her thoughtfully, her face unreadable as she turned and took a seat in a blue overstuffed chair. She raised her feet to the matching ottoman and snapped her fingers over the arm of the chair.

"Come over here, Gillian."

Without either of the women saying so, Gillian understood that she was expected to crawl. Blushing hotly, she did so, stopping right at Madam's draped hand. As she lowered her face, a strange, engulfing and almost luxurious sense of resignation swept over her.

Madam made a sensual sound and stroked the back of Gillian's neck. Her fingers launched a bolt of cool electricity down Gillian's spine.

"You are fully a Disciple now, Gillian," she said. "I welcome you and am honored to call you mine."

Gillian's eyes raised and she caught Madam's sincere smile. Her bearing was as forbidding as ever; and this, Gillian knew, evidenced her sincerity more than any coddling welcome ever could. She knew now, too, that she would not change the lady's strict affections even if she could. Impelled by emotion, Gillian lifted her face and kissed Madam's hand.

This Nemian proprietress had welcomed her for exactly what she was.

"I love you, Madam," she whispered.

Madam inhaled gracefully and bent forward. She kissed Gillian's brow and hugged her face to her breasts.

"And I love you, my sweet." Gillian watched as she looked up to Domme Camille. "You were right, Camille. Most of these young women are grateful."

Domme Camille's face brightened so that the unspoken darkness that had weighted her manner now vanished.

Madam smiled and sat back again.

"Of course, my sweet, you know I have been informed of your liaison at the prison."

Gillian nodded humbly, but she was now more remorseful than frightened.

"This incident caught poor Camille at a bad time, because of another situation, involving two of her sister Leather Wives. Otherwise, I assure that she would have doled out a suitable punishment straightaway. But here you are now, to answer to both of us."

The sense of impending doom descended over Gillian again,

but she did not even think to plead her cause this time. She had been disobedient and she knew it.

"Camille, go fetch my crop."

Gillian's heartbeat pulsed in her temples as Domme Camille stepped to the table beside the bed. At her return, Madam sat up straight in her chair and slid the skirt of her lovely silk gown up over her thighs.

She pointed to the ottoman and said, "Up there, Gillian, belly down."

As Gillian crawled up over the ottoman, Madam told her to keep her legs spread open. Holding Gillian's head between her hands, she directed Gillian's lips between her thighs so that they touched the nest of brown curls at her pubis.

"You will show your devotion to me now, my girl," she commanded sternly, "while Domme Camille punishes you. And if I determine your efforts are flagging, you shall spend the night bound to the Rapture Pillar, after the Warden is brought here and you suck his cock while wearing the dunce's cap!"

She knows I was with him! Gillian blushed so hard that her eyes filled with stinging tears.

Madam trailed a fingernail up the nape of her neck. Shyly, Gillian opened the folds of the older woman's musky sex and kissed her clit just as the first strike of the crop bore down across her backside. She shuddered and the crop swooped down again, scoring her flesh with heat. Again and again Domme Camille flogged her. With tears in her eyes, Gillian licked Madam's clit. It burgeoned forth and she sucked it gently and probed two fingers into the fount of Madam's vagina. How hot and succulent the flesh was there. Even as Gillian's buttocks grew raw and her hips winced under the sensual barrage, she pumped Madam steadily.

Madam's clit swelled and throbbed. With a gush of juices, her body tensed and her clit beat wantonly in Gillian's mouth.

Domme Camille's strikes fell easier for a moment, long enough to allow Madam to recover from her climax. Then Madam pulled Gillian's head back by her hair. She nodded to Domme Camille, and observed as the Leather Wife now flailed Gillian's backside mercilessly.

Gillian tried to keep still, but when Domme Camille began to lash her thighs with the smarting crop, she squirmed wildly over the ottoman. Madam sucked the cries from her mouth with kisses and lifted a hand.

Gillian heard the crop fall to the floor. Domme Camille pried her legs far apart and knelt between them. She buried her face in to Gillian's pussy. It quivered at the touch of her hot mouth, and Madam kissed her deeply just as the Domme's tongue penetrated her sex. Gillian's clit pulsed indecorously. She cried in shame and anxious need. Domme Camille fucked her madly with her tongue, ignoring the craving beats of her clit until suddenly she lapped it once, twice, and an approaching orgasm tightened Gillian's pussy.

Domme Camille abruptly drew back and spanked her sore bottom with a palm. The annulled climax was maddening. Gillian's hips rose pleadingly toward the Domme and her wanton moan filled Madam's mouth.

"No, oh, no," Camille purred, continuing to punish her, "you owe me this passion, mischievous girl!"

Gillian's clit hungered as painfully as her buttocks throbbed. When at length the spanking stopped, she panted desperately at Madam's lips.

Madam drew her face away gently. Her bold, knowing eyes deflowered a part of Gillian she had not known existed until that moment.

At last, Madam smiled and said, "I am aware of the creature that spotted and attempted to seduce you from the circle. And so I've called for one of our most diligent guards to watch over you for a time. Sir Vincent is discussing the incident and your particulars with the man as I speak."

Gillian frowned curiously as Madam continued. "For your own safety, I feel this is warranted. But take comfort in knowing you will be spared the dunce cap tonight. While you are bound to the Rapture Pillar, remember that the unrelieved arousal you feel is a lesson and a passion in itself."

Gillian's mouth fell open. Why did she have to face the Rapture Pillar when the spanking had been so thorough? It seemed so unfair. Yet through the haze of her self-pity, she knew the answer. If Madam proved lenient tonight, she, Gillian, might be forever lost to brazen whims. For this she was grateful, even as she shivered in terror at the thought of being exposed all night long—utterly vulnerable to the attentions of the night guards.

So she tried to take comfort in the kiss Madam blew and regretted it had not the power or intention to snuff the sexual flame deep between her legs.

It had been a long while since Domme Camille had gone back inside the house and left Gillian bound to the Pillar. The guards the Domme had summoned had stripped Gillian utterly and stuffed the dildo part of a submissive's muzzle into her mouth. With it tied firmly in place two of the men lifted her up and pressed her back against the Pillar. The other one had then draped her arms and spread-eagled her legs back so they hugged the Pillar. He tied her wrists and ankles with silk cord. The cords were fastened into the wood with the same kind of metal-toothed clamps used with Alexandra and Lara.

Two of the guards had returned to their usual posts out in the yard, and as the one remaining finally withdrew his probing fingers from Gillian's vagina, she cried silently around the thick dildo filling her mouth. The man had taunted her to the very point of a climax and left her to writhe shamefully against the unyielding Pillar.

When he turned and started walking back, at least the gag helped soften her lingering, pleading moan. His lusty eyes had just begun to caress her again when a sound issued from below the porch. He clenched the handle of his spear and darted to the side and surveyed the hedges below.

"Isn't it a little late for you ladies to be out without escort?"

Gillian raised her humbled eyes. Two women strolled up the steps. By their clothing Gillian assumed at first they were Leather Wives, though the guard's wary look lent some doubt to that impression. They could not have been more dissimilar in appearance; a stout, large-breasted one wearing a short, red dress and black leather jacket. Her leather boots were smudged with dirt and her hair was spiky. The second woman was tall, with dark shiny hair and a lean figure in a sleeveless silver dress. With her dusky complexion, full, swollen lips, and perfect makeup, she could have easily graced any fashion magazine back on Earth, even down to the stock beauty mark flawlessly applied at one corner of her mouth.

The one in red threw an arm about the guard's shoulder and kissed his cheek. "Good evening, Mark!"

He cleared his throat. "You two shouldn't be outside, let alone carousing about the property."

The tall one laughed curtly. "So what? Who asked you?"

The delight that had been in the guard's tone as he had touched Gillian's body dissipated. "You know what I mean, Gina. Perhaps I should send for Domme Camille."

The spiky-haired one swatted his backside. He bristled and pushed her arm away. "Go on, now. Stay out of trouble if you'd like to escape Madam's displeasure."

They both tittered now, as if his threat meant nothing to them.

"Madam wants to be rid of us," the one named Gina said. She stepped to a window and peered in. "We're not goody-goods anymore, you know, already scheduled to return to Earth, where we may contemplate our failures."

Gina's eyes bore into Gillian. Scathing, the look went right through Gillian, as if she were nothing but some unsightly bug not worth the woman's time to consider.

"She might have you brought back," the guard offered hopefully, "when you've proved ready. It has happened before."

The one in red grunted. "We won't be ready until we're too old and creaky to be of any use for the precious Nemi."

"You forget, Rose, old age does not exist here," he argued.

Gina crossed her arms and lifted her chin stiffly. "We'd have to be agreeing. And that, dear Mark, will never happen again."

The guard shook his shoulders. "What can I say, ladies? Appears you have made your choice and are willing to live with it."

Gina regarded him, her feline grin a caricature of amused contempt. "Nemi is not inviolable, Mark. Its self-righteous guardians have enemies, formidable enemies."

"Are you speaking of the Dhjinn-E'noch?"

"No," she said tartly, "they're just as decadent as the Nemian angels, only without the sanctimony."

"She's right," chimed in Rose, "and it won't be long until this stupid outpost will be wiped away forever by powers much stronger than the silly Ur'theriems."

"Bullshit."

"Ooh, hit a nerve?" Gina asked. "It's why we're not scared, Mark, not of going back, not of anything. We know how to approach these enemies, and they are willing, oh so willing, to do us this favor, whether we are here or on Earth."

The guard drew a steady breath, but his impatience with them thickened his voice, "You're insane, Gina, or just as conniving as others say. It's time you two went inside, before I'm forced to call for help to escort you in."

Rose giggled heartily and hugged his free arm. "You don't know if we're kidding or not, do you?" And as she looked awkwardly at Gina and said pointedly, "It's just that, isn't it, Gina? We wanted to leave him with something to smile about!"

Gina sashayed toward him, and stood close, very close, as she smiled innocently and stroked the muscles of his arms with her long fingernails. Anger registered in Mark's features, and as she raised the skirt of her dress up her thigh, he did not flinch, but neither did he resist as she released his arm from Rose and drew his hand to her bare flesh.

"You really don't want to see me go away, do you, Mark?"

She kissed his mouth, but he pulled his hand away. His voice betrayed his agitation, "You go on now, will you? I have more important things to do besides play with disgraced Dommes."

Gina's face scrunched angrily and she sauntered over to Gillian again and slapped her thigh hatefully. Gillian growled to herself as Gina said, "Guarding this, you mean? Hell, Mark, I can do better this abject slut any day of the week! And you wouldn't have to tie me up to have me, either!"

The guard's eyes glittered angrily and Gillian's heart jumped with glee when he grabbed Gina's arm. "It's Sir Mark, and sorry, but I do not care to listen to your bragging, nor do I wish to make an unpleasant situation for you this close to your departure."

Gina laughed and wrestled her arm from his grip. She opened her mouth as if to speak, when the front door swung open and a man's voice boomed out, "Back off from the girl, Gina!"

Gillian could hardly turn her face to see the man who stepped out onto the porch. But his tone held none of the patience of Sir Mark's. "Stay away from her, slut."

His voice was familiar. As Gillian pondered where it was exactly she had heard it before, Gina made a semblance of a pout. "Were you spying on us? Afraid I might hurt this delicate little sub?"

"Get in the damned house and go to your room," he said, and looked at Rose, who sneered like a child at him. "You, too."

"I don't think so," Gina declared and flitted past Sir Mark, taking Rose's hand. "Come on."

Sir Mark reached for them as they rushed down the steps, but only caught a wisp of Gina's hair. Gillian could hear them laughing as they fled through the dark yard.

"It would be best if the other guards were informed they are wandering about," spoke her defender, "in case the fools run into that Dhjinn. I've been assigned to personally guard this Disciple. Go ahead."

Sir Mark nodded and tramped down the steps into the yard. Moments later Gillian heard him conferring with the other guards there, though she could not make out the exchange.

Her defender strode toward the rail and watched, his arms still crossed, his legs set widely apart. She could see him better now that he was out of the porch shadows. His hair was short and dark brown, his neck wide and sensually soft at the corners of his jaws. The sleeves of his white shirt were rolled up to his elbows and even the deep tan of his skin glowed in the dim light. Again she was struck by the sense she knew him. It wasn't until he turned and Gillian saw his face fully that she recognized him.

Bruce!

She could not believe it and had to blink before daring to look at him again. But as she did, the corrections officer's handsome face was still there. His dark brown eyes, which she had always found particularly sexy, were hard and penetrating now as they surveyed her.

As uncompromising as in my wet dreams!

She blushed painfully, tormented he should see her exposed and ripe with passion. And as the moments passed and he still said nothing, she became afraid that she had fallen asleep on the Pillar and was only dreaming. But then he took two long strides toward her, his unreadable face an icon of self-possessed authority.

Yet, the hair on his forearms had tellingly risen.

"You have been a naughty girl, Gillian."

A shockwave of humbled emotions swept through her. How many times had she envisioned him looking at her just as he was now—speaking to her so masterfully?

Reaching up, he adjusted the gag in her mouth and wiped the tears from her face with his fingers. As his hands drew away, he scrutinized her body. He skimmed her hips and thighs with his fingertips, touched the crest of her pubic hair. Gillian shivered hotly, using every reserve of self-control to keep her hips from moving. But then, he unfolded her nether lips and touched her throbbing clit. It pulsated lightly. Into her aching vagina he slid a forefinger and started fucking her with it.

A delirium of wanton desire broke Gillian's restraint. She buckled and moaned silently, imploring him with her straining hips to take her down and fuck her with all the fierceness she had envisioned at his command.

Instead, he drew his hand away and sucked her juices from his fingertip. His imposing gaze frightened her. It tempered her passion so that it simmered; a merciless, voiceless frustration beneath her bonds.

"You are not to trust those women, Gillian," he said quietly, "is that understood?"

She nodded meekly, but her thoughts were only for him and the terrible suspicion that was taking root in her mind that somehow he had forgotten her completely.

What am I to him now, in Nemi? Where he could have any

girl prettier than me in a moment's bidding? And who am I to fault him for forgetting, when I chose to leave Earth and all my ties behind?

He paced the porch for a long time. At last he took a seat and lit a cigarette. By this time, she was too tired to keep her eyes open any longer. But even as her regret gave way to sleep, the weight of his gaze did not move from her.

10

Bruce welcomed the coffee Domme Camille offered, and tried to savor the rich taste, if just to break up the gnawing questions that wore on his conscience all night.

It was early. Most of the Disciples were still asleep in their rooms, and by what he knew, the Leather Wives, too. He was surprised that Domme Camille was already up. She wore a flowered silk robe and her hair was not yet brushed. She looked younger than he recalled. Then again, he had never seen her during the daytime or without makeup. She sipped on her own cup and smiled at the still-sleeping Gillian. The smile whispered of intimacy with the girl or at least interest. At any other time, the thought of watching the two of them going at one another would have been delightful. But Bruce was still ensnared by conflicting emotions about whether to confirm his identity or not with Gillian.

He still felt guilty about not approaching her the first night he had seen her. Of course, if Gillian ever heard the gossip about him and Gina, she might never look at him the same way.

No one had ever looked at him like that, as if he were the moon and stars and heavens consummate.

The day before he had understood that he had wanted to see that look in Gina's face—hell, every pretty face he had ever laid eyes on—and he had spent the entire night wondering what Gillian had thought back on Earth when he stopped coming around. Had she missed him, had she asked about him? There had to be something more than physical passion for that look to remain with her all this time.

When Madam had requested his services in guarding one of her Disciples, he had eagerly accepted. The trying situation with Rose and Gina had made him realize it was time to take the reins of his manhood, instead of just wielding his dick at random. What had he been thinking when it came to Gina? That she would be so impressed with his lovemaking she would be swept off her dominatrix heels, give up her dominant life-style and be the loving sub he had hankered for all his life? It had been a boyish fantasy, impractical and stupid.

And to think, I could have had it all already with Gillian.

The worst part was that he had always been charmed by her, from her demure laugh to her opinions, even the soft way she spoke. It was not just her face or body or even his suspicions about her secret desires. He had liked everything about her from day one. What he discovered while exploring the limits of pleasure-pain with Gillian during the night—a passion that transcended the physical, and was betrayed in the steadfast focus of her lovely eyes—had confirmed his suspicions of her mutual desire. She had probably been too shocked to have known he saw it. Even if she had, there was nothing she could have done to shield herself from her emotions. That was simply against her nature.

He sighed and Domme Camille said kindly, "Why don't you go to the guards' quarters and get some sleep? The Dhjinn are more brazen at night, which is why Madam wanted you here last evening. I will keep a steady eye on her."

Bruce thought about it, but was hesitant.

"I can catch a nap later," he said.

"You will need more than a nap before tonight."

There was reason in that, so he agreed. Eyeing the other guard at the end of the porch, he handed Camille the cup. Gillian did not even rouse as he passed by her, but his cock stiffened to look upon her bound, naked flesh again.

Bruce was awakened by a feminine shriek outside the window. Through the fog of half-sleep, he stumbled out of the bed and jerked back the curtain. The window looked out onto the backyard of Madam's property, and there he saw a Leather Wife pulling a Disciple by one braid over to where a prisoner stood by the edge of a shallow, aqua-tiled pool. The Disciple was deposited at the prisoner's feet, and the man watched with a gleam of mixed vindication and lust as the Domme reprimanded the girl. As she handed her paddle over to the prisoner, Bruce let the curtain fall and rubbed his eyes.

He washed up in the bathroom and put on a fresh change of clothes from one of the wardrobes provided for the house guards. Someone had delivered a tray of food while he slept, and now he grabbed a sandwich and ate it quickly. He found his cigarette pack and matches on the floor and stuffed these into the pocket in the lining of his vest. He stepped to the table nearby, where an assortment of punishment devices—whips, wide belts, paddles, and canes—were laid out. He finally chose one of the newer leather belts, strapped it around his waist, and, taking a quick smoke, headed out.

Sir Kennan met him at the gate of the prison grounds and informed him that Gillian had arrived early in the day with several other Disciples.

"She had been yoked to the granary mill for a couple of hours when the Warden had his trustee escort her back to the household."

Bruce sighed. "Now, why did he do that?"

"One of the Dommes came with the announcement yesterday she'd be commencing a monthlong class on focused attention and deferential display of affection," the guard explained. "It's usually reserved for the girls of the trustees, but the Warden has taken a special interest in that Disciple, so I am not surprised."

A heated prong pierced Bruce's stomach, but he managed to hide the jealousy brewing inside. "Really? He's taken with her?"

The gatekeeper nodded. "She's his type, you know—a wildcat desperate for the taming of an experienced handler. I had a drink with him last night and he mentioned her, said he plans on asking Madam to have her belongings sent to his private chambers."

Bruce tried to forget the angry images that suddenly filled his mind, reminding himself that Gillian was not his to claim now or even ever. He made the trip back to the household and in the foyer asked one of the trustees the directions to the lesson rooms. These were located on the second floor. He passed through without speaking to anyone he met and hiked up the staircase he found beyond the dining hall. Near the landing stood two Leather Wives, talking quietly as they sipped on glasses of tea. The corridor ahead was bright from the light coming through the window at the end. Every door, he saw, had a small window as well.

"Sir Bruce," one of the Dommes piped. She walked over to him.

"Domme Angela?"

"Yes. Domme Camille was looking for you earlier. She thought you probably did not know that the Disciple Gillian is up here."

He smiled wearily. "I do now."

"Yes, and she wanted to apologize. No one was expecting the Warden to enroll the girl."

The back of Bruce's neck prickled hotly. "Is this common? I mean, for the Warden to enroll a Disciple?"

She shrugged apologetically. "Well, no, these particular classes are usually filled with prisoners' girls and the wives of guards or the girls they are about to wed. But he is the Warden."

"I suppose they won't need my assistance, then," he said, his stomach tensing.

"That would be up to Madam, surely. He cannot keep an eye on her here and at the prison, too. I will let Domme Camille know you have come." She smiled sweetly and headed down the stairs.

Bruce scrutinized the doors ahead, wondering which one led to Gillian, and whether he could or even should enter.

"She's in the third to the left," he heard the other Leather Wife say. "You can peep in the window to be sure."

"Thanks."

He proceeded to the door and looked into the window. The room inside resembled an ordinary schoolroom, with small desks where the Disciples sat and an imposing desk up front for the Leather Wife teacher. She held a ruler in her hand at the moment and was pointing to words written on the blackboard behind her. Beside her desk, a man stood with his arms crossed. He was naked except for the mask with eyeholes on his head, so there was no telling whether he was a prisoner or guard. Bruce watched as the teacher turned to the rows of Disciples, but he could not decipher her words through the door.

But then two girls rose from their seats and trotted to the teacher's desk: a redhead with soft freckles and Gillian. Both wore faux-schoolgirl uniforms of plaid skirts, short-sleeved white blouses, and matching knee-high socks with brown loafers. Madam pointed to Gillian and she approached the man in the mask. Bruce watched with mounting anger as she knelt on the floor and kissed his feet. She straightened then so she was kneeling with her back straight and kissed his knees. As her palms touched his thighs, she spoke, and it seemed his mask moved as if he were answering. Gillian inclined her head and kissed his scrotum: one side, then the other. As she lifted his cock to her mouth, Bruce's hands clenched into shaking fists.

He watched her lick the length of the man's cock and loll her tongue over the head of it so that it thickened and grew stiff in her hands. She rose up a little and swooped down, drawing the head into her mouth. She nursed on it slowly, as with the fingers of one hand she cinched and worked the shaft. But she seemed nervous, and after a time, Bruce saw her giggle. This brought a round of laughter from the other girls. The teacher snapped something in a voice that boomed off the walls. Dashing up, she pinched Gillian's earlobe and hoisted her to her feet so that the man's organ flipped from her grasp. His erection had turned dark pink. Bruce growled under his breath and turned away.

He walked to the end of the corridor and lit a cigarette. The Leather Wife kept him company during the hours that passed, sharing gossip and talking about the new construction Madam had planned for the household for the upcoming year. He tried hard to focus on the conversation, but the sight of Gillian going down on that man was burned into his memory.

At long last, the teacher opened the door and the Disciples filed out. The Leather Wife rounded up most of them and led them downstairs, while the man who had been inside emerged, too, garbed now in the uniform of a kitchen trustee. He led two more of the girls down. Seeing Gillian come out with the teacher, Bruce hugged against the longest shadow in the corridor and watched.

"You are to serve and eat at the pavilion," the teacher instructed Gillian as she locked the door. "Sir Peter is waiting in the front foyer to escort you, for you are to help set out the food."

Bruce saw Gillian nod, but he could not determine the nature of the flush in her cheeks. After she had descended the stairway with the teacher, he moved from his vantage point and made his way stealthily to the kitchen and to the door that led out that side of the house. From the eaves, he waited until he saw the majordomo, Sir Peter, leading Gillian across the yard. When they reached the path to the pavilion, Bruce skirted across the grass and followed at a clandestine distance.

He stood about with the outside guards while Sir Peter took Gillian inside. Only when the man had come out again did he approach.

"Hey, can I have a word with you?"

Peter smiled expectantly as Bruce tried to find the best words to bait the man for information. "I wasn't expecting you to wake until later, Sir Bruce."

"Trouble sleeping in a strange bed," Bruce answered. He hoped the next words would make an impression that would reach the Warden's ears. "I'll be close to her the rest of the evening."

"Of course," Peter answered brightly, "we have all heard what happened at the Temple boundaries yesterday. But you may be relieved of that responsibility soon."

Bruce grunted and said darkly, "I heard the morning's gossip at the prison. Don't you think it's a little soon for this new Disciple to be staying there?"

The man's innocuous gaze seemed to penetrate his thoughts. He said confidentially, "All ready to cut a filly from the herd, Sir Bruce? I know you watched her diligently last night, my friend. But it was one night overseeing a gagged Disciple, and from his interest, it's evident the Warden obviously knows her a little more intimately than you, my friend."

Maybe physically, Bruce thought angrily. But then, Sir Peter knew nothing of his acquaintance with Gillian before coming to Nemi.

It is better this way. And better all around if the Warden does keep her to himself, out of my sight and out of my mind.

He realized now it was a gift, really, to get away from the sense of responsibility that wrestled with his guilt. He would absolve himself on some level and be done with regrets forever when Gillian was safely in the Warden's hands. He offered Peter a contrite grin.

"You're right," he said. "I was rather taken with her, but there are plenty more pretty legs where those came from."

Sir Peter laughed and clapped his shoulder. "I understand, really. When the woman I eventually married ended up being sent over to be one of the guard's personal house girls, I challenged him for her. But then, I had known her ever since she first arrived."

Bruce's interest was piqued. "I didn't know you were married. Yet, you live in the household, not the resident's village?"

The man's eyes suddenly grew misty. "She was taken by one of the Dhjinn-E'noch. When we found and laid siege on his lair, the beast had already taken her life. But the Ur'theriems have promised to find her when her soul returns to an earthly life. She'll be returned to me when she is old enough."

Bruce's skin bristled coldly and he wanted to offer some condolence, but the proper words escaped him.

Sir Peter broke the uncomfortable silence. "Ah, but I must get back now. Keep those diligent eyes on her, Sir Bruce."

"I will."

As Bruce watched Sir Peter stroll down the path toward Madam's house, he thought about the painful thing the man had revealed, and it made him realize the gravity of his job. There was no room for envy or guilt here, or any useless passion for that matter. He would do what was required, and soon enough Gillian would be the Warden's responsibility. Maybe then, he could indulge the pleasures he had come to Nemi for in the first place.

He slipped into the pavilion, finding Gillian and another Disciple setting out the dishes and silverware, cups and glasses. He went out quietly and surveyed the grounds and spoke with some of the guards meandering about. When the sun was setting, two guards wheeled out carts from the prison yard. White cloths covered the pans and bowls for the feast, and once they reached the pavilion, one of the others ordered the girls to come out and fetch the food. Bruce hung back against the canvas and watched as they carried the vessels inside.

The musicians, lugging their instruments along, arrived from the residents' village. A young boy was with them, pulling a small wagon that carried their jugs of ale and wine. Guards were prohibited from drinking on duty unless invited to do so by Madam or one of the Leather Wives, Bruce knew.

Soon, he saw the prison gates open again. A line of prisoners came down to the Pavilion under escort of two spear-brandishing guards. These who feasted came from among the prison's general populace; those not yet cured of their contempt or fear of women enough to be allowed their personal servant girls, but not yet proven beyond redemption. As they passed through the entrance, Bruce saw face after face branded with hardened arrogance and hostility for which all Nemi stood for. The perverse grinned with fancies of deceiving the guards and of finding the route to escape. The eyes of the fanatics were lit with visions of using the experience to abet their corrupt agendas, while the eyes of the bloodthirsty and violent shone with a madness that made Bruce cringe.

But unlike on Earth, these prisoners had few privileges. They were never a drain on the finances of the citizenry. Aside from the company of the Disciples who served to educate them, there were only the dull confines of the prison. They knew nothing of the fact they could, and well might be, returned home if they proved unwilling to cooperate—albeit, certainly, of their memories of the time in Nemi that might fuel their hatred. If their evil festered and became more explicit, they could eventually be executed. But the threat of death was considered detrimental for the welfare of their education. They had to accept and embrace development, and so were kept ignorant of executions as well.

The musicians were just warming up their instruments when a bevy of beauties was delivered from Madam. As they were ushered inside the pavilion, Bruce heard a disgruntled groan from one of the prisoners, followed by the snap of a whip across flesh. The prisoner let loose with a flagrant curse at his punisher, for which the guard ordered he be gagged. Bruce stepped in again and saw the unruly one rounded to his feet by two guards while a third strapped a muzzle over his mouth. The prisoner was forced to sit down again. He glared at the table, flinching at the brush of a naked Disciple passing behind him.

Bruce saw Gillian seated now between another Disciple and a prisoner. The man was big and burly, his hair still dripping from a forced shower. But as Gillian kneeled beside him and lifted a tidbit to his lips, his eyes softened and he accepted it. He spoke something to her, and Bruce saw her smile and demurely eat from the grapes on his plate.

Bruce looked away and accepted the plate a Disciple offered. He took it outside and ate the beef and honeyed bread, nibbled on the vegetables. Giving the plate over to another guard, he circled the pavilion again. Finding nothing out of the ordinary, he walked to the pathway leading to the household and lit a cigarette.

It was then he saw from across the meadow two figures tumble out of the woodland and slide under through a loose place at the fence. They giggled as they got up, stifling these sounds behind their hands. When they were composed, they started across the meadow hand in hand. The starlight illuminated their feminine bodies and revealed the mischievous smirks on their faces.

Gina and Rose . . . when they noticed the pavilion guards, their gait slowed to a graceful walk and they inclined their heads formally.

They were given admittance. Bruce threw the cigarette on the ground and hastened back. Inside, he spotted them loading plates with food and ordering two mugs of ale from a Disciple. But as he glanced at the table, he found Gillian gone. His eyes scanned the length of the table as the musicians struck up a lively tune and a little group of dancers began to jig on their bare feet. As Bruce walked by, he heard the bells on their ankles chiming vigorously.

In the shadows behind the table, he spied movement and making his way around the band, tiptoed into a place evidently reserved for private encounters. There was a pallet and a couch here, a couple of stools. On one of these sat the burly prisoner he had seen before. He now had Gillian sitting on one knee, with her panties pulled down to her knees, and was probing her pussy with his fingers. Although Gillian frowned with frustration, Bruce saw that the man's touch made her hips stir and her nipples harden behind the fabric of her short dress.

Bruce closed his eyes. It took several deep inhalations of air before he could control the urge to just snatch Gillian out of the oaf's clutches. He knew it was counterproductive to indulge such a rash emotion. So, he opened his eyes and left them to their shadowed privacy. Gina and Rose were sitting at a place at the table when he passed through. They both were swigging on a jug lifted from the musician's wagon. Their faces were too crammed with cake to notice him.

Gillian knew her manners teacher would hardly approve of her lack of focus now. The prisoner was nice enough, but his skin was filmed with a sour sweat and his groping hands were cold. But she had been told the Warden was determined she learn how to focus her attention and she tried now, tried so hard.

At least I don't have to show this man any real affection, she conceded happily. Affection for the Warden, she felt, would come soon enough. That prospective day would have to be one of solace, for then the yearning for Sir Bruce would surely go away.

But neither her distaste for the prisoner nor the flattering discovery that the Warden wanted her for his personal house girl allayed the thoughts that had preoccupied her all day. Over and over again Bruce's silken words played in her mind, laying her soul bare. The memory of his scorching gaze had bound her concentration as firmly as silken cords had lashed her to the Rapture Pillar. Beside the renewed desire for him, all the others—sweet Clive, tantalizing Alexandra, even the handsome Warden—did not compare. It was wrong, she knew, and ruefully foolish as well. She had not seen him the entire day and guessed the passion he had shown before was only fleeting, something to pass away the time while he was on duty.

"Gillian, come here!"

Hearing the rigid command, Gillian turned her face eagerly from the prisoner's puckered lips. She squinted through the recesses until she saw a woman's outline standing on the threshold of light from the feasting area.

But the prisoner was agitated. "What do you want? I got her fair and square—the guards said I could."

"Too bad," the woman retorted. "Come here now, Disciple."

Gillian glanced at the man contritely, but moved off his lap and pulled up her panties. He caught the hem of her dress in his shaking hand.

"You come back later," he ordered in a mumble.

She nodded humbly, but was glad to get away from him. Only when she had left the shadows behind did she see the woman's features, and all sense of relief abandoned her under the familiar, mocking eyes. Before she could even think, the woman grabbed her hair and wrestled her away to the canvas, where her companion kneeled while holding up the skirt of the heavy fabric.

The one named Gina released her hair. "Squat and follow me under."

Sir Bruce's warning about these two sounded in Gillian's head. She shivered and took a step back from the menacing beauty.

"No. I cannot do that."

The Dommes looked at each other. Gina said tightly, "But you will, if you do not wish another night gagged and bound."

Gillian responded as evenly as she could, "But Sir Bruce has told me—"

"Sir Bruce? This order is not his. We came at the Warden's order, young lady, and I think you have more to fear from disobeying him than some common guard, don't you?"

At mention of the Warden, Gillian remembered the girl restrained on the statue at the prison. It had been humiliating enough to spend a night on the Rapture Pillar; the thought of being bound and gagged at the prison, under the disapproving command of the Warden, tormented her. Emotional now, she thought of turning and simply running to the haven of Madam's house. Gina must have perceived her dilemma, for a compassionate glint suddenly softened her eyes.

"Now, what have you to fear, Gillian? It is only the Warden."

She extended her hand and Gillian accepted it, knowing her fingers were now as cold as the prisoner's had been. She kneeled slowly and crawled under the canvas. Gina followed at once, then Rose, and with each taking one of Gillian's hands, they guided her around the borders of the pavilion grounds, to the path that led from the meadow back to the household.

But as they reached it, they crouched in the shadows by the

fence. A guard came by on his way to the meadow, and Gina pressed a hand over Gillian's mouth. When he was gone, they pulled her roughly on until they reached the avenue that stretched between the woodland and Madam's property. There was another guard standing beneath one of the oaks, and again Gina's hand clamped more firmly over Gillian's mouth. With growing apprehension, Gillian tried to wrest the hand away. Rose's free hand flew to her belt and she brought up a kitchen knife, which she brandished in front of Gillian's eyes. Gillian's heart pounded and she looked to Gina for help, but the smirk on her face glowed with unholy promise.

At length, the guard made one more look up and down the avenue, and then ambled up toward the household. As soon as he reached the lawn, the two pulled Gillian out of the shadows and forced her down the avenue in the direction of the woods. The night provided little illumination in the woodland, and Gillian feared they might stumble at any moment and be injured, or worse—fall on Rose's blade. But the two seemed to know their way around, and presently a hazy light filtered through the branches from the distance, so that even Gillian could see the copse and flowers and roots that they hastened her across.

They exited the woods into a garden area near the high fence that bordered all of Nemi. The jasmine trailing up the wrought iron posts were open even more than she remembered, and their bedewed petals glistened in the strange light that seeped in from beyond the fence. It was the color of deep ocean water. Glancing up, Gillian saw now how the night heaven crowned Nemi like a cap, diffusing at the borders and vanishing into this sea of haze.

The two pitched her roughly to her knees so that her face fell into a cushion of jasmine. She looked up at them, seeing clearly the hatred in their eyes.

"That is the gateway to the universe," Gina said, "or oblivion, however, you may interpret it. The path between Ultimate Reality and the lies of mortality." She grinned and tossed her head so that her hair fell behind her shoulders. "Or at least that's what these decadent liars would have us believe—that reality is what we make it, and we can only make it by embracing their ideals of submission and domination, yin and yang, give and take."

"Take," Rose chortled and admired her reflection in the knife blade. "It's time for us to take, isn't it, Gina?"

Gina nodded, and raised her pretty chin to give Gillian a photo-perfect pout. "I do not accept these inane ideals of reciprocal physical pleasures, and don't give a damn about ethereal accord or spiritual fulfillment. What I can enjoy I will take without worrying about the undeserving or even death. They want us to believe death is but a lie, did you know that, Gillian?"

Gillian turned from the jasmine and sitting up, stared at her mutely.

Gina licked her lips and said in a baiting tone, "You do not know yet the difference between reality and Ultimate Reality? That Ultimate Reality comes when we have embraced the sensual, the loving, the fulfillment of our precious souls—when we become as gods and cannot die or suffer permanent damage. Only long enough to revamp ourselves, rebirth ourselves, even in the same, exact bodies we incorporated before, if that is our wish?"

Gillian exhaled slowly. Secretly, she knew it was all true and was glad for it. Her knowledge resented the mockery of the sacred as displayed by this petty girl.

"Why do you scoff at it, Gina?"

She laughed. "Scoff at it? Oh, no, dear Disciple. I embrace it! But I am tired of playing the slave to the slave-makers. That's all. I should not have to serve as watcher to boot-kissing wretches like you ever again when I can have money and comfort and anything I want."

Gillian blinked. "In the world of lies and mortality? What good is that?"

"What good is it?" They both laughed now and Gina kicked up the grass in front of Gillian, scattering dewy leaves over her knees. "I came here as a prisoner, Gillian, just like Rose. We proved ourselves and won our freedom. In fact, we excelled so well in our rehabilitation that Madam made us Leather Wives. For generations, we served as Dommes and finally we asked for retirement—retirement to Earth, with full knowledge of our enlightenment. But no, Madam could not be so generous. So we decided it was time to stop following the codes of the Leather Wives so rigidly, and devote more time to indulging in the pleasures that go beyond the sexual politics of this place. And how did she reward our choice? By decreeing we are to return to Earth, but expunged of all memory of this place, to suffer mortality as if we had never left. Ignorant, mortal, without a clue of how to claim what we deserve!"

Gina's face glowed pale. Rose patted her quivering shoulder and glared at Gillian, slicing the air with mock strikes of her knife.

"You whores should be the ones left in ignorance," she hissed.

Gina shook her head and her beauty bloomed again in all its shallow glory. "We are ready to go, Gillian, to face punishment for our self-liberation. For the fates have been kind and have brought us new wisdom from a kindred spirit. We are pledged members of a new Discipleship, and the universe—real or unreal—will be opened before us and give us all we ask for."

Gillian sucked back the unspoken fear these mad words created. She tried to shrug indifferently. "Okay."

Rose sneered. "But not before you help settle a bet."

"What bet?"

Rose gestured to her right. "See that space?"

Gillian followed her gesture down the fence and saw between two of the posts a widened spot. It must have taken them hours and the use of stolen tools to spread the iron bars to make a place wide enough that anyone could just crawl right out and into the void beyond.

Gooseflesh popped up over every inch of Gillian's skin and she turned her disbelieving eyes on them.

"No!"

Gina kicked again, but this time Gillian turned quickly and jumped up. She started to run from them, but Gina caught up with her and, leaping on Gillian's back, pulled her down into the flowers. As Gina batted at her with closed fists, Gillian rolled over onto her back. She screamed and kicked at Gina wildly, managing to push her away enough to get to her knees. But at that moment Rose ran up and grabbed Gillian's hair. The point of her knife jabbed Gillian's collarbone. Gina got to her feet, and swatting the leaves and petals from her own hair, bared her teeth as she regarded Gillian.

"Oh, just get up, bitch!"

Rose stood up with Gillian, the knife still pricking Gillian's flesh. Angered, Gillian made a fist and slammed it into the girl's arm. The arm and knife were thrust away and Gillian sprinted past them both toward the woods. They ran after her, and before she reached the first welcoming tree, Gina barreled low and seized her ankles. Gillian spilled to the ground. Gina crawled atop her legs and pelted her back with both fists. Gillian growled and thrashed, trying to turn over, but the next second, the knife blade glinted in front of her face.

Gina straddled her back and yanked her head back by the roots of her hair.

"Bruce seemed to like this blond hair," Gina grunted. "What say we leave him a souvenir, Rose?"

Rose giggled and kneeled in front of Gillian. She lowered the blade and pressed it to her scalp. Gillian shrieked and closed her eyes just as a missile hurtled toward them from the woods. It pierced Rose's back with an ugly thud. Rose uttered a single cry and the knife fell from her grip. As she fell over, Gillian noticed the spear protruding from the muscles just above Rose's shoulder blade, and looking up, saw Bruce come out of the woods.

Gina let out a shriek more shrill and more wounded than her friend's. As Bruce kicked the knife away, Gina's hands sank about Gillian's throat. He bent immediately and slapped Gina backhanded. She squalled like an animal and leapt up, jumping into him with all her weight. He stumbled back over the fallen Rose, taking Gina with him. She growled and seized his balls.

Gillian got up as Bruce twisted and shoved Gina off. But as he scooted back, Gina flew up on him again and seized his neck. Bruce banged his palms against her ears. She roared in pain, releasing him. Sitting up, Bruce grabbed her shoulders, just as she reached forward and clenched his balls again.

Gillian ran forward and kicked Gina's arm. The hold broke and Gina rose and lunged at Gillian, grabbing a handful of hair and pulling her to the ground. Gillian hit the thighs in front of her and tried to bite the flesh she saw. Gina swooped down to both knees and slapped her face. Gillian shoved back at her with open palms and Gina was rocked back a little. As Gina reclaimed her balance, she spotted the knife and raked the grass for it with her fingers. Gillian got to one knee and slapped her. Gina's head snapped back, but in that moment she snatched up the knife. She caught Gillian by her hair and raised the knife high.

Just as the cold blade swooped toward Gillian's face, her eyes closed and she heard Gina scream like a banshee.

She looked and saw Bruce had subdued the girl by the wrist of her hand that held the weapon.

He yanked Gina to her feet, as she clawed at him with her free hand and kicked back, but he shifted on one foot in time to dodge her heel. Letting go of her hair, he spun Gina around toward him and punched her squarely in the face. The blow was thick and awful and blood spattered out over Gina's hair and the front of her dress. She sank at once. Bruce let her go, twisting the knife out of her grip as her knees sank to the earth. Gina's hands folded over her nose and mouth and she stared up at him with a look of incredulous shock.

"You bastard," she sobbed, "you broke my nose!"

Bruce sighed and shook his head as three guards emerged from the woods. One of them lowered his spear at Gina while the other attended Rose. Bruce moved toward Gillian and pulled her to her feet. He looked her over and then pointed to the ground.

"That's their knife," he said to the third man.

The guard seized it and sheathed it in a loop at his belt. He glanced around, and seeing the damaged fence, questioned Gillian, "They were planning to push you out?"

"Yes, sir."

Bruce brushed the leaves and grass from her hair.

"Take these bitches directly to the prison," he said to the guards, "and have them locked in solitary. Have a physician sent for Domme Rose. I take all responsibility for any questions that will, doubtlessly, arise."

The third looked at the fence. "I shall send others immediately to have that repaired." He regarded Gillian a moment. "You will escort her home?"

"Yes. And if you see the Warden before I do, make sure he is reminded that Madam's instructions were that I take whatever precautions I deem necessary for her safety."

"Of course. If not for your vigilance, God knows what these lunatics might have done." He looked at the guard beside Rose and said, "Let's get them out of here."

Gina was ordered to her feet. Then her guard directed her into the woods after his companions who carried Rose.

Gillian's heart began to beat steadily again as she watched them depart. She looked at Bruce, who stood surveying the fence with his hands on his hips. Her heart quickened again, this time not from dread but from having to face the fact she was but a duty to him. Soon the face she had dreamed of kissing and of pressing to her breasts would turn away from her again.

As he kneeled at the fence to inspect the damage, she knew it was more than just lust she felt for him. It was his stalwart personality and unwavering principles that had captivated her, made her desire him so dearly. These things are what had saved her from Rose and Gina, and overshadowed even the Warden's virile appeal. Even if she were only a duty to him, he took his duties as seriously as the other guards. That he sought to guard and protect all the women of Nemi spoke of a chivalry that was real, a virtue few men of her time possessed. It crowned his other, splendid qualities.

Oh, God, it's no wonder I love him.

The unexpected thought caught the breath in her lungs.

She struggled to forget the tormenting thought and came up behind him.

"Thank you."

He looked up at her and the smile that greeted her was the old one she knew so well, boastful and boyishly vulnerable at once.

"You're welcome," he said. He stood up and she was overcome with shyness so that she laughed lightly.

"You have known them a while, haven't you?"

His voice was guarded, "Yes." He smiled tightly and went on, "I feel ashamed to admit to my own stupidity, but I did get involved with them. I was especially knocked over by Gina. That's what I get for opening my heart to the wrong person."

Gillian felt a pang of envy. No wonder he had talked so threateningly to Gina the night before. The woman had wounded him. It pained a little, knowing his protectiveness had been tinged somewhat by a relationship gone sour.

But she smiled and hugged herself. "Well, yes, but I suppose we're all guilty of that."

The humor faded in his eyes suddenly and a flash of pain crossed his face. When it passed, he drew a deep breath and looked at her in a way that made her feel as exposed as she had been while on the Rapture Pillar.

"You speak without permission, Disciple Gillian. Isn't it bad enough to have ignored my warning about them?"

She blinked, astonished by the abrupt change of his tone. She felt humbled, but could not stop the tears that sprang to her eyes. All the sadness she had known when he disappeared out of her life before now came spilling back.

"Why did you run off without a word to me?" she demanded. "You have no idea how I wanted to see you again! How many times I bugged your friends, asking them when you would be back, where you were! Don't you know—" She choked back the next words. They were all charges without reason, for he owed her nothing, not a thing, especially when she had been too shy to reveal her true self to him back on Earth.

She quickly wiped away the tear that rolled down her cheek and stared at him, hating her audacity, her selfishness. "Oh, God, this is stupid! I am so sorry. I have no right, none whatsoever, not when I was too damned shy, too damned ashamed to let you know how I felt!"

He was silent, regarding her in a way she could not read. She wished he would laugh or shake his head at her sappy admission. But he only studied her face, his hands set on his hips, and slowly his brow grew stern and his brown eyes reproachful.

"You will also use unsuitable language? You obviously have no concept of the word 'obey', Disciple."

Bruce took her by the arm and turned about and led her away to the edge of the woods. They walked along the boundary until at last they came upon a small rock bench. He leaned her over and set her hands against the smooth seat. Gillian's heart pumped with growing apprehension.

"Put your legs together," he said and when she did so, he

flipped up the hem of her dress. She gasped sharply, but he peeled down her panties without hesitation and unbuckled the belt at his waist.

He patted her buttocks. At her shudder, he bent forward and said into her ear, "You will hold on to that bench without moving, or the next time that these panties come down will be right before I bind you to the Pillar you slept on last night."

Gillian weakened with emotion, and just as she thought she would fall over from her abashment, he raised his hand and brought the belt down across her buttocks. She flinched from the singular pain and he dealt another stroke.

He touched her smarting buttocks, then strolled his fingers to the cleft between her thighs. He brushed her nether hair for a moment or two and then parted her thighs. With a finger, he entered her pussy. Her hips strained against the impetuous need he incited and her clit fluttered wildly. He drew out and stroked her buttocks once more. She blushed painfully, and he came to stand beside her again, with his feet planted firmly on the ground, and lifted the belt.

He spanked her more strongly now, so that her butt was soon raw. Her hips jiggled under the snapping leather and her wails echoed all about them. She looked back at him tearfully, hoping he would have mercy.

"You will not look back or close your eyes," he commanded and punished her all the harder.

Her head snapped forward and she stared straight ahead as her flesh quivered under the belt's loud, stinging strokes. But her clit beat as soundly as his chastising hand. To her further embarrassment, her thighs grew slick from the moisture flooding from her pussy.

Gillian was breathless when at last he stopped. He touched her backside again. The chastened flesh throbbed.

"Good," he said. "Now you will listen to me, Gillian, and

take my words to heart unless you want me to spank you again. You were wrong in what you said. I am the one who is to blame. I should have ordered you to tell me your feelings. But I was too ashamed, too embarrassed to show you the nature of my desire—how I wanted to take you and chastise you with my kisses, scold you with my desire! To punish you thoroughly at every opportunity and delight in delivering that punishment.

"If there's one thing I have learned from this experience with those two bitches, it is that I loathe the man that I was. So you had best be prepared to accept me back into your life, Gillian. I plan on dealing with you just as I always dreamed—whether we're here in Nemi or beyond that sea-green horizon. What I yearned to do before, believe me, I will do now. With tender discipline I intend to be your sole Master. The Ur'theriems may disapprove, and Madam can be shocked. Damn the consequences, you are mine now."

Gillian gaped. As the words resounded in her head, he raised her hands from the bench and spun her about. She was crushed in his fierce embrace. His hungered kiss stole her last breath and scattered every vestige of doubt in her heart. She had never known such a moment of sublime rightness. The old fantasies dimmed in comparison to this luxurious hopelessness his restraining arms imparted.

He nuzzled her ear and said in a voice so low no other could ever have overheard, "I adore you, Disciple Gillian, and need you more than you will ever know."

She shivered and, looking through her misted tears, touched his chin. He pressed his lips to her throat and browsed the flesh there with electrifying little kisses. Her arms laced about his sturdy neck and she met his lips, kissing him heartily, tenderly, hungrily. He pulled the ribbons completely from her hair so that it spilled over her shoulders, and sitting down on the grass, he pulled her atop his lap. Gillian cupped his face and smothered it with kisses. She tugged his vest from his arms, lifted his shirt, and stroked her tongue across his firm chest. She sighed at the feel of his hair there and nuzzled her nose into his navel.

At his soft laugh, she laced her legs about him and unbuttoned his pants. His cock burst forth, enormous and hard as an oak spike.

Gillian tossed her hair over one shoulder. Kneeling, she lifted his shaft. She flicked her tongue over the great head, relishing the taste of the droplets of cum that seeped out. Taking the root of his cock into her hand, she devoured it, sucking deeply, feeling his hands stiffen against her cheeks.

"Wait," he whispered. He pulled her up and, kissing her again, tore the dress from her shoulders. "Stand," he said. He slapped one of the bells at her shoes, making it ring sharply, and smiled.

"Those you may keep." His hands grazed up her thighs and he kneeled in turn to bury his face between them. Kissing the hair at her pubis, he licked open the folds of her vagina.

Gillian's clit throbbed and she sighed wantonly. With another soft laugh, he slapped her chastened ass.

"Bend over that bench again."

She pouted anxiously but complied. Bruce stood up behind her and massaged her sensitive thighs, then gently inserted his finger into her anus, filling her with delectable discomfort. He lifted her hips upward a bit as the hot head of his cock pressed against her pussy. Gillian moaned and writhed her hips urgently.

"Fuck me, Sir Bruce, please!"

He answered by spanking her upturned ass. A frustrated whimper rose to her mouth, but she suppressed it and tried to keep her hips still. He gathered her dangling breasts and massaged them roughly, pinching her nipples until she moaned again. Her passion was so intense she felt giddy, and when the head of his cock penetrated her, a heated tingle swept up her spine.

Bruce grasped her hair and plunged thoroughly. He fed her

pussy with long, deliberately slow thrusts. Her hips strained to meet each tantalizing stroke. When her moans grew louder, he seized her hips and fucked her rapidly. As if he were deflowering her very body and soul, he hammered, lifting her heels off the ground so that the little bells on her shoes chimed discordantly. Her vagina muscles constricted in eager anticipation and at last his cum rocketed into her.

She gasped with the rapturous climax. Before she could even breathe again, he pulled her up by the wrists. He bound her against his chest so that his heartbeat thundered against her back. Her tender behind rubbed his cock as he cupped her breasts and whispered into her ear.

"I love you, Gillian."

Gillian's elation was unbound. "I love you too, sir . . . oh, how I love you!"

She moaned and undulated in the hot fetters of his embrace, and tilting her head back, she kissed his waiting mouth. Her will gave itself over utterly to his command. A sensation of consummate liberation swept through her; a sensation she had looked for all her life—and one that was hers to keep and cherish for the rest of her days.

11

Bruce was not ready to deliver Gillian back to the household. Instead, he led her to the guards' compound, where, unsurprisingly, he found the Warden standing at the gate. The man was arguing with the compound commander, Sir Karl.

Noticing their approach, Sir Karl gestured toward Bruce.

"There, man, ask him yourself!"

The Warden turned and seeing Gillian, the wrath eased noticeably from his bearing. But when in the next moment he reached for her, Bruce put himself between the two of them. The Warden's face flared and his usual rich tone sounded brittle.

"You have performed well in keeping this girl safe today, Sir Bruce. The disavowed Leather Wives have been put in solitary, and you can now rest assured that your duties tomorrow will not be so demanding. I am assuming custody of the Disciple now and will see to it no harm befalls her."

Bruce felt Gillian tremble and wound his arm about her instinctively. "No harm will befall her, Warden. She'll be sleeping in my home tonight."

The Warden's congenial tone went flat. "And by whose orders, Sir Bruce? I am Captain of all Nemian guards, do not forget."

"My instructions came from Madam," Bruce answered. "And unless you wish to challenge your superior, you will not contest where I decide she stays tonight."

The Warden looked at Gillian for several moments and then smiled courteously. "I shall indeed speak with Madam." As he started to pass by them, he made a low promise, "Whatever her decision, Bruce, this is not done."

When he was gone, Sir Karl exhaled loudly. "I hope you know what you are doing, Bruce."

Bruce patted his arm and answered with only a "goodnight." He would deal with the Warden and any problem with Madam come morning. Soft light strained through the windows of several chalets as he led Gillian through the compound. Music and laughter poured out of the open windows of the taverns. But he had no desire to join his friends tonight. Another time, perhaps, after Gillian had had time to relax from the day's adventures and he had savored her fully.

Alone with her at last in his chalet, he enjoyed the surprise that came to her face at seeing all the modern comforts she had left behind on Earth. He turned on the CD player, finding the last refrains of a haunting ballad lilting through a channel.

Gillian stood bashfully on the plush throw rug on the floor, her hands held tightly in front of her. With her disheveled hair and the youthful dress, he thought she looked like a mischievous girl.

But that's what Disciples are supposed to be, he thought.

He laughed happily and lifted her off the rug. Carrying her to the sofa, he sat her down. He knelt in front of her and kissed her again with more relish this time, slowly stroking every inch of her soft flesh as he disrobed her. He even removed her shoes this time, and kissed her small toes.

His cock stiffened. "Yes, I think you shall stay naked for a while."

Her lips spread out in a lazy, glorious smile and she kissed him shyly. Laying her down, he parted her thighs and massaged her musky delta until it soaked his fingers. He pulled her down off the sofa into his lap.

"Touch me," he said, pressing her hand to his cock.

The commanding tone made her eyes widen nervously. But she obeyed, stroking it gently with her fingers, then massaging it firmly with both hands. His need was too great to bear. He clasped her firmly about the waist and raising her up, impaled her upon his eager cock.

"Ride me. Fast and hard!"

Her pert breasts jiggled as she obeyed and he pinched the stone-hard nipples so that she emitted a wanton moan. She was so wet and as incredibly taut as earlier, her face adorably strained by her mounting pleasure. Just as he sensed she was about to climax, he squeezed her clit between his forefinger and thumb. She shuddered violently, and her head fell back, her vagina quivering. He pressed her between the sofa and his thrusting loins. With a remorseless harshness he fucked her, coming with an exhilarating force.

As he lay down breathless on the floor, she licked his balls and penis clean with her tongue.

"Come here," he whispered. She crawled to him, smiling, and lay down in his arms. Soon she was asleep. As Bruce drifted off as well, he thought of the coming day, and all the new and exciting ways to love her.

With the arrival of morning, Bruce threw some bread into the toaster, brewed coffee, and fried up some bacon and eggs while Gillian slept. He took a long shower before waking her. After they had eaten, he watched as she bathed. He even observed while she brushed and ribboned her hair. He had no clean garments to offer her, but that didn't matter. He was proud to show her off, naked but for her braids, as he escorted her outside.

He walked with her through the woodland surrounding the compound for a time, and gave her permission to speak as she wished. They discussed their mutual reasons for coming to Nemi and the strange and often exhilarating things they had experienced. Gillian's eyes softened sadly as he explained how the Saphorian's invitation played on his sense of adventure and gave him hope of finding that fulfillment he feared to pursue on Earth. And as she told him of her encounter with the Ur'theriem, Xaqriel, Bruce had to force away the jealousy that knotted his gut. But as they talked, he did not doubt that she loved him or that she had for a long time. The troubled knit of her brow vanished completely when he told her again how much he loved her. They held hands as they strolled, and even as they returned to the compound, he did not care who saw how he kissed her palms or how he grinned like a smitten schoolboy.

He took her to the café and ordered her a mug of spiced water. He smoked as she sipped it, admiring the firmness of her breasts and the way her bangs sculpted her face. He wanted so to see those breasts dangle and her hair spill wildly. When she related the distasteful encounter—or near encounter—with the soured prisoner in the pavilion the night before, a wonderful idea came to his mind.

As they left, he told her not to speak again until he allowed. At her timid nod, he led her through the pathway past the last of the chalets to the wide common area situated at the back of the compound. Here stood the commodities store, the leather and iron smithies' shops, the weapons shack, and other buildings used for storage. But the area was also used for displaying girls, from a polished rotating oak wheel, cross-beamed and shafted into a sturdy hollow steel pole that had been driven and cemented into the ground.

Two girls had already been set upon the wheel: they were suspended with their bellies down, their arms and legs spread apart and secured at wrists and ankles by leather-padded brass cuffs dangling from chains that draped the wheel. There were wide stools nearby and presently a man sat on one of these. A flail with suede thongs lay across his lap. Seeing them coming, the man rose and shook Bruce's hand. He scowled at Gillian and gave a rehearsed growl. It was believable enough to make her gasp and hide behind Bruce. The gesture made him smile, but nevertheless, he grabbed her hand and pulled her out before the man.

"Your girl needs a little contemplation time, sir?"

"Oh, yes," Bruce replied. The man nodded and positioned a stool under a free area of the wheel. Bruce ordered Gillian to step up, and together the men lifted her. Her eyes filled with frightened tears, and as they cuffed her, she began to sob openly.

"No, please," she whimpered.

She looked so deliciously helpless suspended from the wheel. Bruce spanked her breasts roughly, making her moan as she wept. Reaching between her legs, he touched her pussy lips. They were moist and so warm, and as he smacked the exposed little clit, it beat hotly against his fingers.

But her crying grew loud and more agitated. He stood back and regarded her with a deliberate coolness.

"Oh, Sir Bruce! Have mercy, please!"

He grimaced and gestured to the man. He raised the flail and commenced to lash it over her breasts and stomach. The thongs produced only the lightest of pink stripes across her flesh, but Gillian flinched and screamed as if the man was flaying her alive. But when Bruce said it was enough, he saw that the pout on her tear-stained face came more from confusion and humiliation than anything else.

"I am going for a cup of coffee," he told her firmly, "and leave this man to punish you for the least infraction."

"Sir Bruce," she started to wail, but he covered her mouth with his hand.

"This is not punishment. Not yet, anyway. I enjoy seeing you this way and so you should accept it."

She frowned crossly but at last she nodded, and he left her for a time to think of what he had told her. He hoped she would learn a little obedience from the display, but as he headed back down to the main pathway, he heard her let loose with a vexed wail. She did not stop and he turned, growing angry now, and marched back.

She writhed frantically under the overseer's spanking flail, but her screaming did not stop—not until Bruce assumed the instrument himself and dealt out a volley of heated strokes across her flesh. She gasped again and tried to suppress her crying. He punished her breasts and thighs until they glowed like rose-dust. When he deemed it was enough, he handed the flail back to the overseer. She was panting softly, her falling tears forming a puddle on the ground. Without a word he turned his back and left her to her punishment.

He did not hear her protest once during his leisurely visit to the café.

It was almost midday by the time he finished his coffee and lit a cigarette. He stepped outside again, feeling an urge to get to the household soon. He wanted to talk with Madam about obtaining Gillian for his own house girl. But Gillian's recent behavior made him realize she needed to be humbled further before he approached Madam, in case the proprietress raised any question of his fitness to be the sole possessor of a Disciple.

So, he went back to the common area. The other girls still hung there and he saw their masters looking on from the door of the weapons shack. He helped the overseer unshackle and lower Gillian. Her face beamed with relief at her release, but that relief was short-lived when she saw the disapproval in his face. Saying nothing, he threw her over one shoulder and carried her to the café.

On the outer grounds stood two wooden staves facing the tables set outside, each bolted near their tops with chains that hung midway down the wood. Each chain was tethered with leather cuffs. Bruce set Gillian down between the staves so that she kneeled facing the tables. He buckled a cuff to either of her wrists. Going inside, he got a strip of cloth from the owner. On returning to Gillian, he used it to bind her ankles tautly together.

He stood in front of her, and her eyes lowered as he quietly observed her. Her eyelashes were damp and her breasts still suffused from their recent chastening, but he could spare no mercy.

"It's time to eat," he said.

She bit her bottom lip nervously, and he continued, "You will beg for your meal, by beseeching each man you see to feed that pretty little mouth of yours."

She cringed and started to weep again. "Please, no!"

He shook his finger at her. "It's this kind of behavior that brought you here, Gillian. You will be better off to learn quickly that to protest against display or punishment will earn you only the severest of consequences.

"Now, you will call out 'Feed me, sir, please,' to every man who passes by. If they are generous, you shall, of course, thank them modestly. And if I see you have failed to beseech any one of them, I will use my belt where it does the most good. Do you understand this, Gillian?"

"Y . . . yes, sir."

He patted her head and went inside then and ordered a sandwich and a bowl of boiled potatoes to be brought out to a table. Returning outside, he took a seat at one of the tables and watched as Gillian asked her humbling question to the first guard who ventured in from the pathway.

Her voice broke with tears, "Feed me, sir, please?"

The man smiled but shook his head. "Not now, pretty one, maybe another time."

He walked inside and soon other men were passing in and out. Gillian made her request to them all, and when the serving boy delivered the plate from the kitchen, Bruce relished his meal with a delight unmatched. At length, one guard did show Gillian interest. Bruce watched keenly as he lowered his pants enough to pull his aroused organ out and offer it to her mouth. She accepted it shyly and sucked until he climaxed. She did not forget to give her gratitude, and as he buttoned his pants, he spoke something too softly for Bruce to overhear. The guard continued on into the café and Bruce saw Gillian's eyes dart his way. Her hips undulated ever so slightly, but he pretended to look away, and when again he looked at her, saw she was sulking.

Gillian fed on the cum of five guards before Bruce decided to free her. She smiled shyly as he released her wrists and pulled her to her feet. Immediately, he took her home and gave her water to drink before ordering her to lie across his bed.

A trembling, mischievous angel she was to him. He lifted her so that her head settled on the pillow, and kissed the strands of her blond hair and stroked the crumple from her brow. Then, straddling her shoulders, he smoothed her pink lips with his thumb.

"Suck me off now, little Disciple, and do it as well as you seemed to do for those men."

She smiled voluptuously, and he guided his hard cock to her mouth. Her lips closed about the head and she sucked energetically. His eyes closed, and his pelvis moved forward and back.

As he fucked her taut, obedient mouth, he hoped her lesson had been enough to make a lasting impression on her. For as exciting as it had been to watch her go down on those others, he vowed that never again would she give another man pleasure.

His orgasm was intense. Afterward he held her for a time, lavishing kisses on her and blowing on her belly until she giggled. She was soon pouting, though, and dared to beg him to fuck her.

"Behave yourself," he whispered.

Rising from the bed, he closed the door behind him as he went into the front room. He lit a cigarette and inhaled slowly, and as he stared out the window, meditated on the words he would soon need. They had to be phrased in the most convincing, frank, unyielding, and yet polite manner he could muster—if he was to stand a rat's chance in Hamelin of securing Madam's consent to keep Gillian.

12

Gillian had been dismayed and apprehensive when Sir Bruce gave her one of his shirts to wear and told her they were going to the household. Although she sensed he planned more than just delivering her back, his tenseness had played on her imagination. The Leather Wife who met them at the front door had a most annoying look of disapproval on her face. Even Madam's personal guard who escorted them to the door appeared to be sizing Bruce up, as if at any moment he might assault Bruce with his stave. Gillian knew these ideas were probably only nervous fancy, but when at last they were allowed entrance into Madam's room, she was shocked to find the Warden there. The hostility between the two men infused the atmosphere. Worse, Madam was not in a good mood.

She sat in a fan-backed wicker chair, looking almost like a queen, with her hair gathered in tight curls high upon her head. She wore a loose-woven gown of deep red that accentuated her exotic features. Her eyes narrowed upon them as they entered. At once, she snapped her fingers. "Come, Gillian, and bow your head to the floor!"

Gillian obeyed immediately, casting a single look over her shoulder to Sir Bruce. Madam snapped her finger again as she approached and told her to face the chair as she bowed.

Madam sighed as Gillian's brow touched the floor. Sitting up, she lifted the shirt and smacked Gillian's naked bottom. But it was the men Madam addressed, and her tone was thin, exasperated.

"Sir Bruce, our Warden has told me of last night's events—at least from his viewpoint. Of course, he was not party to what happened with Rose and Gina. I would appreciate you explaining to me your version of this conflict, as well as why you kept Disciple Gillian in your home all night."

"And all morning," the Warden added in his velvety drawl.

Despite his suave manners and intimidating looks, Gillian felt only a vague fondness for the Warden now. Even though she was flattered that he was challenging Bruce to claim her, she simply wished the man would forget all that had happened between them.

"That's enough," Madam reprimanded him sharply. "You may wait in the foyer until I call you."

The Warden lifted an unbelieving eyebrow. "But Madam, I must insist—"

"You charged in on me, dear Warden, without the civility to knock. You have made charges without permitting Sir Bruce the benefit of being here to defend himself. Now you shall wait while I listen privately to his side of the story."

Gillian was surprised Madam had let the Warden come in at all, but she was not surprised to see the vexed flash of his eyes now. Nevertheless, he apologized and stepped out. It was only when he was gone that Gillian noticed a figure standing very still near the black veil canopy of Madam's bed. It was Domme Camille. She smoked a slender cigarette in a lengthy filter and looked at the floor as if very bored. Yet the true feelings of this hard and beautiful woman had always been difficult to ascertain. Gillian could not help but wonder if her motive for being in the room was to temper the wrath she feared Madam might demonstrate toward Bruce.

Madam's fingers trailed down the length of Gillian's back slowly, and when she reached the end of her spine, she smacked Gillian soundly on the ass. The sound rang crisply against the walls, and though Gillian tensed expectantly, Madam stayed her hand.

"Now, explain yourself, Sir Bruce," she said.

He told her everything, from the events in the pavilion to his taking Gillian to his chalet in the guards' compound, giving blunt, logical explanations for all of his actions. When he was finished, Madam responded to his logic with a question that rationality could not answer.

"Ah, Sir Bruce, you are infatuated with this Disciple, are you not?"

Gillian could not see his face and the moments seemed to lengthen into hours as she waited to hear his response.

"I knew her on Earth, Madam," he admitted. "And I wanted her then. Like any coward, I pretended not to understand she wanted me as well. But in Nemi I've grasped the true nature of myself, and as heaven has seen fit to bring us together again, I intend to keep her."

"Knew her," Madam repeated softly. "Is this true, Gillian?"

Made nervous by the sudden question, Gillian said faintly, "Yes, Madam."

"Well. And so you have claimed that you did not know her feelings then. This requires more consideration of the matter. Gillian must be sure before any decision is reached."

"Sure of what?" Bruce asked and then blurted out, "We love one another. It is enough."

Madam's face brightened with impatience. "I will not be spoken to in that tone by someone beneath my station, Sir Bruce. It may be that she does love you. All considerations for her declaration and your declaration will be taken into account. For now, she will remain here in the household—confined for a while so she may have time to think, away from both you and the Warden."

Bruce's voice shook, "You can't do this. She is mine!"

"I can do whatever I deem proper," Madam retorted. "Now, return to the guards' compound and resume your daily routine. I shall certainly see to it that the Warden does not deal unfairly with you over this."

Gillian's heart sank. She raised her head defiantly and looked at Bruce. His hands were knotted into fists at his hips and his brow heavily furrowed. She feared he would yell at Madam and lose in a single heated moment all they had rediscovered. Forgetting everything else, Gillian stood and looked Madam directly in her eyes.

Madam's reprimand was low but cautioning. "Gillian!"

Gillian shook her head. "I love Bruce," she declared. "I do not wish to be anyone's Disciple except his."

Madam's face was hard, but Gillian saw what looked to be a suppressed smile on her lips. Her eyes were patient. At length she asked, "Do you think you love this man?"

"I know I do!"

Bruce strode to Gillian's side. He took her hand, and she held fast to it and felt the burning tears gush over her cheeks. "I love him! I cannot bear to be away from him. Nor do I care for any pleasure—in this world or any other—except to be his and his alone."

Madam's eyes closed, and the smile ripened full and sweet on her lips. When she looked at them again, a flash of amber glowed in her eyes. Gillian felt uneasy, as if for a fleeting moment, she was looking not simply at Madam, but someone else she knew but could not place. Power, gentle and subtle, radiated from the woman, tempering the atmosphere with a sweetness as unrefined and unearthly as the Ur'theriems' angelic powers.

"So, Sir Bruce," she said, "you love Gillian and you say she is yours. What does this exactly mean to you?"

Bruce's brow darkened. "She is mine to love, mine to discipline, mine to cherish. I cannot, will not, let any other man . . ." His words trailed, but the intensity of his declaration hung in the air.

"You two leave us no choice," Madam answered. She closed her eyes again and let her head fall back on her shoulders. Her arms raised heavenward. At once, the morning skies outside the windows darkened. Lightning flashed in the distance, and the scenery outside the household vanished before their eyes. A flood of rainbow-colored light waved over the glass panes. Gillian heard a crackling of soft sound and saw the wicks of all the candles in the room kindle to flame. No one had touched them, but the flames glowed full and radiant. It was the last thing Gillian saw before darkness engulfed the room.

She clung to Bruce and felt his steady lips press her brow.

"We're together," he whispered. "I will not let you go."

In seconds the darkness began to pale. Shadows fell over them and soft sunlight danced through these across their limbs. When her vision cleared, Gillian saw that they stood together in center of the Temple of Purity. The golden altar had been moved to the north quadrant and before this altar stood Madam and Xaqriel. For a moment, Madam's skin glowed an intense white. When the moment had passed, she now wore a regal gown of purest white, with a high stiff collar that shimmered with tiny garnets and pearls. Gillian saw again the amber glint in her eyes and something told her that time did not exist in this moment and place. Only the inner, true meaning that was Nemi existed, and they all stood now in the nucleus of it.

Xaqriel spoke to Bruce, "You wish this woman to be your sole and beloved Disciple?"

Bruce took a deep, steadying breath. But his voice was undaunted as he answered. "Yes. Yes, I do."

"And you, Gillian, have found the master of your pleasure and heart in this man?"

Gillian's breast beat resolutely. "Oh yes!"

At Xaqriel's nod, Madam turned to the altar. A slim silver box lay there. This she lifted and turning, spoke, "As in the flesh, so in the spirit. Union of one soul with another so they may be as the god and the goddess: One Eternal. As you were drawn from the Beginning, so forever shall you be drawn. Return home and accept this gift and know that you are blessed among men and women through the reciprocal desire that expresses union of the eternal."

Madam held the box out to Bruce. With a relieved look, he released Gillian's hand and accepted it. At once the light grew dusky pink and a temperate wind buoyed the branches of the trees. Xaqriel's wings appeared, and clasping Madam about the waist, he ascended from the ground. Toward the cloudless sky he sailed with her, winking out of sight in the next second just as suddenly as they had all been whisked from the household.

Gillian turned to Bruce and threw her arms around his neck. His kiss was gentle upon her cheek and he laughed softly.

"For a moment there—after she said return home—I thought she meant Earth." He set the box down upon the altar and pulled his shirt off Gillian completely. His hands slid down over her hips and skimmed over her bare buttocks. He squeezed them and lifted her from the ground so that she felt his hard cock rub against her pubis.

Gillian gyrated greedily and ran her fingers wildly through his hair. "It doesn't matter. Wherever you are is home for me."

"Yes," he said, "but I'd as soon enjoy you in Nemi for as long as possible."

He kissed her again, and her body felt as if it were melting against the very flame of creation.

"I want you now," he murmured, "but let's get home and see this gift."

Frustrated, Gillian wanted to resist. But she did not mind the idea of being alone with him in his chalet. Here, she feared the Ur'theriems might be listening; in the chalet, she could share her vow in privacy and show Bruce how truly she would honor her words. So she nodded and, retrieving the silver box, took his hand. Together they left the Temple and took the path that led home.

Once they were alone in the chalet den, Gillian opened the silver box. Inside was a piece of jewelry: a black leather cord sleeved by golden filigree.

"A choker," Bruce said. He lifted it from the box and held it up to the sunlight coming through the windows. "Or more precisely, a love slave's collar."

Gillian blushed and he bade her to pull her hair aside. He strung the choker gingerly over her head and pinned the antique clasp at the back of her neck. The filigree tickled her throat slightly, but she liked the snug, cool feel of it. Bruce lifted her hair and let it fall slowly over her shoulders as he admired the choker.

"Naked and properly collared," he mused. The lusty smile that came to his lips made Gillian tingle. But she wanted to say something very important and the moment seemed perfect. She sank to her knees on the rug they had made love on before and lowered her cheek over his shoe.

"I am your love slave," she vowed. "I have loved you before I knew you, such a long time! Now it is unbearable to think that we may be separated. I vow to you, Bruce, that I want no other. I shall never seek any other master of my heart. You are my only love and desire."

The love shining in Gillian's eyes nearly took Bruce's breath away. She was sincere and intelligent, vibrant and adventurous. All the important things he had ever really sought in a woman. No woman had ever looked at him the way she did now—as if life was nothing without him being there to share it. And he wanted the same. So lovely, body and soul. It humbled him. His gratitude was boundless. The realm of Nemi had given him this second chance.

He cupped her face. "You are everything I want, Gillian. My fidelity is only to you. I will spend the rest of my life loving you, enjoying the sound of your voice and your company. Whatever may come, in this world or any other, I will be your champion, friend, and lover."

Bruce pulled her up and held her close. The feel of her trembling, desirous mouth was the greatest possession a man could enjoy. He massaged her pussy. Her cleft was damp to the touch and as he treasured the silken heat against his fingers, Gillian moaned and her nipples swelled into hard pink nodules against his chest.

"Oh Master!" She touched his hard cock and moaned again. But Bruce smiled and pulled her hand away.

"No, young lady," he warned. "You may touch me only with permission."

Her eyes flew open wildly. "Master, please?"

It was wicked delight to have her so frustrated. He turned her about by the waist and inclined her back against his shoulder. He stroked her clit until her pussy was sticky and her tight ass undulated fitfully against his hip. He loved how her upturned cheeks warmed him and how her deepening moan resonated with animal need.

His own need was growing dire, too. But he wanted so to see her frustrated a little more. So he led her by the hand to one of the leather-seated stools that stood at the bar.

He pulled it back a ways and said, "Lean across this seat and take hold of the legs. And don't you dare let go until you are permitted."

Gillian obeyed, all the more anxious because she could not see what he was doing. She felt his hands grasp her ass cheeks; he plumped them a little, and then gave her a hard spank. A pang of heat spiraled through her. His strong fingers cupped over her pussy. He stroked her clit until it beat wildly. Her moans were decadent and she could not keep her hips from moving shamelessly.

"Oh Master, fuck me!"

He did not answer, but continued to torment her until she was breathless. His fingers delved into her pussy a time or two, and then he parted her ass cheeks and, bending over, blew on her little anus. It tickled, but then he probed a finger inside. An intrusive sensation bolted through her. It was strangely pleasurable and intimidating at once.

His voice was husky, "This body belongs to me, doesn't it?"

"Yes, sir," she crooned.

"Yes, sir, indeed. It pleases me to see you so frustrated, Gillian, to feel you so wet and anxious, and to know that you will know no satisfaction until I give it to you."

She moaned wantonly as he stepped back. Her flesh seared for more of his touch. She heard him undress, and when she tried to look through the stool legs to catch a glimpse, he made a disapproving sound. At once he laid one hand on the small of her back. With the palm of the other, he spanked her thoroughly. She began to cry, though whether from the pain, humil-

iation, or from raw need, she could not guess. She held tightly
to the stool legs and listened with chagrin to the echo of the
crisp spanks against the walls. When at last he seemed satisfied,
her buttocks were flaming. But she did not try again to peek
and kept her eyes dutifully to the floor.

Moments later she felt the head of his warm, hot cock press
against her fount. He grasped her hips and lifted them a bit,
then drove into her. He was hard and enormous inside her. He
fucked her with strong, fast strokes. She moved her hips as
much as possible to meet each slapping thrust. Deeper and deeper
he seemed to drive into her. Her pleasure intensified and suddenly she climaxed. The power of it was incredible. And still
his cock rocked in and out of her, until at last he came with a
low groan.

Gillian's nether lips were still shuddering with sensation as
he lifted her up from the stool. His mouth moved down her
spine as he went to his knees behind her. He imparted several
loving kisses across her thighs and the backs of her knees.

"Gillian," he said, "you've mastered me entirely."

She was giddy with happiness. Turning in his arms, she bowed
and kissed the top of his head.

"Shall I spank you now, Master?" she teased.

His dark eyes flashed. "I see I still have a lot to teach you
about suitable behavior," he said.

He stood up now and smacked her ass lightly. But he was
grinning as they embraced. "I suppose you know that I will enjoy
every moment of your education, my dear Disciple of Pleasure?"

"Oh yes," Gillian sighed. She closed her eyes and inhaled his
fragrance until her senses felt close to bursting. "And I plan to
enjoy every moment just as much, my Master!"

It was early morning when Gillian awakened to the delicious sensation of Bruce's lips grazing her throat. He threw

back the bedsheet and suckled her nipples, then, unfolding her thighs, rubbed her pussy until she was, very soon, wantonly wet. He watched the emotions on her face as he tantalized her, smiling in that proud, amused way that made her whole body smolder.

"You're mine, all mine," he whispered.

Gillian's hips strained toward him, and she touched his cock, finding it hard and ready under her caressing fingers. She whimpered earnestly. "Please, Master," she begged. "Take me, please . . . !"

Bruce pulled her fiercely into his embrace and kissed her mouth. "You possess me, slave girl!" he sighed. "Mount me now and ride, but slowly. I want to savor the feel of that pussy bouncing up and down on me."

Gillian got to her knees and straddled him. His huge organ penetrated deeply, and it was all she could do not to ride fast. Slowly she rode, her body awash with sensation, her soul craving his firm hand with her. But his mouth parted ever so slightly, and his hips lifted so that his cock pierced her to her wanting core. He seized her hips and thrust her up and down rapidly. Gillian cried out, and her body flushed as her sensations coalesced into a violent orgasm. Bruce's hips drove against her shuddering sex, and she felt his own climax deep inside her.

Breathless, Gillian gazed down at him in repose. Triumphant. Her heart panged and she swept down to deliver a dozen fevered kisses to his lips. He growled low and pulled her down upon the mattress again. With his fingers he touched her slick pussy and caressed her throbbing clit.

"Oh, Master," Gillian moaned.

He kissed her tenderly now. "I love you so much, Gillian."

"I love you, too," she said. "More than anyone can ever know."

They snuggled together in the love-dewed sheets, until the first rays of dawn shone through the bedroom windows. Bruce eventually went back to sleep with his face pressed against Gillian's breasts. For a long time she combed her fingers through his short dark hair. But at length she felt a hunger pang and thought she'd go to the kitchen for something to eat.

Kissing his forehead, she slid softly out of bed and found one of his plain white guard's shirts laid across a chair nearby. She slipped this on and touched the collar at her throat. Exquisite it was, a black leather cord sheathed by golden filigree—an honored gift from Madam when a few nights past she and Bruce had avowed their love in the Temple of Purity. Gillian thrilled to remember those sacred moments. Smiling, she silently thanked the Creator for her fortune and padded out of the bedroom and made her way through the chalet den and into the kitchen.

Doughnuts. The other thing she craved. There were several stacked on a plate and covered with a glass dome. Gillian removed the dome and, taking a doughnut, ate it quickly. She was amused at her hunger, which was more ravenous than usual.

"He sure knows how to give a girl an appetite," she said aloud.

She was sleepy still as she took out a second doughnut and went to stand by the tall narrow window. The view overlooked a fountain pool here in the guards' compound. The water was placid, the surface shimmering with the tangerine and purple reflections of dawn's first light. Gillian nibbled on the doughnut as she gazed at the water and contemplated her present situation. How very fortunate she felt—and how very loved. Gillian had been brought to Nemi by an angel of delight to be a Disciple of Pleasure; and in the end, had found it in the man she'd thought had abandoned her on Earth. Nemi had given her and Bruce a second chance to own up to the mutual desires they'd always hidden, even from each other.

In the end, Bruce had measured up to everything Gillian had

hoped for, and more. She was Bruce's personal love slave, and he her beloved master.

Gillian finished the last bite of doughnut and yawned. She was ready to return to bed, and her drowsy mind filled with fantasies about Bruce. She returned the glass dome to the tray and just as she started to go out the kitchen, a movement of light from the window caught her attention.

It seemed that the sky had changed drastically. Curiously, Gillian stepped to the window. Indeed, the sky was different from what she could see, the beautiful prisms of morning muted and the clouds covered over by what appeared to her eyes as heavy yellow smoke that descended over the fountain outside. The water in the pool whipped haphazardly. Whirls of smoke curled over the outside of the pane. Uneasy, Gillian backed away, and then she saw something manifest on the inside: what appeared to be a moist circle cut into the glass. Curls of smoke infiltrated the design and entered the house. It reeked of sulphur, this smoke, and at once Gillian felt a sense of terrible dread at the smell of it.

"Sir Bruce!" she called. As the tendrils of smoke moved toward her face, she felt whipped by them. At once she was afraid, and she tried to run to the door, but her body was overcome by the need to sleep. She felt herself slumping against the wall, and knew she was sinking but there was nothing she could do to stop it. She heard the shattering of glass, and the next moment it seemed the entire tawny sky whipped through the window. Gillian was blinded by a sulfurous haze. She tried to scream, but the sound was soft as a lullaby in her ears. "Sir Bruce!"

Gillian could not see, not even squinting, and the smoke took substance all about her. It gripped her hands, and though she tried to knock it off, it clung all the more. Her nostrils smarted from the smell, but when she coughed, it receded and a perfume like wilting flowers filled her senses.

A voice, raspy and paper-thin, croaked nearby, "Disciple!"

The startled cry that came to her mouth was silenced by an unfamiliar mouth. Its leathered lips pressed into her own, burning them like live coals and filling her throat with a flavor of rotten eggs just beneath the taste of perfume.

She struggled against the force, and as she flailed at this thing, felt substance and shape in the haze. Limbs, torso, a long, muscular back, all encased in leathered skin.

As the arid mouth began to sweep down to her neck, invisible knees forced her thighs apart. She felt large hands open her vulva. Terrified, she screamed and beat against whatever hallucination or dream had taken possession of her. At once, its unseen hands grabbed her arms and pressed them to her sides. The mouth swooped over her left breast and sucked the whole of it into its hollows. A great cock crushed into her vagina, wounding the delicate inside flesh with its sharp, scalding head.

Screaming again, she rocked left and right in the effort to break the hold of the evil hallucination. A spare laugh emitted from the vaporous throat.

"There is no escape, Disciple."

And as the mouth sucked her next breath, the invisible cock hammered into her.

"No!"

Gillian heard Bruce call her name, and then his footfalls rushing toward the kitchen. The nightmare entity stilled and growled low in its throat. Gillian was able to glance to the door and tried again to shriek. The hateful mouth descended over hers again. It inhaled her breath rapidly, and the haze thickened so she could see nothing but a yellow mist.

Just before she lost consciousness, she heard Bruce run in. But his anxious voice sounded miles away, and his features seemed to dissolve before her eyes. Gillian tried to grasp his hands, but she seemed to be tumbling away from him. Into an oblivion of darkness she tumbled further, into a sleep without dream or desire or even fear.

Bruce still couldn't believe what was going on; Gillian was gone, obviously taken by someone. The kitchen had been filled with a yellow mist when he'd come in answer to Gillian's cry. This mist and the shards of broken glass from the window were all he'd found. At once he'd ran outside the house and called on the aid of other guards. As they had searched he had checked the chalet. But neither he nor the others found her, or any trace of who had taken her. Bruce and his neighbor, Sir Wes, had then gone to Madam's household and told the Dommes there what had happened, or what seemed to have happened.

Bruce wasn't accustomed to the feeling of desperation, and it made him surly. If Madam or the Dommes or other guards noticed, however, they didn't comment; their concern, of course, was to find Gillian. Madam's first task was to send the Dommes and guards on a search of the household and its grounds, the woods beyond, and even the Temple of Purity. When neither Gillian nor any evidence of her recently having been in these places were found, Madam withdrew to her chambers to call Xaqriel for a private conference, returning with a frustrated look in her exotic eyes. Nevertheless, she spoke with the same calm and resolution as always as she summoned her private men to bring the Warden to the household. Bruce suspected him already, and when the man arrived his genteel bearing could not hide his lingering resentment toward Bruce. But as Madam questioned the Warden it was evident to Bruce that he was just as stunned as everyone else. He claimed to know nothing about what had happened to the Disciple he was so enamored of.

Bruce asked Madam to send her men to inspect his own quarters. He joined in on the search, but nothing suspect turned up. Sir Peter, Madam's majordomo, then led the search party on an inspection of the prison. The guards here helped in the search, but by late afternoon it was apparent Gillian was not anywhere in the building or on the grounds, and Sir Peter returned with discouraging news. Madam's next course of action was the ordering of a scouting party to go to the residents' village. Sir Wes volunteered to lead this quest, but the village lay some miles from the household, and Bruce knew it would take many hours before any news from there was heard.

Bruce was pacing the household grounds when the first shadow of evening darkened the sky. Domme Camille joined him and suggested he go get something to eat in the kitchen. He could not think of eating, though he did accept the pack of cigarettes and lighter she'd brought.

"You are not doing Gillian any good," she sighed. "You should go home and rest until we hear something."

Bruce lit one of the cigarettes and stuffed the pack into his inner vest pocket.

In her cropped pants and black tank top, the warm breeze tossing her hair, Bruce thought Domme Camille looked more vulnerable than when dressed in her regular Leather Wife clothing. And again he thought of Gillian—taken against her will; maybe hurt or worse—and he felt both impatient and angry that this could have been allowed to happen.

"The damned Ur'theriems are supposed to protect the Disciples," he grumbled. "So much for divine beings."

Camille frowned uncomfortably, but she didn't respond to the remark. "I'm sure she'll be found, Bruce," she said.

She was being kind, and he was thankful for her companionship even as he felt the need for action. And as he stood there wondering where to go, where to look, he couldn't dismiss his anger at the Ur'theriems. Archangels, he thought sourly, protectors of Nemi.

Suddenly Bruce knew exactly what had befallen Gillian. The

biggest peril to any woman in Nemi: she'd been taken by one of the Dhjinn E'noch. Gillian had told him about the Dhjinn who had spied her while she contemplated in the Temple of Purity just a little while after her official Dedication. Considering the nature of that race, if the Dhjinn had seen her he must have been enraptured. And if so, the Dhjinn surely wouldn't have hesitated to ask the help of any who might be willing to give information about Gillian. Madam's household provided some protection against their intrusion; but Bruce's chalet was as vulnerable as most anywhere else in Nemi. If a pursuing Dhjinn was determined, he would certainly wait out his time until the moment when he could elude detection by the Ur'theriems and infiltrate Nemi long enough to capture the woman in his sights.

Bruce's heart beat swiftly. He was sure that Xaqriel must have already guessed what Bruce now understood. Perhaps he and his brethren were on the tracks of the offending Dhjinn E'noch even now. But Bruce understood something they might not have even guessed—he knew, somehow, who had directed the creature to Gillian.

"Camille, tell Sir Peter to meet me back at the prison," he said.

Domme Camille looked troubled. "What is it?"

"Just tell him, and make it fast," Bruce replied. He started to run toward the prison grounds, his fears growing more anxious with each long sprint.

Bruce was downing a second beer, contemplating ways of entering Madam's abode unseen to take possession of Gillian, when someone pounded on his front door.

He opened it to the sight of more than half a dozen speared guards. Not even the usually courteous Sir Peter asked him for entrance; they simply shoved him aside and entered. The majordomo remained at Bruce's side, with a spear pointed at his chest, as the others began to ransack the place. Bruce demanded an explanation, and the reply Sir Peter gave knocked the breath from his chest.

When they did not find Gillian, Sir Peter announced they were taking him into custody, just as they had already taken the Warden.

Bruce's thoughts spun and he sat down on the sofa, shaking. But his anger got the better of him soon enough and he told Sir Peter and the rest of his bunglers to go to hell. They said nothing but forced him to his feet. Then he saw Domme Camille standing in the doorway. The Leather Wife was distraught; the understandable accusation in her eyes so different from the self-centered kind he had seen not so long ago in the eyes of the former Domme, Gina.

Suddenly the hairs raised on his arms.

Sir Peter gestured to the door with his spear. "Madam will speak with you before Lord Xaqriel arrives."

Bruce took an even breath. "Not before you take me to the prison. I think I know who is behind this."

The majordomo shook his head impatiently. "I've already told you, the girl is not in the Warden's chambers, and he has already been escorted to the household. But just as your friends and associates are questioned, so shall his be. We will find her, Bruce, be assured of that. And if it comes to a forced confession as to her whereabouts, so be it."

"The Warden is no more part of this than I am," Bruce replied. There was nothing to back up the suspicion that drummed in his thoughts, but he wasn't going to ignore it or let them pass it off. "Take me to the prison, now!"

Sir Peter regarded him steadily. "Very well. To the prison, after all."

Sir George, one of the prison guards, had met Bruce and Sir Peter at the front entrance and now led them through the solitary hold. It was dark except for the light of George's lantern. Silence pervaded the place as the three of them walked over the brick. The echo of their footfalls sounded unnatural against the walls.

George stopped and lifted the lantern. Its amber light illuminated the door that stood before them.

"There," he said.

Bruce felt the unease of the other guards who stood watching from out on the staircase landing. His own heart beat unevenly as George unlocked the cell door.

He cleared his throat as the guard pulled it open. Before the lantern light could make its entry Bruce heard laughter from within. He grabbed the lantern and stomped past him, finding under the waning illumination Gina lying on her stomach on a cot, her chin propped in the cradle of her palms. Her beauty would be restored, he knew; the guards had bandaged her nose with gauze and tape, and he knew the prison physician made daily rounds. But that beauty was shallow, more brittle than porcelain. And now she acknowledged his presence with a smirk as cold as her heart.

"Well, Bruce," she snickered, "have you missed me?"

George and Peter flanked Bruce as he confronted her.

"Tell me where the Disciple Gillian is," he demanded.

She pursed her lips in that way he had once found sexy. "Lost her? How would I know where your slut is?"

"She's vanished," he said slowly. "And I think you know what took her. In fact, I think you helped what took her."

Gina yawned and fluttered her eyelashes as if bored. "Really, idiot? You truly think I found a way out of this hole and summoned something to take your slut? Get real!"

His hands balled into fists and he slammed them down onto the mattress beside her face. She flinched and her lips pressed together so hard they blanched.

"Tell me, bitch! What has happened to her?"

She sat up and backed away from him as far as the mattress allowed and looked at the others innocently. "Please, sirs, is it not enough that I am confined here—must I be this man's scapegoat as well?"

Bruce's patience snapped and he yanked her by her hair back down onto her belly.

"Tell us, Gina! If you have one shred of compassion left in you, tell us where she is!"

He felt George and Peter grab his arms. They forced him away from the cot and shoved him to the doorway.

"Control yourself," George roared. "She is right. There's no way she could have been involved in this."

Bruce struggled against the other two men, until Peter pointed his spear at him and George raised his dagger. With a grumble, Bruce exited and Peter followed, while George closed and re-locked the door.

"Think," Peter said. "That woman couldn't have got out of here to design some revenge against Gillian. I think you should go get some rest, Sir—"

The majordomo's next words were silenced by a cackle nearby. It was so low and horrible it hardly sounded human. Troubled, Peter glanced about and asked the others if they had heard it.

George grimaced. "It's just the voodoo woman," he said. "She gets a little wild some nights."

"That other female prisoner?" Bruce asked. "The one suspected of summoning evil spirits against Nemian women?"

George nodded. "Yes."

Peter sighed as if anticipating Bruce's next question. "Gillian isn't here, Bruce. The prison has already been thoroughly checked."

Bruce ignored him. "Which door?"

But George shrugged and pointed to a certain door. "Bitch is in there, awaiting the Ur'theriem court to take her back to Earth. There's no chance of rehabilitation for that one."

Bruce snatched the lantern and ran to the door. Peter and George followed and watched as he threw up the bolt of the panel, slid it open, and peered inside. A sickly light flickered from inside the cell.

George frowned. "None of these prisoners are allowed candles!"

Bruce stood aside. "Open it."

George jabbed a key into the lock and turned it. He rushed in, with Peter following and Bruce at his heels.

In the center of the floor the woman sat, wide-shouldered and crowned with a dirty mop of brownish ringlets. She was huddled over a hollowed brick she had managed to pry from the wall. In the hollow a shred of her dress and bedding from the cot's mattress were burning. Bruce saw two minute pieces of flint lying on the floor beside her.

"What goes on here?" George demanded.

She looked up at them, and her face was disfigured by an insane grin. But she did not speak and turned her eyes back to the brick.

George knelt and quickly drew something out of the fire. He tossed it from hand to hand until it cooled, then held it out and inspected it.

A doll, fashioned of some hardened putty. It was blackened from the fire, but as George turned it over Bruce saw it was not one sculpted figure, but two.

"May I?"

George handed it to him. Bruce turned the figure over in his hands and examined it. One of the dolls had been constructed of raw materials: hair of straw and tiny green stones for eyes, coarse thread for a mouth, smooth stones for breasts, blood for the outline of the vagina, breasts, and buttocks. It was the other figure fused by the fire to the putty doll that sent a bolt of nauseous horror through Bruce's stomach.

The figure was sewn up within the skin of an albino toad. There were dusty markings of ash and blood over the crudely sculpted flesh, traced in a way as to resemble scales.

"My god," Peter said under his breath, "it looks like one of those damned Dhjinn E'nochs!"

Bruce's breath quickened. He turned the thing over in his hand and stroked the smoking straw hair of the putty doll. His legs felt weak, and for the first time in his life he wished he could say he had been wrong about something. How he wished that the Warden had taken Gillian, and that this thing was nothing more than a madwoman's toy.

But when the weird prisoner looked at him again he saw the madness was diminishing, and behind the madness glowed vainglorious contempt. Her thin lips turned up in a smile of fathomless mockery. A mockery not only of the cell that confined her and the guards who watched over it, but of all that Nemi stood for, and the very Disciples her captors were avowed to defend.

Gillian's sighs were crushed beneath a ravenous mouth. Its lips were smooth and hard; its taste could only be described as scalding virility. The large hands that stroked her limbs and combed eagerly through her hair were scorchingly hot. Instinctively, Gillian sensed the fevered force that motivated them, even though it was alien and cryptic to her understanding. She opened her eyes and beheld the cheek of the face of he who kissed her. Perspiration dewed his marbled, stonelike features. His great, sinewy body molded over her and emanated the oddest musk—at once virile and tinged with an odor reminiscent of flame-singed bricks. His hands explored her breasts and thighs. Roughly, adeptly, he massaged her sex. He spread Gillian's thighs and lightly touched her anus, sending a bolt of blushing fire up her spine. The caresses prompted her passion, and soon her hips raised, her wet orifice throbbing in shameless pleading.

Lost in sensation, Gillian welcomed the kissing mouth and touched the lithe, naked arms and back. The texture of his skin was like satiny scales. His loins pressed against her stomach, and she knew a moment's terror at the size of the manhood that loomed above her pubis. Then, as he lifted her buttocks so that she arched toward him, her panic mingled with her passion. Her legs thrashed wildly, and her fists beat into his hard, hard chest. He leaned over her carefully, pinning her wrists down, and with his legs, unfolded her resisting thighs. A droplet of his sweat fell upon her brow as his cock plunged into her.

He filled her utterly. His pelvis thrust hard, driving her hips into the solid surface beneath her. Her moan echoed in her ears, and still he pumped her. Again and again he prompted her to an orgasm, until her whole womanhood shuddered with ecstasy and her mind knew nothing but the coursing tides of sensation.

Through half-closed lids she saw his clenched jaw and she felt his own pleasure tiding. Then she felt him tense as if deliberately holding off his orgasm, but he continued to thrust in and out of her at a slow pace, until, with a little shriek, she climaxed again.

As the spasms coursed through her, Gillian saw how flushed his strange skin was now, red as a ruby. A strange, dry mist escaped his finely molded lips. A sound permeated the mist: guttural, articulately spoken words that she felt as they spilled forth. They pervaded the air, creating an aura that pulsated with a fiery rapture. The inflections of each pealed syllable singed Gillian's flesh. With a last echoed sigh from his throat, the aura suddenly burst apart and a culminated passion ripped through infinity.

An orgasm, she thought, but no orgasm of a mortal man! As hard as Gillian tried to comprehend its source, she could not.

But she was exhausted, more than she could ever remember.

And as his muscles relaxed, images poured into her mind, so quickly that she had no time to sort them. They were familiar, these faces and memories that seared her heart with a lifetime's worth of emotions. She knew they were her own, and as she sought to focus on them, a devouring mouth covered her lips and every last poignant image was snatched away.

She was left with the need to sleep and a soft but recurring spasm deep in her nether regions. He smiled at her, amazing her with his gentleness despite his monstrous features. Kissing her forehead, he rose and told her to rest.

For once in her life, Gillian knew nothing of resistance. His voice touched her like the song of creation itself, filling her with a sublime comfort and lifting all concern for anything except the desire to sleep.

You have pleased me. I am glad you are strong enough to love so passionately.

Gillian nodded compliantly and felt him move away. And just as her eyes closed, she glimpsed—for what seemed the first time—the natural ceiling of red slate with its bluish veins above their heads.

Gillian awoke with a sharp, tingling pain in her head. It passed as she sat up, but she was sure that her vision was playing tricks. She closed her eyes and raked her fingers through her hair, but when again her eyes opened, panic stopped her breath. She wasn't in the pretty little room she shared with other Disciples. This certainly wasn't her dormitory room on Earth with the cheap bed and squeaky mattress. It was no bed at all she sat on, but a wide slab of marble, and she was utterly naked.

She was not in a room, either, in the proper sense of the word. Rather, it seemed more of a chamber hewn within a cavern. It was as large as a good-sized chapel, with greenish marble walls and ceiling and floor. The air was hot and dry, and as she studied the wall nearest her she saw beads of moisture covering the surface. She got up from the slab and ventured closer, and realized that what she had taken for moisture was in fact tiny gems formed throughout the stone.

In the center of the chamber stood a pedestal of some ivory-hued stone. Upon this stood an old-fashioned copper lamp. As small as it was, the flame that rose from its spout shone like a diamond under illumination. Its light filled the entire chamber with a weird glow.

There was no sound to be heard. Even as she stepped closer to the pedestal, the soles of her feet made only the softest echo across the stone floor. As she stood staring at the lamp with its unusual flame, she began to feel frightened.

"Wake up, Gillian," she told herself. Reaching down, she pinched the tender flesh on the underside of her left knee. It stung, but even after the second attempt, nothing about the outlandish scene changed.

She stood and drew a long breath. Folding her arms instinctively about her bare breasts, she turned about slowly to survey the chamber. There was nothing else here besides the slab and pedestal with the lamp, nothing except the glistening walls. Her mind sought for the last conscious thought she'd possessed before going to sleep. She didn't even know what day it had been when last she'd laid down in bed.

Her skin tingled as she stuggled for her last recollections.

She remembered going into work at the steak house and succumbing to an intense desire for a cigarette. And she had been anxiously waiting to see the correctional officer, Bruce, who frequently came in. He had been away for some time and she'd had no idea when or if she'd ever see him again. His absence had touched her deeply, though she'd never spoken about that to anyone. Not seeing him had cast a pall over the delicious fantasies about him that had accompanied her to bed each night.

Now, it seemed that she had stepped out to the restaurant parking lot to catch that quick smoke. Yet, oddly, she had no desire for one now.

As her eyes pored over the strange chamber she grew more confident that she'd just been in the parking lot . . . and she remembered, vaguely, a woman approaching her, the one her co-workers had nicknamed the Goth queen. The woman had made a most incredible offer. For some reason that Gillian couldn't recall, she'd accepted.

There were other images in her mind, or the sense of images that should have been easily recalled. Dim but sensuous. As she tried to clarify them in her mind's eye, a sharp pain struck her temples. There was only one image she could clearly make out from the haze before the pain compelled her to release it . . . an ethereal being, winged and magnificently virile. This being had somehow prompted Gillian for validation of her acceptance of the Goth queen's offer.

But her head ached too much to recall anything else . . . and besides, she seemed totally alone at the moment, lost within the unfeeling walls of this cavern chamber.

She heard a soft sound behind her, and looking back, she gasped to see a panel-shaped portion of the wall move slowly inward. Bright light filtered in from beyond and two tall silhouettes stepped upon the threshold. Instinctively, Gillian covered her breasts and sex with her arms, and watched nervously as the pair passed through the fully opened doorway.

"Oh," she heard a masculine voice say, "she is already awake."

The one who had spoken drew closer. He was a young man, rather good-looking, with brown eyes and black hair falling over his shoulders. He wore a vest and breeches of billowy, gauzy white cloth, and nothing else. His skin was richly tanned. But he was completely bare of facial and body hair, as if he had been shaved.

He offered Gillian a tender smile as his companion walked

up beside him. This one was dressed just the same, and was just as clean-skinned. But his hair was pale flaxen waves that flowed down to his waist. Despite her fear, Gillian couldn't help but admire their smooth, boyish good looks.

Their demeanor seemed harmless. Yet all the same, Gillian felt vulnerable before their eyes, and her hands and arms worked all the harder to shield her exposed flesh.

"How sweet. She tries to hide herself," the flaxen-haired one mused.

The brown-eyed one nodded. For a moment he simply gazed at her, and then she heard him snap his fingers at his hip.

"Come here, Gillian."

13

Gillian frowned, thought again that she was surely dreaming. And ignoring them, she pinched the side of her left breast beneath her hand. It twinged, but nothing changed. Cursing to herself, she closed her eyes and willed herself awake. But when she looked again the young men stood where they had before, with the light cascading over their outlines from beyond the doorway. With a sigh, she tried to believe they could not touch her, not harm her, for she was doubtlessly asleep and they were only figments of her imagination.

"Go away," she said, "I have no need of you."

They did not vanish, nor did the room around them waver or the door disappear. All that changed was her increasing nervousness. Perspiration dewed her limbs, chilling her skin as it evaporated in the dry air.

"You must come with us," the flaxen-haired youth said. "You were brought here to serve in pleasure—you cannot resist now."

The words brought back to Gillian's mind the offer of the Goth queen, or at least whatever dream had inspired it. She inched away from the youths until she collided with the pedestal.

They bounded forward at once, grabbed her forearms, and pulled her away so quickly she had no time to struggle. They flanked her and each pinned one of her arms behind her back.

"Stop it," she hissed, even as the voice in her head cried out clearly that none of this was a dream.

"You should be more careful," scolded the flaxen-haired one. "You could have caught your hair afire."

The two young men looked at one another, and Gillian heard the brown-eyed one whisper, "Her memory has been damaged."

Suddenly, the flaxen youth grasped her right breast, sending a ripple of unexpected sensation through her. He massaged it and stroked her nipple until it was hard, then the other breast. His fingers drifted down her stomach teasingly. When his hand cupped over her nether hair, her thighs clamped, but still he was able to probe his fingers through the curls and touch her clit. Despite Gillian's reluctance, the small organ roused, and, as he began to strum it between two fingers, it was all Gillian could do to restrain her hips from moving in undignified response to the passion he stirred.

Gillian felt herself blush from head to toe. It angered her, and the anger pushed her fear aside. With a cry of rage she lifted a leg and brought her heel back into the shin of the flaxen-haired one. He made a shocked sound of his own. She delivered another kick to the brown-eyed one, and raised her foot again to attack the flaxen youth, when he released her and stepped back. As she struggled to resist his companion, the flaxen youth, brought a length of rope out of his vest pocket. Before she knew what was happening, he sprang down and wrapped the rope around her ankles. As soon as Gillian felt it, she tried to kick him away, but his deft hands quickly cinched and tied the rope so that her legs were bound.

The brown-eyed one now had her wrists. Gillian closed her eyes once more and inhaled deeply. This time she refused to look at them again, though, and instead mentally ordered herself to wake up. She thought of the lamp on her nightstand at the dorm, how close it was to her bed, how easy it was to turn it on and surely throw off this disturbing, seemingly endless dream forever.

And then she felt herself lifted off her feet. Her eyes flew open just as she was thrown over the shoulder of the brown-eyed man. He turned and marched to the doorway. Through her tumbled hair she could see that the flaxen one followed closely.

At last she realized that it was all too real. Her heart pounded wildly, and her fists flailed at the back of the young man who carried her, and her legs beat the air.

"Put me down! Put me down now!"

As he exited through the doorway her eyes smarted at the sudden intensity of light. It seemed he carried her down a long, wide stone corridor ablaze with torchlight. Her thick blond hair blinded her as his pace increased, but she could hear the flaxen one attempt to calm her.

"Ssshhh, it will all be all right. There's nothing to fear."

But Gillian's panic would not let her quiet down, and as she felt the boy make a sharp turn in the corridor her fists thrashed against him harder than before. She screamed for help, though from where that help might come she had no idea. Her captor ignored her, though she heard him mutter disapprovingly under his breath. Just as she would have scratched the back of his fine legs, he stopped in his tracks. Her face was lifted just as suddenly between the hands of the others. His blue eyes sparkled as he raised a finger to his lips.

"Hush, dearest," he whispered. "You are perfectly safe, I promise."

Unwillingly, she found comfort in his voice. She heard a rapping upon stone and heard a door open nearby. Again, she was struck with the realization of her nakedness, and thought to beg these young men to cover her with something when her captor proceeded to carry her into another room. She could just imagine others seeing her secret parts exposed and clamped her legs together. But the next moment the youth set her down on the floor. It was a thick carpet her soles touched, and her gaze lifted to behold a great circular room full of women regarding her with a mixture of expressions. Aghast, Gillian gasped and tried to cover herself. But the brown-eyed man captured her wrists and pinned them firmly to the small of her back.

Gillian felt close to crying. "Stop it!"

Even as she struggled to wrestle from his grasp and heard the ripple of laughter this elicited from the other women, Gillian was overcome with a dreamy, inexplicable sense that somehow, she might have once felt a keener reaction of shock and outrage at this public captivity.

At least the flaxen youth now removed the rope from her ankles. He rose to his feet and returned it to his vest pocket, when one of the women approached. She loomed over Gillian. She was a tall blonde dressed in leather pants and boots; her puffy-sleeved black silk blouse had silver trim on the collar and cuffs.

"Who are you?" Gillian demanded.

The woman frowned, looking over her head and addressing the young men. "She remembers nothing?"

One of them must have made some gesture, for she began to shake her head. "Unfortunate when this happens. Ah, well, they all come around eventually."

The woman reached out to Gillian's hair and swept it back from her face. Her light brown eyes seemed to inspect Gillian now from head to toe. Her demeanor was determinedly confident, and when again Gillian demanded to know who she was, the woman met her eyes for only a fleeting moment.

"She's very different from his last few, don't you think? I never expected him to choose one so fair."

Gillian heard the two young men murmur in agreement. Agitation flickered in her veins. "Answer my question, damn it!"

The woman's lips tightened, but at last she met Gillian's eyes solidly.

"My name is Martine. I am the Overseeress of the harem."

Gillian blinked, unbelieving. "Harem? What kind of ridiculous game is this? Why have I been brought here? Where is this place?"

Martine patted her cheek. The smooth pads of her fingers were as hard as porcelain. "Your memory has been temporarily affected by the passage between the elemental worlds. I am sorry that it is sometimes this way. You should be flattered, however, to know that you were selected by our king himself. This brings, of course, greater expectations as to your conduct and harem training than the others. But be assured, I am consistent and not daunted by a girl's title. And I expect your ready and willing obedience to our rules. The breaking of rules will not be tolerated and insolence can very quickly fetch you a stay in the Disciplinary."

The woman's response and Gillian's increasing foreboding made her speechless. She regarded the other young women in the room; they were whispering among themselves and eyeing her as if she were a sideshow. But they were almost all as scantily dressed as Gillian—standing or sitting on benches, their arms adorned with sleeves of shimmering gossamer cloth, cinched with gold bands on their upper arms and wrists. They wore pantaloons of the same material. These pantaloons cuffed about their ankles and again about their thighs. These outfits varied in their rich colors, some of them in lavender, others in silver and deep green. They all wore dainty, curled-toed jeweled slippers upon their feet, and gleaming gold bands about their busts. Brassieres of a sort, with half-cup plates in the front that scooped up their cleavage so that their breasts were held firmly forward. Their jutting nipples were clamped with loops of silver or gold and coinlike discs that jingled with their every movement. Most of the young women wore only these revealing garments, with their buttocks and private regions exposed; their pubic nests were oiled and combed into attractive curls. A few others wore chastity belts of finely molded gold. Thongs of what looked like rigid steel mesh were attached to the belts, which plunged tautly down to cup and shield the flesh between their thighs. When one of the girls turned to whisper into the ear of another, Gillian got a good look at her chastity belt. She saw that the thong was sealed so firmly over her nether region that while the girl could easily relieve herself through the mesh, it was impossible for her to pleasure herself.

Gillian blushed and looked away. Her heart fluttered with a flux of embarrassing emotions. She hated the aloof look on Martine's face, and she tried again to wrest her arms free of the smooth-chested youths. To her shock, Martine slapped her face. It only stung a little, but the disapproval in the woman's eyes subdued Gillian's protest. To her own disgrace she began to cry, which only made her angrier.

"Take her to the pool here to bathe," Martine said. The next moment, Gillian's captor released her wrists and scooped her up in his arms. Her body was grateful, though her anxiety only increased as he carried her across the room. At least the other young women moved aside, and when she heard Martine order them to mind their comportment, she knew a tiny moment's vindication.

It was an alcove the young man entered. Small and lit only with candles set about in deep niches of the cavernous walls, the sound of trickling water echoed all about. He lowered Gillian to her feet upon the bank of a shallow, natural pool. The bottom shimmered like beaten brass through the clear water. She could feel the heat of it lifting off the surface, and marveled at the slender rivulets of water that wept down the stone walls cradling the pool. Looking up, she saw that the walls soared into utter darkness. The scene made her giddy, and she started to lose her balance. But the youth's quick, steadying hands saved her from falling straight into the pool.

"You are fatigued," he said softly.

He held her hand and led her into the pool. The water was very warm, almost hot. He guided her to sit down, and the exquisite liquid immersed her to the tops of her shoulders. Gillian felt at once the tenseness loosening from her muscles.

She was all too aware of her escort. He waded over to the closest wall, and leaning with his back upon it and his arms folded over his chest, he observed her. Blushing again, Gillian's eyes lowered. She saw the fabric of his breeches waver with the stirring of the water. His thighs were lean beneath the fabric, and she saw that his cock was slightly erect.

"Can you bathe yourself?" he asked, "or would you like me to help you?"

Just then someone else entered the alcove and, embarrassed by his offer, Gillian was relieved to see it was one of the other young women. She carried several folded thick towels, and these she lay upon the bank beside the pool. Gillian noticed the way she looked at the young man. Despite the demure little smile on her heart-shaped lips, Gillian saw the flame of desire in her eyes.

"Hello, Abraham."

"Good evening, Jeya. How are you?"

When Gillian dared look, she saw the tenderness in his own eyes for this Jeya.

Jeya's smile broadened and her cheeks flushed deeply. "I am well. Martine sent towels."

"I see. Thank you."

She looked at Gillian. "I apologize for the rude welcome of the others," she whispered, "they can be such boors at times."

Gillian did not know what to say. She longed to beg this kind girl to tell her where they were, to explain what happened to her. But she suspected that to ask for such information could make some trouble for the girl.

"I have to go," Jeya said. She glanced at Abraham again. Their eyes locked for a deep, timeless moment. Then Jeya turned and departed.

It was only her and Abraham again.

"Where am I?" she asked him. "I don't understand why I'm here . . ." Gillian heard her voice break under the weight of overwhelming emotions and the solid certainty that somehow this was all a mistake.

"You are in the keep of our king," he said. "You truly don't remember?"

At the shake of her head, he continued patiently, "He is king of this world, and a powerful—perhaps the most powerful—Dhjinn E'noch. You may know them better as genies, spirits of the element of fire. They are similar to the angels of air, but of a different temperament. And this is his private domain.

"He evidently laid eyes upon you, for here you have been brought. They are creatures of obsessive desires. Once aroused, their passions are never dispelled. So you will be a member of the harem, and likely, will be groomed to be his suitable love slave. He is not so scattered in his emotions as his brethren, which is why you'll have few rivals, if any."

For a moment Gillian thought this was all only a nightmare, that at any moment she'd awaken in her own humble bed in her campus room. But the boy's sober mien was all too real.

"A genie," she said, her voice tittering without humor. "You mean like a genie in a bottle?"

"Yes."

She shook her head and stared at her tightly folded legs beneath the water's surface. How hard they were shaking!

"So, why is he not in a bottle—or under obligation to some enchanted object?"

"Because he was set free, Gillian. And having been set free

after servitude to mortals, his power is on a par with that of the archangels."

The image of the ethereal being glinted in Gillian's brain. It was fleeting, but it seemed so familiar, a titanic winged figure of ravishing masculine beauty. Nothing like what she surmised this Dhjinn E'noch surely looked like . . . and she wondered if perhaps the Goth queen had been conjured from her fantasies as well.

"He kidnapped me, then."

The youth's brow creased, but his voice held no certainty. "I would imagine not, as kidnapping is generally viewed in your mortal culture. You must remember," he continued in a warning voice, "that world, which was mine at one time, too, does not hold the last word on ethics, Gillian. Earth is a battleground of religious conflict, of temporal greed, of psychological immaturity. I consider myself fortunate to have been taken from it, and you should think yourself the same."

"Perhaps, if I'd been asked," she said. Again she thought of the Goth queen, and she felt very confused. "He came to me through that woman? The woman in the parking lot?"

The youth shrugged. "I cannot say where he found you. You remember a woman when he claimed you?"

Gillian nodded, but she was uncertain.

"It is probably a dream you had, a dream during the flight. I would not worry about it. You are here, and that's all that you should be concerned with. And pleasing your lord, of course."

These last words struck Gillian as condescending, and she said coolly, "Oh? What will he do if I spurn his obsessive desires? Am I safe?"

Abraham glanced toward the entrance, then knelt in the water. "I think our king realizes now that mortal women are fragile creatures compared to his fortitude." A grave shadow crossed his face, and he glanced away a moment until it was gone.

"But for those who have not accepted our king as their lord

and husband, there awaits the crystal sepulcher," he sighed. "I would not wish to see you entombed there, Gillian."

"Entombed?" The word hung on Gillian's lips, and a horrible half-vision tried to form in her mind.

Again, Abraham peered toward the entrance, and now his voice was hardly more than a whisper, "All he seeks is love, Gillian. And it is not so hard to love those who adore you, is it? Besides, you will never age while you are here. If you accept him, you'll never lose your beauty, nor know the sorrows of mortal life. I am not part of the harem, but I have accepted my state, and thrive and am happy. You can know this, and more, I am certain, by just giving in to the simple restraints of his passion."

This is madness, Gillian thought desperately. But the sincerity that shone in Abraham's eyes was not.

As he lowered and kissed her brow, a sudden longing to see the correctional officer overcame her. The longing was imbued with more emotions than the old regret that she had been too shy to get to know him. Emotions that defied logic.

She stared at Abraham, her eyes filled with bereft tears. Rashly, she envisioned herself forgetting her misery in his touch. How sweetly sensual he was, and his gentleness belied his authority over her. Knowing that compelled her to her knees, and she reached for his crotch. He made a surprised murmur when she touched his cock through the wet fabric. Yet he neither scolded her nor moved away. She caressed him so that the length of his cock stiffened under her touch. Slowly, her fingers drew down the length of his shaft and she dandled his tightened scrotum over her fingertips.

Abraham looked nervously at the entranceway. "You should not," he whispered, "we could get caught."

She stroked him and licked his balls. With a low moan he bent at the knees and pulled her to her feet. He kissed her breasts and licked her nipples until they were hard pink stones.

His hands clenched her buttocks, massaged them while his cock pressed against her dripping fount. Gillian explored his body with greedy hands. What a tasty contradiction he was, all supple skin and firm muscles. He kissed her mouth, and her wet body ignited with yearning.

But it was not Abraham she wanted. And she could not deny this even as her pelvis rocked hungrily against him and the heated moisture inside her trickled over her thighs.

"Oh, pretty one," he whispered finally. He drew her hands gently to her sides, and nuzzled her throat with a rueful sigh. "Our king has chosen well, but I cannot put you in jeopardy because of my own weakness."

He urged her to kneel again in the water, and assured her that their king had no equal in virility and soon would pacify the desires that tormented her.

She wondered if she should hope this was true and ached yet to forget her fright in his arms. This alien, cavernous place, with the sensual ambience that permeated the dry, hot air only added frustration to her fear. It seemed she'd been brought here to serve in some sexual capacity . . . so why was it forbidden to indulge those fantasies? Especially when they had taken away her chance of ever seeing Bruce again?

Whatever the answer, she didn't want to make trouble for Abraham, especially when he had been so kind.

She let him wade back to the wall without following. Into the soothing water she sank to her shoulders, and turned her back to him slowly, hoping to obtain a little privacy for her thoughts, at least. She looked up at the fathomless maw that stretched above them, and gave in to the silent tears of desolation and intimate frustrations. They ran down her cheeks and spilled into the water, making tiny ripples on the glassy surface.

When later Abraham escorted her back to the chamber filled with women, Martine directed her toward a chair near the back of the chamber. Upon it was laid out an outfit like the ones the other harem girls wore. Gillian felt an objection rise to her lips. But there was nobody here to rally to her cause, and she thought again of that place Martine had alluded to: the Disciplinary. A new dread welled up inside her, which vanquished the calm imparted by the hot bath.

"We took your measurements while you slept in the welcome portal," she heard Martine say matter-of-factly.

The pair of gauzy sleeves that had been laid out were made of a shimmering indigo fabric, and completed with a pair of matching thigh-cinching pantaloons. There was a golden breastplate with the partial cups to elevate her breasts. Gillian shivered as Martine snapped the little clasp together at her back. The metal contained her breasts very snugly, so that her nipples bulged over the rims. Gillian was grateful that the Overseeress didn't seem to notice the deep flush on her face. And onto her nipples Martine attached golden loops. Golden coins dusted with diamond powder dangled from the loops, and they jingled as Martine had her sit down and handed her a pair of black satin slippers with curled toes.

Abraham was standing close by. When Gillian was dressed, he brought a comb to Martine and a wide band of indigo cloth. With deep, soothing strokes, Martine swept the teeth of the comb through Gillian's hair. She made a ponytail on the crown of Gillian's head, and this she cinched in place with the band.

Now Martine told her to rise from the chair and to turn about. Gillian complied, very aware of how the adorning pantaloons left her sex visible and that her nipples jutted provocatively in their golden breast cups. These things seemed to draw focus to her sexuality, and the pinch of the loops only intensified the feeling. She felt more exposed and captive than when she had been naked.

At least the other girls were paying no attention. They were involved in their own private conversations. Except for Jeya,

Gillian noticed. The girl stood by herself to a sideline of the room. Her gaze was transfixed on Abraham; her expression at once animated and tormented. If Abraham noticed her gaze, he did not acknowledge it as he stood beside Martine and watched while she lifted Gillian's ponytail and released the strands slowly so that they cascaded over her back and tickled her skin.

"I think our king will be pleased," Martine commented. "What say you, Abraham?"

It did seem to Gillian that his attention was elsewhere. Nonetheless, he smiled and murmured in agreement.

Martine told Gillian that she might sit where she was and relax for a while. The overseeress walked away with Abraham then, and they took a seat together on a plain wooden bench far from the others. Despite the fact she did not like the high-handed Martine, Gillian felt more uncomfortable than ever sitting alone. The atmosphere of the room was one of patient expectancy, and she wondered what exactly everyone was waiting for.

As her tension increased, ideas of escape raced through her mind. She scrutinized the walls for a possible route out. But the door was firmly shut, and the only other passageway visible was the one to the bathing pool.

Slowly, she realized she was being watched by the other members of the harem. There was a variety of emotions in the faces of these women; some looked at her as one would gape at some oddity, while the faces of others were twisted with smirks. A few offered friendly smiles. And there were two or three among them who ogled her with blatant lust. Gillian was shocked, but heard an unexplainable inner voice scold that such shock was wrong. When she turned her face away, her eyes met an even more disquieting sight.

A throng of the harem girls had risen from the floor where she had previously thought they were simply clustered in a circle to talk privately. But as they scampered off into the crowd,

Gillian saw the couch they had surrounded. Another girl was lying there on her stomach, and her mouth was filled with a large silver ball that was tethered by a leather band behind her head. The girl's hands had been bound at the small of her back with a thick braid of black. Her ankles were bound together similarly. Her eyes were reddened, and her brow knit with chagrin. Gillian noticed, too, how her backside glowed scarlet as if it had been punished very recently.

Gillian's breath faltered, and as she stared at the girl, she felt a little quickening between her thighs. It was embarrassing enough to make her look away again—but she couldn't stop thinking about the bound girl and especially the telltale shade of her buttocks.

A loud clap got her attention, and raising her eyes, she saw that the door had been opened and another male youth with long fair hair stood at the threshold. Martine came up to him and as they spoke the frivolity of the harem was silenced. Martine turned and gestured to three of the girls, who immediately flocked to the door. Then she looked at Gillian and waved for her to come forward.

Gillian tried to rise from the chair, but her legs seemed strangely heavy. She was almost relieved when she heard Abraham's voice next to her ear, "It is all right, Gillian. You're going to be introduced."

He helped her rise and she plodded to where the others awaited in line. Martine squared her shoulders.

"Stand straight," she fussed. "You are going to be introduced to the brothers and freed kin of our king. So stop looking so glum. This is an honor for any new girl."

As Gillian wondered what these freed kin were, the girl standing in front of her made a disgruntled sound. At once Martine's palm slapped her buttocks smartly. The girl jumped with a startled yelp.

"Your master is devoted to you, Gigi. Why do you have to be so snide to Gillian?"

"I apologize," Gigi murmured. She bowed her head humbly, but Gillian thought her words sounded grudging.

"Very well. Gillian, you must be on your best behavior. Any impertinence will be reported back to me."

Gillian refused to comment. She was still determined to find a way out of the cavern. But as the youth led the four out into the corridor, she could not shake the smoldering image of the girl on the couch. It had kindled some familiar, warm, and delicious excitement in her that made her cheeks flush now as brightly as the girl's behind.

The chosen harem girls were led to a room with walls of real cream plaster and dark wood molding and paneled ceiling. Hotter and drier than anyplace else Gillian had been so far in the cavern prison, there was, strangely, no hearth fire, nothing that indicated where the heat manifested. But this did not make her as curious as the men who were sitting around the great round, stone table.

They were very tall, every one, with long arms and powerfully muscular legs. Their hair—of various shades of silver and burnt orange—was long and flowing. Each was garbed in an outfit that reminded Gillian of the fashion worn by gentlemen during the Romantic era. Their features were extraordinary. Some looked serpent-like with mottled or yellowish scaly skin and down-pressed noses. Others looked like gargoyles to Gillian, with skin of slate gray and strange features that could have been chiseled straight out of stone. Most all of these titanic beings were attractive in an unworldly way, but there wasn't any doubt that they were hardly human.

They were playing a game with slivers of geodes painted with pictures in luminous colors. At the feet of one player knelt another young woman. She was dressed in a leather thong and collar, and seemed to be watching with much interest as the player pored over his cards. Gillian saw his hand dip down and pat her hair like a man would a loyal pet.

"Ah, you are on time for once, Attendant," commented one of the players. He regarded one of the harem girls and his hard brow seemed to soften.

"Come here, Belinda," he said, and the girl hastened to him, giving a little squeal as he embraced her.

The other two went to stand beside two of the other gargoyle-men, while their attendant led Gillian to a single unoccupied chair.

"Who is this morsel, girly-boy?" demanded one of the players. Seeing how the face of the attendant blanched, she felt an immediate dislike for the speaker.

The youth managed a breezy smile. "Our king's new acquisition, my lord."

Then he bade Gillian to kneel beside the chair. She was appalled. Was she some animal to kneel anywhere—especially in a room full of men who were not men?

But the attendant must have sensed her unwillingness and gave her a look that warned that this wasn't the time or place to resist. With a heavy sigh she relented and took her place on the floor. The other harem girls were allowed to stand or were invited to sit on the lap of this or that player, and it was obvious that they were well acquainted with the men, who caressed them frankly.

The youthful attendant quietly exited the room. As the door shut softly on its stone hinges, Gillian's chest swelled with terror. Her place on the floor seemed suddenly a welcome refuge from the scrutiny of the inhuman males. She hugged the leg of the huge chair and turned her face away from the table, staring at the wall behind, hoping they had forgotten her entirely while they talked and played their game.

Then she heard one of them speak, "Did you know he had taken a new one?"

"He doesn't confide in me these days," replied another. "He is preoccupied much of the time."

A third snorted thickly. "And with what? That Queen Marianne again—and King Marcus's ridiculous threats?"

"How would I know?" retorted the second speaker. "But it is not my concern, nor yours, brother."

"It is the concern of us all," said another balefully. "Yet, I suspect he might just keep the pretty queen for himself. That would show Marcus!"

There was a deep grunt from one. "Ah, but this is not the time, my brothers . . . our ladies are here. And I am interested in how long this new little pet will last him."

"You mean survive him?" spoke another in an undertone.

The first speaker told him to hush, but an icy sweat already covered Gillian.

Almost to her relief she heard one of them scold the girl at his side, "You are not wearing the jewel I gave you?"

The girl stammered, "M-Martine would not let me keep it. She said it is too valuable and I must wait . . ."

The creature's voice grew surly. "The overseeress is trying to overstep her position again. You will inform Martine that next time you are brought to me and I do not see the jewel on your finger, she will answer to me."

The girl's voice was shaky, "Yes, my Master."

Then Gillian heard a loud smack and the girl whimpered. A chair was scooted back from the table, and she heard the creature rise from his seat. The girl made a languid little moan and the man stood and led her from the table. Gillian watched furtively as he directed her to a couch in a dark corner of the room. The girl lay down on her back, and her Master raised her knees with her thighs parted. She moaned again, a sound mingled of both timidity and passion. Beneath the idle talk of the others he gave her some order that brought a sultry curve to her lips. And slowly, hesitantly, the girl's hands crept down into the nest of soft brownish curls between her thighs. To Gillian's shock, she began to masturbate under her Master's rapt and approving gaze.

A sharp, pleasurable twinge shot through Gillian's belly. With a gasp, she covered her eyes and turned her head to the shelter of the chair. She tried to think of nothing, but the creatures at the table were fondling the harem girls at their arms. The girls' amorous sighs lilted the air, and the one in the corner began to moan. Then one of the gargoyle creatures remarked that Gillian's hair was blonder on the mountain than at the valley, and her cheeks blazed. Fervently, she prayed that the attendant would return soon and escort her from the room.

But more so, she wanted something to take her away from the disturbing sense of normalcy she felt amid all she heard and saw.

What is wrong with me?

The next moment one of the beings rose from his seat and came round toward her sheltering chair. Before she knew what to do, he grabbed her up by the arms and raised her to her feet. Her head reeled with panic. With his huge hands, he lifted her by the wrists so that her feet only brushed the floor. As inhuman as he was, his eyes gleamed with earthy lust. She squirmed in his grasp and desperate tears sprang to her eyes. But they fetched no sympathy from the gargoyle-man; he simply lifted her higher, and turning, dangled her before the others.

Their hungry eyes roamed over her. Gillian's face scalded with humiliation, and without thinking, she lifted a foot and drove it back so that her heel struck her captor's thigh. He laughed, and when again she kicked, he was obliged to swivel his hip before she struck him fully in the scrotum.

"A feisty one!"

"Bring her here, Ghi," purred one of his companions. This one scooted his chair away from the table. Gillian let out an agitated squeal, and again kicked back at the captor. But her efforts were useless against his agility.

"I would enjoy training this one, yes." His brazen words agitated her deeply. Against her will, she felt her sex ripen. Mortified, she struggled to loosen herself.

Then to her utter disbelief he carried her around the table to where the other one sat. This one greeted her with a lick of his lips. Gillian's agitation intensified. When he reached out and touched her leg, she screamed and kicked him squarely in the chest. The impact made a soft thud, and a disapproving frown creased his brow. Gillian cringed with remorse for the stupid move, knowing full well that she was no match for any one of these creatures, let alone half a dozen of them.

The next moment this one seized her legs. With a leer, he yanked her legs wide apart. She struggled with both legs to break free, but like her wrists, they were well constrained.

"I could break your legs off, pretty one," he said softly, "as easily as a child snaps off a butterfly's wings."

His wicked threat halted her struggle. Gillian felt close to fainting with terror; and yet, as she saw him peering at her nether mouth, an undercurrent of excitement passed through her shivering limbs.

"That's better," he said. Leaning forward in his seat, he pressed his stony lips over her tenderest flesh. His skin felt like baked leather against her fount. His tongue flicked over her pubic lips; it was a leathery, snakelike thing that inflamed her against her

will. His devilish tongue parted the folds of her labia; Gillian felt
her clit stir and a trickle of moisture seep from her trapped sex.

"You must not," she panted.

"Hush," cautioned Ghi, "or we can gag that little mouth."

Tears of humiliation flooded her eyes so that his face was
only a misted image. She struggled to restrain her hips as his
mouth continued to ravish her, and as his tongue entered her
fount, her entire sex convulsed madly. Her nipples hardened
within the pinching loop clamps. The soft tinkle of the bangle
coins seemed an ornate and mocking song of her helplessness.

His tongue plunged in and out of her, turning her pussy into
a swollen, starving, pulsating orifice. Wantonly, her hips arched
toward his cruel face and her clit pulsed wildly. As her head
lolled back, she saw Ghi watching with much amusement. Seeing her, he winked. Gillian blushed and closed her eyes. The
other continued to lick her clit, and her pussy ached enviously,
growing wetter as his tongue teased the aroused organ again
and again. Mounting pleasure coursed through her body. Gillian's
hips bucked wildly in the air, and her moans rebounded inde-
cently against the cream walls.

And then she heard a door open. It seemed a faraway, unim-
portant sound. But the one who held her legs looked over his
shoulder. Her sex throbbed for his tormenting mouth even as she
felt the sudden change all around her. He lowered her legs suddenly, so that she swayed on her unsteady legs. If not for Ghi
holding her wrists, she would have fallen.

The other one growled thickly under his breath. Following
his eyes, she saw another titanic figure standing at the open door.

He was as humanly male as these others were only hulking
caricatures. Gillian's entire body shuddered as he stepped in,
and when his eyes set upon her, her quickened breath stopped.

He was the single most beautiful man she had ever seen. With
a smooth complexion and fine features, his skin had a subtle,

exotic over-sheen of olive. His mane of silvery-blond hair was long and silken and there was a widow's peak on his high brow. His clothes were fashioned similarly to the others, except his were cut of a more refined fabric and his boots were of dark suede leather. Through his gossamer hunter-green shirt she could see his lean torso and the sinews of his long arms. But it was his deep-set eyes that most keenly defined his looks. Pale and blue as the sky, they regarded her like two hard, brilliant aquamarines beneath his heavy silvery brows.

Only the hard set of his mouth indicated his displeasure. Gillian heard the gargoyle-man in the corner tell his girl to be quiet, while the others at the table rose from their seats. In two great strides the newcomer was at Gillian's side. The one who had ravished her stood up immediately and shrank back. Ghi, however, grasped her wrists all the more jealously.

In an uncertain tone he challenged the one that looked like a man, "It is custom to share, brother!"

Brother! Gillian could not believe it. Surely, she thought, this is only a turn of phrase they used when addressing one another.

The newcomer replied in a voice melodious as well as fierce, "In my domain you will follow my custom. Now, release my woman."

When Ghi hesitated, he uttered a threatening, eerily light sound. A ripple of terror crawled up Gillian's spine. Ghi did not back off, but returned the sound with his own guttural challenge. She winced to see the baleful glint in the newcomer's eyes. They lowered a moment, however, and registered her frightened gaze. And confronting Ghi again, his hands clamped into fists and again he uttered another dreadful growl.

The air was growing insufferably hot, and Gillian felt the others edging away to the recesses of the room. The women were pressed protectively behind the palisade of their forms.

And though she was terrified, Gillian could not take her eyes from this newcomer. She heard Ghi speak some words that brought a flare of color to the handsome one's cheeks.

Then to her amazement, flecks of heated amber glowed in the surface of his blue eyes. Fear like a cold blade cut through her belly, and the room reeled as a sickening sense of familiarity swept over her. She smelled him now—the faint tinge of sulfur beneath his virile scent. It seemed to strangle her, and the half-memories that flooded into her mind suddenly were precious things that ravaged her heart. She felt Ghi finally relent and release his hold, and the newcomer's hands clasped her shoulders to steady her.

She tore at those hands, pushed away from him, and pressed herself under Ghi's towering form.

"You," she gasped, "you are the reason I'm here!"

She didn't know how she knew this, but she did. His now gentle regard did not fool her, nor did she know comfort as the amber flecks in his eyes softened and faded as if by will. She perceived an emotion like hatred chafing at her consciousness, and an instinctive knowledge that he was dangerous.

Sprinkles of pain filled her head. All the horrid reasons for her hatred deluged her mind. Memories of Nemi and of Madam; of the lush forest surrounding the household. She felt the handsome Warden taking her over the sofa; heard Clive's honeyed words in her ear. She saw again the Ur'theriems, the prisoners, the coolly passionate Leather Wives.

And she remembered Sir Bruce. Her Sir Bruce.

This was the Dhjinn E'noch who had tried to seduce her outside the Temple of Purity. She recalled the shatter of the window in the kitchen at Bruce's chalet. This creature's phantom presence and ghostly caresses came back to her, as did the stifling odor of the acrid mist in which he'd carried her off.

She ignored the pretty mask he donned now. Her entire body shook with hatred. He'd kidnapped her from Nemi and, worse, her true love. This creature had corrupted the only happiness she had ever known.

The hatred bled with violence into all of her memories.

His features blurred into a thousand angry, crimson dots before Gillian's eyes and her surging blood roared in her temples. She thought she moved toward him; she definitely felt her nails sink into her palms as her hands drew into fists. She hissed and raised her arms to strike when consciousness seeped away.

14

_____

Gillian's eyes opened to a scene of lavish pagan delights, of nymphs running through a lush, flowery field, the sun gilding their streaming hair and voluptuous bare limbs.

For a moment she thought she'd returned to Nemi and her heart lightened. But then she realized it was only a frescoed ceiling above her head, and that she lay on a bed draped with a red satin spread. The pretty slippers they'd put on her feet were gone, and her hair loosened. She looked above her, seeing an astonishing headboard, a great arch of yellowish marble that touched one golden frame of the ceiling. Four pillars of the same stone cornered the great bed.

As hesitant and suspicious as Gillian was, the tantalizing aroma of food tempted her to sit up.

It was with great disappointment that she realized she was simply in another cavern room in the Dhjinn E'nochs' abode. The walls were glimmering russet stone and the floor was covered by an ornate rug. The light emanated from a framed square globe of thick glass situated high in the wall to her right.

But the sleeping place was an antechamber, divided off from

what appeared to be a private sitting room by two tall screens of latticed woodwork. Peering between them, Gillian flinched to see the Dhjinn E'noch in the sitting room. He reposed on a heavy sofa upholstered in black damask, his face turned away from her.

Desperately she thought of what to do next . . . when suddenly the Dhjinn E'noch's eyes lit upon her. His seductive mouth turned up in a lean smile.

"You're awake." His smooth voice seemed to penetrate her skin and make her shiver. "Come here, Gillian. I have had some food brought in."

She was still dressed in the scanty garments she'd been given, and for a moment she was determined not to comply. But her stomach betrayed her with sharp hunger pangs. With a sigh she crept off the bed and walked through the screens into the sitting room. There were two more of the framed light fixtures on the wall here, too, flanking a wardrobe of carved ebony. As she stepped around the couch she found a low table, also of smooth ebony. On it a golden platter had been laid out with small, open-faced sandwiches and candied figs. The Dhjinn E'noch offered her a stemmed glass filled with what looked like dark wine.

"Thirsty?"

Gillian shook her head. Though she avoided looking at him, she felt his gaze, and instinctively she folded her hands over her pubis.

He laughed softly. "So you will garb yourself in modesty?"

Her face warmed angrily.

"It is a natural reaction to the unexpected, and so I will overlook it. From now on, however, you will not try to hide your charms." His authoritative attitude agitated her, and yet, his languid voice made her feel drowsy and weak. Her arms fell awkwardly to her sides.

"Good," he said. "Sit down now. I know you are hungry."

She complied again, almost grateful to be able to keep her legs together and hide herself a little bit. He set the glass on the table and slid the platter toward her. Despite her hunger she eyed the figs and sandwiches suspiciously.

"What is it?"

"Beef and cheese on bread. Figs, too. Common victuals among your people. But no, nothing has not been drugged, as you fear," he said. "And Gillian—you will speak to me respectfully at all times. Address me as 'my lord.' "

She was almost painfully hungry now, and looking away from him, tried one of the little sandwiches. She couldn't help thinking she had no idea what poison was supposed to smell or taste like. She sipped the wine as well, and detected nothing amiss in the bouquet or flavor.

From the corner of her eye she saw him grimace.

Without meaning to she wondered how he'd changed his appearance from the demonic image he'd presented on Nemi.

Probably a natural talent among his kind.

And then she realized he'd read her mind concerning her suspicion of poison. It hadn't been the first time, either: he'd done the same in the Temple of Purity. Gillian's mouth felt parched as she ate. She wanted to avoid thinking about it and feigned indifference as she looked around at the furnishings.

On the wall to their left hung a large pyramidal mirror. Beneath this stood a cabinet about two feet high. Fashioned from a creamy beige wood, it resembled a doll's wardrobe, and Gillian presumed it was a liquor cabinet, given the lock hanging on a chain between the little doors.

Looking around, she saw a niche hewn into one part of the room. It could have made an excellent closet, but it was bare. And a beam on the ceiling supported something odd: a large metal hook with metallic loops hanging from it by short chains. At first she wasn't sure what purpose this hook served, and then she saw the long metal canister bolted to the niche wall. A suede-sheathed crop was propped inside this. A twinge of alarm compelled Gillian to turn her attention back to the food. She nibbled on a fig, and hoped the Dhjinn E'noch did not sense her disquiet.

He watched silently as she finished the sandwich. She suspected that he was trying to penetrate into her thoughts, and tried to keep her conscious mind separated from her intention to find a way of escaping his abode and making her way back to Nemi.

"You are certain that I have kidnapped you," he said at last, "made you an unwilling hostage."

The statement was true, though certainly not a solid thought in her mind during the last little while. She refused to willingly look at him, and took some vindication in the exasperated sigh he gave.

"That interpretation is subjective, of course. You are mine because I took possession of you—but I would not have been so infatuated had you not been so desiring of possession."

Gillian's anger flared, but she remained poised. He came nearer, and it seemed his very breath was a dangerous entity shadowing over her.

"Ah, you try to ignore me in an effort to insult. This is the testimony to the shallow training that Nemi gives to its Disciples."

The insinuation roused Gillian more deeply than she would have thought. She cast him another quick glance, unable to keep her brows from knitting.

He smiled softly and the blue in his eyes was warm. "And you would defend Nemi and the Ur'theriems even now. A human woman of perfect readiness and inclination to enjoy all fleshly delights. You believe they satisfied your true penchants and awakened your real self. But it is not so, Gillian. They merely used those desires you denied yourself too long. I, on the other hand, will appreciate them. I will refine and polish them. Soon, you will be a brilliant, faceted gem, instead of a mere chip among many on the jewel-cutter's wheel."

The determination in his voice troubled Gillian. She was racked with dread of what exactly transpired when he'd kidnapped her. Had he besieged Nemi in other ways, and most importantly—had he harmed Bruce?

And then she sensed the Dhjinn E'noch's calmness drain away. His cheeks flushed slightly and anger imbued his close aura. She heard his knuckles pop as one hand clenched tightly.

"The fragile mortal man is unharmed," he said in low tones. "And for the present, I have no intention to lay siege to the Nemian stronghold."

Gillian looked boldly at him, careless of the angry amber lights dancing in his eyes. "I have no proof you speak true, kidnapper!"

His voice thickened so that the air shook with his suppressed rage. "Unlike mortals, my race does not fabricate, woman."

He snatched her wrist suddenly. His skin was so hot it almost burned. She attempted to twist out of his grasp, but it was impossible. Grabbing the length of her hair, he pulled it back so that she was forced to look at him. The horrible thought of the otherworldly beast snapping her head off her neck made her tremble.

But his voice resonated with what sounded like an effort toward patience. "I only wish you to not worry for your acquaintances on Nemi. And I assure you, my dear, that while I may punish you, never will I damage what is mine."

"But I am not yours and you had no right to take me!" she cried. "I belong on Nemi, where I chose to serve as a Disciple of Pleasure! I never asked for you!"

He bowed over her so that her upturned face was shadowed under his glowering regard.

"It is enough I chose you! You should feel honored. Grateful! I have delved into your thoughts and all the desires of your heart, Gillian. I know the secret of your soul. You sought a

Master inflexible, reliable, and desirous of your devotion. The Nemians only offered the outward satisfaction of your desires, and only for their benefit. I am the real thing, the Master you have longed for all your life."

"Not so. They gave me love and security, and for that I am grateful," Gillian seethed. "As for a Master, I have already chosen one!"

His eyes flashed and his lips flooded crimson. Then his eyes closed a moment. He drew a long breath, and when he exhaled his features were again composed. He released her hair and drew his fingers down the length of her spine.

"You were already a Disciple of Pleasure," he murmured, as if speaking aloud his thoughts. And looking at her again, his eyes shone tranquil blue again. The half-smile on his lips was assured and firm.

Still holding her wrist, he stood and pulled her up to her feet on the floor. Under his full height and lofty gaze Gillian's heart raced. She felt like a small child looking up at him, her arm a doll's limb in his hand. He touched her cheek and the pads of his fingers singed her flesh. Catching her chin, he bent and kissed her mouth. Her nostrils detected a blazing virility that swept away the traces of sulfur. When she squirmed and tried to wriggle away, he pulled her captive arm to her back and hugged her against his hard body. Her entire body quivered; her pussy swelled and moistened against her will.

He uses my training against me!

His mouth drew back, and to her shock her lips felt almost bereft.

"Perhaps I do use it against you," he replied. "But it will serve to help to teach you the difference between what you were in Nemi and what you will come to be very soon—a true passion slave, and *my* disciple."

He seemed bent on possessing Gillian's will, determined to crush entirely her every last objection. Aghast, she shrieked, and kicked his shin with all her might. He grunted, but only that, and suddenly he lifted her up and threw her over his shoulder just as Abraham had done earlier. His shoulder pressed into her pubis, and he patted her buttocks firmly. A tremor of heat filled her pelvis even as she pounded his back with her fists.

"Let me go!" she screamed.

He carried her into the adjoining chamber and sat down on the bed. At once she fought to crawl off him, and even made it to the mattress, but he captured her ankles and pulled her back over his lap. Gillian twisted and kicked, but his strength was incontestable. Snatching her wrists, he pressed them against the small of her back. She writhed fiercely and tried to wriggle away, to which he answered by giving her backside a single, smart spank.

"You cannot escape me, Gillian. My fortitude exceeds that of mortal men, and even if you were to free yourself, my men are outside the door."

She grunted and kicked again, which brought a harder spank. Again, it was only one stroke, but Gillian sensed the warning behind it and tried to keep silent as his chastening hand moved to her pubic hair, which he brushed slowly with his great fingers. Her thighs were clenched, but a moment later, with only the slightest of efforts, the Dhjinn E'noch separated them. He patted her exposed nether folds and opened them gently. With a finger he traced her fount, and then her clit. Against her will she grew slick, and as he drove a finger slowly into her fount, her whole sex swelled with sensation.

He worked her more rapidly. Gillian's breasts heaved helplessly over his lap, and her pussy grew wetter, hotter with need. The nipple clamps pinched into her swollen nipples. To her deeper chagrin the little coins chimed daintily.

"Please," she whimpered, struggling yet to free her wrists. How humbling it was to know he watched her bare buttocks undulate and enjoyed the slippery heat of her pussy! But under his devilishly sensual torment, her mind and senses seemed to drift back to Nemi. She imagined it was Sir Bruce's lap she was over. An anxious moan escaped her and her back arched wantonly for something more . . .

She heard a masculine grunt, and the exploring hand drew away. The Dhjinn E'noch lifted her and set her upon her belly onto the mattress.

Before she could think, she was turned over onto her back. The Dhjinn E'noch was hovering over her now and his smoldering eyes had turned into two deep amber pools. He was physically flawless, and her entire body tingled as he unbuttoned his breeches. Splendidly endowed he was and she reproached herself for even acknowledging it. She closed her eyes and welcomed memories of Bruce.

I can bear anything because you're the one I love . . .

"Look at me," the Dhjinn E'noch ordered, "or I will chain you to that fixture in the niche."

She complied, but it was not his glowering, lusty regard she saw, but Bruce's sensuous face.

He draped over her, clasping her wrists down to the bed above her head. He suckled her right breast roughly, then the other, chafing each manacled nipple with his feasting lips. His knee parted her legs and the crown of his swollen cock bulged against her fount. It rubbed against her this way several seconds, and then he penetrated her. She felt engorged by his great cock. With slow, careful strokes he moved in and out of her, creating a decadently delightful sensation that spiraled through the pulsing depths of her orifice. It filled her with remorse, even doubt of her love for Bruce, and even as her hips rose to meet his plunging loins, she wept.

"You will forget him soon enough," the Dhjinn murmured, and his face glowed with sweetness as he kissed her mouth.

Poignant sensation filled her mouth now, too. The Dhjinn provoked the same needy physical passion that Sir Vincent and the Warden had. How very close they had come to fulfilling her utterly! And though Gillian had come away from her time with them without the spiritual appeasement she found with Bruce, she would never forget those moments.

The Dhjinn's hips thrust harder now, quickly intensifying her already fevered pleasure. A climax spread through her like runaway lightning. All her strength drained and she panted languidly as her hips moved in synchrony to the Dhjinn's rutting. Yet, it was not the Dhjinn who made her wanton and flushed with adoration—it was the memory of Bruce, which overshadowed even this being's divine talents.

He positioned himself on his elbows over her and slowed his thrusts. His breath was sweet cinders, and sweat dripped from his hair over her breasts. Her pussy contracted lazily about his cock as she waited patiently for him to get up and be done with her.

But he kissed her throat savagely. "No," he whispered, "it is not done yet, my slave."

He turned over on his back. With her hands released, Gillian rolled over onto her side and wondered what he meant by this.

The answer came only a moment later when he gathered her by her hair, and rising from the bed, pulled her off and onto her feet. His arms swept around her and he kissed her hungrily. Plunging his hand between her thighs, his scorching fingers met her wet pussy.

"Touch me!" He pressed her hand to his cock. It felt like a silken rod, its base drenched with her juices. He guided her hand to stroke him, and the head of it pulsed against her fingers.

"Yes," he whispered, "yes . . ."

He turned Gillian around now and told her to bend over and hold onto the mattress. Her buttocks were thrust out, and now he slapped the mouth of her pussy and ran a finger down her spine. To her sweet despair, he clasped her clit between two fingers, and as he stroked it, her passion roused once again. She moaned, for it was all she could do to keep her hips from undulating and disclosing the sensation he rekindled within her.

He made a satisfied sound that frustrated her further.

"This is my ravenous little pleasure-mouth," he spoke and Gillian felt ablaze with both anger and sensation.

He entered her sore nether mouth with a strong thrust. His hips worked feverishly, driving deep, slapping strokes that punished her needy core. Gillian cried out, the golden coins rattling melodiously against her quaking, hard nipples. When the Dhjinn reached around her hips and stroked her clit, it burst with sensation. She moaned and fell limp over the mattress. The Dhjinn did not stop. Bowing over her, he gathered her hips and raised them, and continued to stroke her quivering orifice.

She climaxed again, with an intensity that made her every muscle shudder.

Yet, all Gillian could see was the one she truly loved. And as the Dhjinn E'noch lifted her up to her toes and raised her hands high above her head, his breath fell hot upon her shoulders. She felt his discerning thoughts as clearly as his scalding hard member against her buttocks.

He spun her around into his rough embrace. He kissed her, his hands possessively roaming over her limbs and breasts.

"You will love me yet!"

His hands clamped upon her buttocks, and his cock pressed into her navel. His kiss was almost savage, and when he released her at last, he cupped her shoulders and pushed her to her knees on the floor.

Gillian was shocked by her own primal desire. Her body ached with mindless passion, her panting mouth moistened. The Dhjinn's gaze was intent as he stroked her bottom lip with a thumb.

"Love me with your mouth," he said, and though her body ached to do just that, the word "love" struck her as a cruel mockery.

Her lips opened and she drew the unearthly head into her mouth. Its sweat was spicy to her tongue, and as she started to suck, her whole mouth and throat tingled. But his member was huge, impossible to take fully, so she sucked the head and forefront of the shaft. The effort acted to intensify her desire. Her hips rocked and she moaned, though whether this was for his touch or the desire to release him fully, she wasn't sure. And it pleased her in a carnal way to see his features tighten, his eyes closed as he enjoyed her. Her vision blurred then, and all she saw was Bruce's face.

Yet, he never came, and when several moments later he withdrew, she felt devastated. She knew it should be a triumph of a kind that he had not climaxed, but then she recalled the earlier spanking, and winced with dread of his disappointment.

But he only regarded her with an uncertain look that accentuated the physical desire he'd expounded.

"Up now, my willful, pretty disciple," he bade, and wrapping her hair about his hand, guided her to her feet.

He led her out of the bedchamber. As he passed the sofa, Gillian realized he was leading her toward the place with the niche with the metal hook and chained loops dangling from the ceiling. She panicked and whimpered, to which he responded by lifting her about the waist and carrying her into the niche.

The loops, she saw now, were in fact iron manacles.

"No," she whispered, and her eyes flooded with frightened tears.

"I am patient, Gillian," he said soberly. He released her hair and grasped her hand instead. His clasp was immobile, she found, and suddenly she almost regretted remembering Bruce . . .

"But your willfulness is stronger than I'd imagined. You will spend the night thinking about the consequences of willfulness."

Gillian's body quivered with a burgeoning frenzy that strangely heightened her fear and resigned her to it.

"You know my men wait outside. Now, you shall either raise your hands, or I shall have them raised for you."

As irksome as the vainglorious Dhjinn was, the thought of others coming in to help him bind her and see her helplessness seemed insufferable.

She frowned darkly but lifted her arms. The Dhjinn inhaled deeply and opened the manacles, one and then the other. He closed one about her left wrist and Gillian's heart jumped. When she heard the metal snap about her right wrist, her mind reeled and she gasped for air.

"Please," she wept. "Oh, please . . . I will behave, I promise to behave!"

His grim features lightened a little, and a rueful smile crossed his lips. He smoothed the errant strands of hair from her face.

"Your misconduct is deep-rooted, my dearest. Far more deeply than you know. But I promise it shall be corrected. Soon, I suspect, your psyche will be cleansed, and you will submit willingly, passionately, as you are expected."

Her tears flowed heavily down her cheeks as he stepped back into the sitting room and opened the wardrobe. From it he took a long strap of leather. As he strode back into the niche, Gillian's eyes widened to see the oblong leather bit attached in the center.

"Open your mouth, Gillian."

She twisted her head this way and that, and heard him sigh.

"Do it. Either of your own accord, or I shall compel you with that whip on the wall."

She saw the canister where the whip was placed. Her pussy quickened and her heart beat harder.

Her voice trembled, "Please, have mercy . . ."

With his fingers the Dhjinn gently pried open her lips. And as the bit entered and stuffed her mouth, immodest warmth flushed through Gillian's thighs.

He tied the strap at the back of her head securely. "I am nothing if not merciful."

She stomped her feet and pulled at the binding manacles. He regarded her coolly a second or two, then he took the whip from the canister. Gillian's terrified shout was a muffled noise.

He cracked the whip against his palm. Gillian jumped; her body shivered hotly.

"I may whip you in a little while. I may wait to do so in an hour or so," he said. "It is not for you to know, but to dread and contemplate upon. Such thoughts will help subdue your will and make you more ready to demonstrate acceptable behavior."

Gillian glared at him, hating him and this place where he was sovereign. And yet, his cool beauty seemed overpowering in itself. She wept harder, stomping her feet again in protest against all she'd experienced, and more so, for the rampant desire he'd managed to evoke in her.

But he left her then, taking the whip with him. Gillian turned as much as possible, but the chains would not give enough. All she could see was the stone wall of the niche.

After a time Gillian was overcome with fatigue. Her head fell upon one shoulder. But the day's unsettling events were beginning to fade away. Uncertain but tender images filled her mind and all thought of the Dhjinn left her. Even the bothersome weight of her body upon the manacles seemed to belong to a different reality.

She almost was asleep when the first stinging blow of the crop fell across her buttocks and roused her to a new frustration.

15

Life in the Disciplinary had taken on a rhythmic routine for Gillian. Hours of labor on the mill interrupted by whatever arousing torture the guards fancied for the day, followed by more grinding hours at the mill. She fell asleep each night with her backside scalding and her sex wet and pulsating, craving more, wanting the ultimate sensation. Her heart beat with trepidation at sight of the guards. She held no antipathy for them, only respect for their talent to bring her and the others to full arousal without climax. Not once while in their custody had she been truly harmed.

The other prisoners came and went, and one day Gillian was awakened for breakfast to discover that none of her original Disciplinary mates were still there. Some of the new ones she recognized from the harem. But she never had a chance to speak to any of them, even on the few occasions when the guards removed their gags and herded them in single file to the shower room. Renier, the guard, had masterful eyes that lorded over them while they entered the stall, two at a time. Silent they remained, blushing and wet as they soaped and scrubbed one another.

At least, Gillian consoled herself, it was not so frustrating or intimidating as when the Mistress had governed her in the shower.

By morning Gillian was awakened by the guard Dylan telling her that it was time to get up. He was raising the pillory when her eyes opened, and this time he unfastened the gag himself. As he helped her to sit up, Gillian saw the Mistress standing close by. The woman had her back to the pillory as she spoke very quietly with Renier. Gillian's heart skipped a beat, but she stifled a whimper as Dylan led her to the chamber pot.

The steady, deep breathing of the other girls revealed that they were still asleep in their pillories. And when Gillian had relieved herself, Dylan took her by the hand and led her to the Mistress.

It was this Mistress who had taken Gillian to the Disciplinary. Sister of the Dhjinn host, this fiercely beautiful being was lithe and majestic of height, with a perfectly oval face and dusky golden skin. She donned now a sleeveless black dress and leather boots that soared to the thighs of her long legs. Her long-lidded hazel eyes regarded Gillian.

The Mistress's smile was almost warm. "Here is my brother's spoiled betrothed," she said. "Your time here is over. I trust you have learned a lesson that will not be shortly forgotten?"

"Yes, Mistress," Gillian quickly answered. Her head bowed as swiftly, as if the gesture had become second nature.

Gillian was naked as she followed the Mistress through the hall that led to the heart of the harem. It was just as Gillian remembered, even to the weepy faces that peered at her through the spectacle portals down the exterior wall. But once they'd entered the harem chamber, she felt something was different. As she followed the Mistress through the little groups of harem girls, she realized what it was: Martine was gone. Esther was still there, bossing the girls lined up for their morning bouts in the exercise wheel. And in the very back of the room, sitting in a high-backed chair that allowed him to survey all the room at once, sat a man Gillian did not recognize. He appeared to be a man, anyway. But as she followed the Mistress toward him, she realized this being possessed more Dhjinnish features than human. He was slighter, more refined of features, with hair and thick eyebrows of blue-sheened black. But the scales of his face and hands gave him away. On one of his earlobes was clasped a fan-shaped piece of silver filigree, dotted with tiny dark gems. He wore a wondrous clingy robe of black, over which hung a silvery iron latticework cloth. As he rose to meet them, this latticework, Gillian saw, was not actually part of the robe, but hovered close to the fabric.

The Mistress snapped her fingers toward the floor. Gillian got to her knees in mindless response, and it was then she caught the bitter little dimples at the corners of the creature's mouth.

"This is your temporary harem Master, Gillian," the Mistress said.

Gillian had an uncomfortable suspicion that Martine was not far away facing her own type of punishment.

"So it seems," the Master remarked.

The Mistress's eyes narrowed and Gillian could almost feel the antipathy between her and the Master. A bland smile spread across his face, and he reached down and touched the crown of Gillian's head. His fingers brushed through her hair. His touch was much gentler than his bearing.

"Very pretty," he said contemplatively. "Our king chose well."

The Mistress said impatiently, "As I said before, have her prepared and ready this evening."

"I will not forget."

The Mistress replied in a hard, silky tone, "You had best not." She stepped close beside the master, and whispered something in his ear. Gillian saw her hand flit to his crotch and fondle his scrotum. He tensed, and his head bowed just as Gillian's own had a little while earlier.

"I will not forget, Mistress," he promised again.

The Mistress turned and walked out, and Gillian felt the master's arm tremble as he parted her hair over her neck and stroked the nape. He seemed thoughtful as he watched the Mistress depart.

But then he smiled sardonically. "If she were only male, eh, Gillian?"

Gillian flushed. She wasn't sure what he meant, but the words brought back the memories of the Mistress's imperious manner at the shower. Suddenly Gillian realized she might never be alone again with the dominating woman . . . and an unexpected heaviness filled her heart.

"But I will have you clean and lovely for our comely host," the Master went on absently. "In the meantime, be sure to behave yourself."

Gillian did obey, and after the morning meal, the Master told Esther that she was to be given a break from the morning workout. So instead of waiting to take her turn inside the exercise wheel, she was at liberty to reacquaint herself with her budding friendship with Lil, Holly, and Summer.

They were all kind enough not to ask about her time in the Disciplinary, nor mention the fact that she, of all the harem girls, had been allowed nothing to wear that day. From time to time Gillian's eyes wandered over to the wall where those serving their time in the spectacle portals knelt. The line of pink backsides brought heated, mingled emotions, so lenient did this humiliating punishment seem compared to the Disciplinary.

She remembered the gag she'd worn and a part of her seemed lost without the leather bit glutting her mouth.

Once, she saw Esther order two girls, a tall redhead and an ample-breasted blonde, to go up and heighten the punishment of those kneeling. With deft hands they stroked the reared, exposed pussies, until the hips of the punished wriggled and writhed, and their hands clawed at their captured necks. Their tormenters slapped their swaying breasts and pinched their nipples. Esther brought them a long, thick dildo of leather. The pair took turns using it to spank the nether mouths they had excited, until the wet slapping sounds made them rock with laughter. And then, to Gillian's alarm, the redhead pressed the dildo into the anus of one of the punished. As she worked the leather back and forth in her victim's orifice, the blonde massaged the punished one's breasts. Gillian stared at the three, and she saw the slick juices that trickled down the thighs of the punished girl. Her body was suffused all over and gilded brightly with her own sweat.

"Do not feel sorry for her," Lil said. "Jeya has been nursing a snappy mood for days now. The portal will cure her tart tongue!"

Jeya? Gillian had not recognized her face down the hall. Of course, their faces had all been so red and wet with tears. Gillian could guess the cause for her mood . . . and wondered now how Abraham fared, and if ever he would have the chance to have Jeya for himself. She sensed now that indeed her suspicion had been right and that Jeya returned his love. Contemplating this, Gillian's resentment for what she had been robbed of returned in force.

She didn't know that she wept until Lil drew her aside from the others and offered her a cloth for her tears.

"You need to stop grieving for this man," Lil whispered, "it will never gain you the trust of our king."

Gillian was surprised, and asked with a sniff, "How do you know what's on my mind?"

"It's as clear as your eyes. You must be happy, Gillian . . . most of us are." Lil's voice took a cheery lilt, "You should know that the king can be most generous. And oh, think on how handsome he is. Surely you didn't forget this while you were away?"

Gillian shook her head. She confided very quietly, "I don't care, Lil. I love another!"

Lil frowned and rubbed her shoulder. "Ah, but you can love our king as well. He will be a master most affectionate if you let him."

"I have a master," Gillian said despondently. "Can't you understand that? I have a master, and he is the only one I will ever love! The king stole away that which I treasure more than anything. He severed me from the other half of my very soul!"

The uncertain expression on the girl's face was telling. Gillian squeezed her eyes against the next stinging tear and said, "You've never loved anyone besides your Dhjinn Master, have you?"

"No." Lil kissed her cheek. "Oh, Gillian! I hope you will come to know love with your Master. But if you can't, at least, I wish you pleasure."

Gillian couldn't help but smile a little.

After the harem had all taken their customary afternoon naps, the Master escorted Gillian to the bathing pool. He had brought along a basket of bath supplies and towels, and told her that she was to clean herself.

"Without abusing the privilege, of course," he added with a hard smile.

Inside the cozy cavern with its gem-encrusted walls the pool beckoned to Gillian. All she desired was to wash away the sweat of the Disciplinary. Hidden light imparted a tranquil blue shade to the water, one that Gillian hoped would help give her a little peace from the acute and lingering passion the guards had provoked during her incarceration.

The Master set down the basket and towels and asked, "Now, how do you prefer the temperature of your water?"

"Very warm when possible, Master."

He knelt down by the poolside and stretched an arm over the water. His forefinger touched the surface, making a soft indentation. She heard him utter some unfamiliar words.

"There," he said, rising. "I will be back in a short while. I must order the Dame of Wardrobe to bring something very special for you to wear tonight."

Gillian felt a twinge of new dread, and asked quickly, "May I have permission to speak?"

He gave her a smile that so thoroughly softened his features that for a second he looked human to her. "I know already—you wish to know the meaning of the occasion?"

"Yes."

"A banquet our king has ordered in honor of Queen Marianne's departure tonight. Are you acquainted with the good queen?"

"Yes." Gillian felt a blush creep into her cheeks.

"As I hear it, it was for this alone that your release from the Disciplinary was ordered. So be sure, pretty Gillian, to act with utmost grace tonight. This is your opportunity to impress the king's more simple-minded brothers—to show them all that you are indeed worth the possible danger he's put us all in by taking you from Nemi."

Gillian was startled by the words. She'd almost forgotten about the Ur'theriems. She wondered suddenly why they had not yet come to challenge the king and demand her back. The Ur'theriems were supposed to defend against those who would steal Nemian women. Why had they not come?

And as she looked at the Master's face, she wondered, too, about what he'd just revealed to her.

"Do you not resent me, Master?"

He looked at her, and his countenance was sublime tranquillity. "Why would I? In our world—our realm, our element, as you might say—passion is the foundation of existence. Our king's passion for you is a hallowed thing. I respect him for this, unlike many of our kindred who have transcended the planes of our primary existence. Their limited mindsets refuse to appreciate that which was, is, in all planes and times."

Gillian frowned and thought on this. *True,* she thought, *and yet I am afraid of those others, the freed kin. And where, oh where, are the Ur'theriems?*

Yet, she was torn by a sudden vision of violence and death.

"However," she heard the Master say quietly, as if he were thinking aloud, "he himself is limited by other ingrained beliefs."

She didn't know at all what he meant by this. And she was overwhelmed suddenly with guilt. "I am a danger to you all. It would be better if I were to die!"

He lifted a stern brow as he regarded her. "Why should you wish such a thing? There is no real death, Gillian, only the illusion of mortality. As a Disciple of Pleasure, I'd think you had learned that by now." His countenance softened and he patted her chin affectionately. "You are a component of the Eternal Ones. Your fantasies, those things to which you are drawn, are integral parts of their reality. Whatever your most secret desires, they will manifest, if you only know they will. So enjoy the saga, Gillian—enjoy being. We are as the Eternal Ones wish us all to be. It is when we reject that wish that we divorce ourselves from Them and wed the Great Lie, which is death and its deceits"

Gillian hoped he was right. She was sore with yearning for Bruce and a shadow of guilt still weighed on her.

He gave her a startling swat on the buttocks. "Now, get into that water and bathe. I may be only a retained priest and part-time Master of the harem, but I can be a disciplinarian when the need arises. Now relax and get clean, and forget all those pointless feelings of guilt."

He gestured for her to sit on the poolside, and watched as her legs slid down into the water. It was almost hot, but wonderfully relaxing, and she let her knees give way until her body was submerged to her shoulders.

"You like?"

At her nod he waved a cautioning finger and said with a faint smile, "Just don't forget, I am much more attentive than my predecessor!"

The Dame of Wardrobe was waiting at Gillian's bed when the Master returned her to the sleeping quarters. Another female Dhjinn E'noch was there. With a shower of gold hair that splayed in thick curls about her shoulders, she was not, Gillian thought, as beautiful as the Mistress. She was dressed in a simple wool gown of deep green and black slippers, and her skin was a shade of mottled gray. Unlike the king, his sister, and the Master, the outline of her scales were quite vivid. As far as Dhjinns looked, Gillian thought, this Dame was rather plain.

Yet she greeted Gillian with a warm smile that brought an attractive liveliness to her chiseled features.

Her voice was a hiss of buoyant mist. "I have brought you the most perfect ensemble, little Disciple."

The Master spoke behind them, "I will go see if the Mistress has arrived."

The Dame gave him a sidelong glance. "Ooh, a confrontation? And I'll miss it!"

To Gillian's surprise the Master laughed. "I'll have to disappoint you this time," he said and patted the Dame's shoulder. "However, as I have our Mistress to thank for taking me from my rightful station and putting me in charge here, I shall make it clear that I will brook no interference."

The Dame shrugged. "Ah, but she has been a good, strict

Mistress. No doubt she's instilled into this young lady a little more appreciation for rules of conduct."

Gillian glowed with humiliation. Did everyone know of her one indiscretion?

The Master nodded. "I cannot fault her there, no. But I had no desire to oversee the females, no matter how lovely they are. And she knew this. It is only her way to get even."

"It is only that you wounded her pride," remarked the Dame. "After all, he was her slave, you know . . ."

Gillian was intrigued by the pair's discussion and saw a blush of yellow imbue the Master's features. A glint of the distinctive Dhjinn hardness shone in his eyes.

"Yes," he sighed, "But if I find my suspicions are correct, and he wishes to be mine . . . then I will find the way to convince the king to grant me this."

The Dame idly played with Gillian's hair as she said, "I'd be careful with whom you speak of this, my dear. Most especially your regard for the youth's own desires. They will think you have grown too human! It might be better to simply take him hostage. Such an action would appeal to the king's empathy, and more likely gain his forgiveness."

"Perhaps so," he replied. And he went away then and left Gillian alone with the Dame.

The Dame pinched her cheeks giddily and patted the edge of the bed.

"Sit," she said, "and I will have you soon looking as exquisite as Queen Marianne!"

First, the Dame brushed out her hair until it was full and wild and sprinkled it with gold dust. Then Gillian's skin was oiled, and lightly dusted, too, so that she shimmered from head to toe. The ensemble was a lovely variation of the customary harem outfit: the usual ornamental pantaloons and billowy sleeves had been made of ruffled black gauze, the ruffles edged with gold cloth. There was a breastplate of polished black metal, and the scalloped half-cups were of gold. The Dame then painted her nipples a shade of deep coral rouge, as well as her lips and the intimate folds of her sex. And for her thighs she provided cuffs of strung black pearls, attached to one another by a very short shackle of entwined black iron and gold. The last item of the outfit was a wide choker of black velvet edged with gold lace.

When the Dame was finished dressing her, she stood up and told Gillian to get to her own hands and knees.

"I am sorry. I know you are new to this," the Dame said.

Gillian got down as commanded, and saw the Dame take something long and shimmering from the mattress. It looked like a leash, with a black velvet holding loop at one end. The Dame bent over and showed her the other end: a very slender, long dildo set upon a golden knob about the size and width of a quarter.

"Once this is in I will turn the knob so it can't slip out," the Dame said. "This won't hurt, but it will make you uncomfortable until you are used to it. Now, look straight ahead, and do not squirm, or I'll have get the Master to assist me."

Uneasy, Gillian nonetheless looked straight ahead. The Dame's warm fingers touched her buttocks, and lightly tapped her anus. Before Gillian knew what had happened, the dildo slid into her anus to the knob hilt. Gillian felt her body shudder with the unexpected intrusion, and then she felt the Dame turn the knob. At once something ballooned inside her tightest orifice.

"Oh!" she cried.

The Dame patted her backside. "All over with," she said soothingly. "It is snug in place, and will remain expanded for a couple of hours, perhaps three. I know it feels much larger than it really is. The exterior is mildly medicated, but it will not dull your other physical desires."

Gillian blushed as she'd never blushed before. She bowed

her head, so that her hair veiled her face. She knew not how she could ever look at anyone with the slender dildo inserted in this undignified way and for so long. And then she felt the Dame move about behind her, and the next moment she parted Gillian's thighs as far as the pearl cuffs allowed. Gently, she felt about Gillian's pussy, and captured her clit between the fingers of her hand, applying some oily concoction. Ripe with a heady perfume it was, and it wasn't until the Dame removed her hands that Gillian was aware of warmth brewing over her clit. Quickly, her clit was pulsating with heat. The organ swelled, and her thighs and sex were acutely aroused. Her nether lips grew slick and her pelvis wanted to undulate. And when the Dame tapped the golden knob, Gillian's whole body was overcome with raw desire.

"She looks ready."

Gillian's face lifted miserably in response to the Mistress's voice. She was a towering statue at the entranceway, her implacable face cold and lovely. She wore a long black silk jacket with a high neckline, and underpants of black silk. She carried a long-handled crop of pure black leather. Part of Gillian wanted to scramble under the bed, to find shelter and hide her humbled dignity. But as the Dame handed the leash over to the Mistress, another part of Gillian softened with a desire more potent than even the aphrodisiac oil.

The Mistress lifted the leash a little so that the dildo moved languidly inside Gillian. The Mistress laid the end of her crop to Gillian's thigh, so that the tip caressed her shimmering skin.

"You've done well, Dame. One wouldn't know that she was just returned this morn from the Disciplinary."

She moved the crop so that the tip invaded Gillian's thighs and tickled her sex, prodded the opening of her damp private lips. Gillian whimpered softly, and the Mistress told her to lift her face.

"Don't try to hide under that hair," the Mistress scolded,

and with her fingers, combed the veiling tresses from Gillian's face. "Yes, I am sure my brother will be pleased. You will kneel beside him at the banquet, and do not forget that you are his treasured prize. As such, it is proper that you show him the most earnest devotion and deference. Now rise and come along, Gillian. The hour grows late."

16

It was to another passageway unfamiliar to Gillian that the Mistress directed her. The path rose steeply for some time, and steadily grew wider until they reached a vast chamber with a tiled floor. Monumental pillars—as wide and tall as redwood trees—stood about everywhere between the floor and a domed ceiling far above their heads. Garlands of wide cloth wound about the pillars, which were strung with fiery little bulbs that much resembled Christmas tree ornaments. Their footfalls echoed ominously as the Mistress continued.

At length Gillian spotted a wall ahead, with a granite stairway. Two men stood at the top of it, one to either side, before a great curtain that hung from a marble arcade. At least twenty feet long and forty feet wide and overlaid with tiny mirrors of intricate designs, the velvety maroon curtain swept the landing of the stairway. Gillian couldn't take her eyes off it as the Mistress headed her up the stairway. The men flanking this wore only silver pantaloons and slippers, but otherwise they were the most fearsome men Gillian had ever encountered: they were at least seven feet tall, and their every muscle seemed to ripple.

Each man bore a sword in a fine scabbard upon his back. And beyond the curtain and the fierce guards Gillian heard the sound of cymbals and pipes and laughter.

The guards did not move or flinch as the Mistress and Gillian approached, though Gillian had no doubt the men certainly saw them. Her legs weakened as they approached the men. The Mistress was right on her heels and, cupping Gillian's shoulders, directed her to one side of the curtain and then pushed her through.

Gillian's heart skipped a beat as she passed between the wall and the cloth . . . and the scene she entered upon made her cry out with astonishment.

It was a huge semicirclular deck they had come to, as large as a ballroom, with a clear dome rising up from the stone casing. For the first time in weeks Gillian's eyes looked upon light, real light. Sunlight was just sinking behind orange clouds in the distance beyond the deck, and stars peeked through a pinkish indigo haze above her head. She was so pleasantly surprised she could not move. There were others on the deck—couples sitting cross-legged on cushions around low tables set about the mosaic tile floor; several freed kin, as she supposed them to be, standing about talking over glasses of drink. A band of musicians sat to the eastern side. A dozen or so dancing girls draped in ribbons of amber and lavender swirled about in sensual movement to their melody. But all of it seemed a galaxy away as Gillian gazed at the heavenly spectacle. She even forgot the dildo hidden snug inside her.

Mistress smoothed her shoulder. "Beautiful, isn't it?"

Gillian was too delighted to respond. Her eyes drank in each facet of the clouds, relished every glint of parting sunlight.

"More than I recalled," she whispered. If the Mistress heard she did not reply.

The next moment something streaked out of the encroaching night above their heads. It was a sphere of ornamental brasslike metal aglow with a fiery aura; it hovered for a millisecond above the dome before it sped across the sky and disappeared behind a wisp of claret clouds.

It had come and gone so fast that Gillian didn't even know how it had startled her until the Mistress spoke, and the words sounded faint behind Gillian's racing heartbeat.

"This is the aerial dome. And there, Gillian, awaits your master."

Gillian followed her eyes across the room to a table positioned upon a dais. Queen Marianne sat there, with her slave youth naked and kneeling at her side. The queen was enchanting as ever, wearing a silver gown and a slender diamond tiara upon her brow. Two male Dhjinn E'nochs sat across from her, and at the far of the dais cushions were strewn. Two other harem girls reclined eating great dark cherries from a silver bowl. From the interior of the dome behind them all a circular length of veils was suspended. If there was anyone within these shades Gillian could not tell. But at the queen's side, sitting straight and regal, was the one Gillian wanted to ignore, the Dhjinn abductor and their king. He had already noticed Gillian, and his intense regard weighted upon her.

Master of masters.

His invasive inner voice addled Gillian's nerves. She was outraged that he still played his mind games on her. And yet, the mere sight of him eroded her rightful resentment. Resentment she'd thought unshakable. If it was possible for a being to be more beautiful than the king, she simply couldn't envision it. Straight he sat, wearing a silk robe of royal blue. His luxurious silvery hair fell loose about his shoulders, and his face was as flawless as ever. His demeanor seemed much more mature to her than the last time she'd seen him, as if his vitality had been renewed, somehow, and was now both honed and raw with purpose.

The Mistress pressed her forward, and Gillian deliberately

gazed at the floor as they walked. But as they passed the queen and approached the king, she remembered that she was expected to kneel and show him devotion and deference. The Mistress, however, did not give her time to even consider, for she pressed Gillian's shoulders firmly until she sank to her knees before his cushion.

"Oh," she heard Marianne say, "your naughty Nemian trophy! How splendid she looks tonight!"

The queen caressed her back so lightly that a shiver raced straight up to Gillian's skull.

"Thank you, sister," the king said. Out of the corner of an eye Gillian saw him take the leash from the Mistress. He wrapped the end about his hand and tugged on it gently so that the dildo ever so subtly compelled her to crawl closer to him. It was he who now stroked her back, and she was struck by the smoothness of his great fingers. She had almost forgotten these things; but now the evening in his chambers flooded back into her mind. She felt helpless, at his mercy, and terribly aware of how fragile a human being was compared to a Dhjinn E'noch. As the Mistress walked on to the other side of the table and sat down, panic swelled in Gillian's chest. She knew she wasn't supposed to hide her face, and yet she did, taking a moment's comfort in the security of it.

The king's fingertips lifted her chin, and with his other hand he moved her hair aside. She felt his lips press against her forehead.

"Rise up on your knees, and lift your eyes," he said softly.

As she obeyed, she found not the fierce displeasure she expected, but a look she'd never seen on his face before. Thoughtful and almost tender it was, and the longer he gazed at her the more relaxed his countenance became. Then he took a tidbit from his plate and put it to her lips. Her trembling lips opened and she accepted it without protest. He fed her more fruits and bread flavored with saffron, and offered his own goblet, filled with a delicious spiced wine. Gillian fought to keep her unspoken feelings from shaping her thoughts. No shade of her resentment or grief for Bruce could she bear for the king to steal again, no hint of how just being close to him stirred her primal desires.

After a long while the king's attention turned back to his guest, and pouring himself some fresh wine, made a toast in her honor. Gillian watched the others raise their goblets, and noticed the hard, undertone of red on the Mistress's face. The look on her face reminded Gillian of someone trying to feign boredom. But her smile was candidly unenthusiastic.

The queen reached over and touched Gillian's choker.

"I almost regret you are so fond of this one," Marianne said to the king. "My dear husband doesn't have too many blond courtesans. Maybe if I brought this one home, he'd acknowledge that I do notice his existence."

The other male Dhjinns laughed, but the king said soberly, "You should sell his courtesans, my dearest, and then he'd have no doubt!"

Gillian felt the Mistress's regard, and when she glanced over, the woman gave her a reproachful look. Her stomach quivered with dread. The king didn't seem to notice as she inched behind his shoulder enough to evade the Mistress's eyes.

"And she won't be blond for long," spoke one of the other males, "my brother will have her to wed soon enough, you know."

Gillian was confused by the statement, and forgot even the Mistress as Marianne replied, "Oh yes, the crown of the Chosen One. I forgot. What a pity, I love her natural shade!"

The king made an amused sound, and turning, stroked Gillian's hair. "It is beautiful," he said matter-of-factly. "But I am old-fashioned in some ways."

Gillian was startled when Marianne leaned over. The queen

reached a hand between her captive thighs and touched her pubic hair. Gillian's vulnerable nether mouth quivered under her petting fingers.

"And this, too?"

"Yes," answered the king. Gillian fought back the vision of him shaving her.

"Red hair is the mark of a beloved queen," the Mistress said dryly, "at least among our nobles, who cherish their women."

Gillian shuddered with relief. But the Mistress's dig was not lost on her, and she saw Queen Marianne's wounded frown.

One of the males lifted his goblet again. "Friendship," he said quickly, "may it always be thus between our king and his lovely Marianne."

As goblets clinked, Gillian saw the Mistress's eyes drift again about the room. Gillian wondered about her obvious antipathy toward the queen. Yet Gillian's curiosity dimmed quickly enough, for her sex tingled more acutely than ever, and the anal dildo only worsened the passion that possessed her. Again and again she found herself looking at the king, admiring him with blatant lust.

But soon he ignored her entirely. Of course, she dared not move from her humbled position because the Mistress was so near. But her body ached for his touch, his regard, as much as she despised him for it. Her labia swelled cruelly, and her thighs were damp and sticky; yet there was nothing she could do but kneel here and wait for him to notice her. She was ashamed for this need, the potent animal lust that seized her despite her love for Bruce.

At length the dancing girls left the floor and one of the musicians commenced to play a strange instrument that produced a sound very like sitar music. Soon he was accompanied by others playing pan pipes and tambourines. Some of the other guests advanced to the floor in couples. The dance was sensual, the steps slow and graceful. The music made Gillian's desire more potent.

As the king rose from his cushion and asked Queen Marianne to dance, Gillian felt a great twinge of envy.

She couldn't bear to watch them, and as her head turned, saw the pained look on the face of Marianne's slave, who was kneeling with his palms pressed to the floor. The candlelight from the table gleamed against his lithe, sinewy limbs. She could see the pink welts across his back and thighs, and little bruises of passion upon his throat and chest. For the first time Gillian noticed the leather collar buckled taut around the base of his cock. The organ was fully erect, and Gillian realized that the collar was designed to keep it so. His eyes were cemented to the king and queen and glinted with unshed tears. Gillian might have found this kind of despair unnatural for a man, if she didn't suspect his honest passion for the queen.

There is no shame in that kind of devotion, she thought. "I'll never see Bruce again," she lamented, so quietly she hardly heard her voice beneath the tempestuous music.

Gillian looked timidly again to the dancers, and tried to focus on Queen Marianne's graceful movements. She danced with an indefinable exuberance, which in its complex beauty outshone the fire-elemental Dhjinn E'nochs. How refined the queen remained even as her body undulated in time to the pagan rhythm. She was a bastion of stability beside the king.

When they returned and sat back down at the table, Marianne cupped her slave's hands between her palms and kissed him. His immediate relief rippled like water through his tense muscles. The queen glided a hand down between his thighs. She squeezed the tip of his cock, so that a few drops of fluid dribbled out over her thumb. A deep, shameless moan came from him.

The king had joined some conversation with his male guests, content to stroke Gillian's hair idly. Gillian's sex had become a well of heated desire. She could hardly keep her hips still for want of rubbing her thighs or rocking her hips in some shameful manner. She dared not look at the king and kept her furtive eyes on the queen and her slave.

She saw Marianne drain the remainder of wine from her cup. The lovely woman was smiling lushly now at her love-starved slave. And at length Marianne stood up and went to the circle of veils. She pulled a drape of them aside, and Gillian saw the bed of cushions piled within. At Queen Marianne's nod the youth crawled quickly from the table through the little passageway. He knelt beside the cushions with his hands behind his back. As Marianne let the drape fall back into place, Gillian's eyes narrowed. She watched the shadowy image of the queen lower down upon the cushions. The queen adjusted one of them behind her head so that it was raised, then motioned with a finger for her slave to approach. Eagerly he did so and reverently kissed her slippers.

At Marianne's whispered command, the young slave crawled forward and kneeled on his haunches at her side. She ordered him to keep his hands behind him, and reached out and grasped his cock. Her hand moved slowly up and down the length of the collared organ. When he moaned again she cautioned him to be quiet. The pinnacle of the organ bloomed a vivid scarlet under Marianne's continued ministrations and his face turned as ruddy. His mouth fell open and his breathing grew urgent and desperate.

Gillian expected to see the hot seed spill over the queen's tormenting hand, but before that happened, Marianne released him. She slid the hem of her gown upward, slowly revealing every curve of her shapely legs. She wore no hose tonight, Gillian saw, and the skin was creamy; her thighs ample and flawless. Marianne's hand now dipped between these lovely pillars, and her hips moved ever so gracefully as she stroked herself.

"Your mouth," she ordered softly, "love me with that divine mouth—and perhaps the whipping I give you later shan't be so ardent!"

The youth's mouth glistened as he nodded, and he got down again and crawled over the cushions between her legs. Onto his belly he dropped, and carefully spread her knees. Gillian heard his wet kisses upon Marianne's secret flesh. The queen stroked his hair wildly while her cheeks suffused with color and her hips swayed up and down to meet his attentive mouth.

Gillian hardly heard her own jealous moan until the king abruptly snatched the length of her hair. She let out a mortified shriek. He pulled her to him, clamping a hand about her mouth. Her whole body went numb as he pulled her close. Yet, even half-paralyzed with fear, her aching desire was only exacerbated in his restraining arms.

"Ogling is ill-mannered, my dear," he said in such a way she couldn't tell if he was angry or not. His breath singed the side of her throat for a moment or two, then suddenly he let go of her mouth and spun her about on her knees. His arms laced about her waist. Pulling her close, he kissed her. His pungent sweetness took away her breath. How sorely her body craved him now. She felt like a crumbling vessel of sand in his arms.

All the same, she rued this overwhelming lust. She envied the slave with Queen Marianne. The queen was humane as well as sensual. These characteristics were wedded upon her very being, attributes that Gillian respected. Her lust-possessed body felt a twinge of grief to know that once this night was over she might never see Marianne again.

With that thought she felt the king's arms stiffen and his lips grow cool. He released her body and grasped the ends of her hair tightly. She raised her eyes timidly, and knew by the stony regard she met that he had perceived her feelings only too clearly.

A moment later she heard the Mistress speak anxiously, "I should get your betrothed to bed now, brother. She needs to recuperate from the trials faced these last days, and let to slumber for a night or two without stimulation. It will help her become one with the lessons learned in the Disciplinary."

He studied Gillian a moment longer. But she could see that despite his jealousy he was trying to stay rational. His expression softened a bit, and he touched the ends of her hair now to his cheek.

"Yes," he replied thoughtfully. "Make sure she rests for two days, and then bring her back to me."

As the Mistress said good night to the other guests, the king embraced Gillian roughly. He kissed her, and the virile taste of him and the firmness of his lips weakened her. In a delirium of acute, mindless desire she watched as he handed the leash over to the Mistress.

The Mistress gave the leash a little tug that brought Gillian to her feet. As they left the dais Gillian thought of Queen Marianne. As much as she wished to, she didn't look back at the veils or the table. Her heart and body were raw with need, but which demanded the most she dared not wonder.

17

During the trip back to the harem court, Gillian could feel something was not quite normal with the Mistress. But she said nothing to Gillian at all, not even as she turned her back over to the care of the Master.

The others who had not returned from the banquet, or had remained behind, were already asleep in their narrow beds as the Master took Gillian to the bathroom and helped her to undress. Gillian was so tired. She was surprised to find that she felt little embarrassment for this particular male to see her naked. Very gently he deflated the phallus and removed it, and once she was undressed entirely, washed away the oil that had driven her mad all night.

As Gillian lay in bed, she thought of Marianne again. The thought of the queen leaving the king's domain frightened her. With Marianne's departure, Gillian might be forever lost in this world with its underground halls that led always to new and more forbidding doors.

And as she drifted to sleep she thought of the Mistress briefly, and pondered over what could have had prompted the dark woman to whisk her away from the king. The Mistress had obviously perceived that her brother could read Gillian's troubled emotions. She had saved Gillian by subverting his wrath with her quick thinking. As much as Gillian feared her, she couldn't help but be grateful for the woman's gift for observation.

Later Gillian was awakened by the sense of someone kissing her throat. For a moment her drowsy conscious thought it was Bruce kneeling by the bed, and her heart leaped with joy. She turned over eagerly and her arms opened to his stalwart embrace. But it was a mouth flavored like anise and ambergris that enveloped her own and made her unspent passion burn hotter than ever. Hands, firm in the softest way, pressed her shoulders back down on the mattress.

"Sweetest Disciple," the Mistress crooned in her ear. "I am your ally, never forget!"

Gillian was too astonished to speak. The Mistress pulled the blankets aside, and shy goose bumps spread across Gillian's flesh. Her eyes began to make out the Mistress's familiar features, and she lay silent as the Mistress stroked her belly, gliding a finger over her hips and again up her belly. Gillian could feel her inflamed juices dampen the mattress. In the darkness the Mistress couldn't see her blush, and it was all Gillian could do to force her hips from making some inadvertent movement.

The Mistress rose to her feet then. As she crawled into the bed, Gillian saw that she was naked. Her hard nipples were black against her shadowed flesh. She kissed Gillian's brow, and lifted Gillian's hand and pressed it to one of the great dusky breasts. She smelled of honey and spice to Gillian, and her lips curved in a soft smile. With a hand she skimmed the surface of Gillian's stomach. Her fingers delved into the thatch between her legs, and just the touch of her hot fingertips over her vulva made Gillian's sex singe.

Gillian could feel the Mistress grow hotter, too, and the air was thick with her Dhjinn musk. When the Mistress kissed her, Gillian's mouth was electrified. The woman's lips were succulent, with a taste like the exotic fruit. And then she released her, and giving Gillian's nose a fond little stroke, turned about on the mattress. She straddled Gillian's middle and Gillian admired the sensuous length of her back and firm buttocks. The Mistress lay down then over Gillian, and with her fingers unburied her sex beneath the nest of curls between her thighs. She parted Gillian's hidden folds and pressed her lips to the hood of Gillian's clit. Her tongue roamed over the unveiled flesh, and this the Mistress kissed, too, sweetly, so lovingly. It had been long since Gillian had felt such tenderness. Warmth spread through her that soothed her soul as much as it excited her body.

Gillian clasped the firm thighs above her shoulders, and kissed the dark flesh. Above her face the Mistress's arched pelvis moved back and forth in faint rhythm. Her long, crimson pussy glistened under its black pelt, and Gillian's mouth watered to taste it. Shyly Gillian tugged the Mistress's thighs, and to her relief the woman's hips nestled down so that she could lick the beautiful nether mouth. She kissed the lips as the Mistress had kissed her own, and relished the taste as her tongue wandered over the heated folds and darted into the tight seam.

And then the Mistress drew Gillian's clit into her mouth; she sucked it until it was aching hard. Gillian's legs strained and her hips went taut, and she felt then the Mistress's tongue encircle the organ, suck it again, nibble it. Gillian moaned deeply and in turn devoured the Mistress in the same way.

"Aahh," the woman moaned and suddenly stopped what she was doing. She peered back at Gillian, and her face was contorted with pleasure.

"No, you must stop," the Mistress whispered.

Gillian wanted to continue to lavish affection upon the succulent flesh, but the Mistress's stern look stopped her. She was panting, her heart racing; but she lay obediently as the Mistress returned to her own feasting. The woman's face moved back and forth slowly, as her tongue lapped now at Gillian's clit, now stuffed her hungry orifice. Gillian's legs strained and her hips twisted, and her moans sounded low and pitiful in the night. The Mistress's cherry-red clit peeked out of her jet curls with the rocking of her thighs. Gillian hungered for one last taste of her. Moaning, she turned her face against the Mistress's thigh. Her lips fell open against her, and when at last a climax spirited through Gillian, she screamed hopelessly into the smooth flesh.

She was half-blind with sensation as the Mistress lapped the juices that squirted out of Gillian's pulsating sex. The dark woman turned about and crept up beside Gillian. She kissed Gillian's mouth, her temple, her hair.

Her voice was loving. "Now you may sleep well, precious disobedient one."

With the last ripple of ecstasy coursing through Gillian's pelvis, the Mistress enfolded her in an embrace and lavished kisses over her face. Gillian returned these timidly, relieved the woman allowed herself this affection. Gillian couldn't understand why the Mistress had held back and denied herself that same satisfaction she'd given. At least she allowed her to play with her breasts a little and stroke the dusky nipples until they were hard under her fingertips. Gillian kissed her again and her tongue probed deep into the Mistress's mouth. Gillian heard her make a sound much like a purr. Gillian's arms glided about her and took delight in the woman's solid warmth against her face. Like a dusky panther, the Mistress seemed to Gillian now . . . a fierce and beautiful creature demanding of respect, yet feral and unswayable in her devotions.

At last the Mistress got up from the bed, and bending down once more, kissed Gillian's brow.

"Sleep now," she whispered. "When you wake you shall

find your heart's desire. Not me." She padded away in the night as soundlessly as she'd come.

For a long time Gillian stared into the shadows behind, wondering what she meant. Never again would she begrudge the Mistress's discipline. The Mistress had dared disobey her brother to relieve Gillian's frustrated desires, without demanding solitary devotion back. It was the kind of selfless affection Gillian had thought alien to the Dhjinn-E'nochs.

"Things are not always what they seem," she said quietly to herself.

Gillian's thoughts turned to the masterful king; not of how his almost sinfully delicious scent and looks had incited her, but of the time when she'd been alone with him in his private chambers. He'd taken her so wildly then, and in several ways. He had succeeded in making her orgasm with a force that could properly be termed volcanic. And yet, she recalled, for all his possessive passion, he had not climaxed—or at least, not allowed himself to. It made no sense, this restraint of the Dhjinns. But there was a reason for it, though she cared not what it was. This, she was as sure of as the contours of her true lover's face.

Suddenly she was overwhelmed by the single desire to be with Bruce. In anger her tears flowed and she visualized the Mistress coming to her again, and listening with sympathy and compassion as Gillian shared her most earnest plea. It was the only thing Gillian ever wanted to ask of one of these creatures, and if she didn't say it now she feared she would never again have the chance.

Her whispered voice shook with emotion. "You may be a free Dhjinn, Mistress, but you are a Dhjinn all the same. Please, if I mean anything to you, grant me this one request—let me be with Bruce!"

She was enveloped in darkness, the kind of darkness that seemed to have a life of its own. Gillian whispered the petition again and again, until it became a mantra on her lips. And after a time she perceived some shift in the pulsating void. There was a gradual softening of the darkness, and Gillian felt a warm breeze against her face. The air smelled different, too; imbued with freshness, and a whiff of the sea and of flowers. She heard the distinct sound of a distant tide, and was aware that the soles of her feet touched earth.

She was nude and divested of every ornament of the Dhjinn king's claim. Above her, a great orange sun broke through heavy ivory clouds. Several gulls passed overhead and they called to one another with fervent cries. The breeze tossed Gillian's loose hair over her eyes, and as she pulled it back she now saw that she stood upon a beach. There were great rocks strewn down the shore, and the light of the new sun glinted hazily upon their uneven surface. Gillian stepped toward the shore, delighting in the feel of the cool sand. With the next tide the water lapped over her feet, immersing them in foam that was as white as the sea was turquoise. She wondered if she was alone, and the sea offered silent assurance that she was also free of the Dhjinn King.

Gillian was overcome with gratitude. The Mistress must have taken mercy on her. Although she did not know where to go or even where she was, as she turned to breathe in the beautiful fields of flowers beyond the shore she had no fear. One way or the other she would find a way to face whatever trials this wild new land had in store.

As this assurance settled over her Gillian noticed a movement in the distance. She lifted a hand over her eyes and peered over the stretching beach. A figure was running toward her, bathed in bronze by the morning sun. And as it drew closer she made out the familiar stalwart physique; the warm, manly smile; the dark and ravishing eyes. Gillian's heart leapt. With a joyous gasp all thought of the Dhjinn washed away like the withdrawing tide. She forgot about the king and even her gratitude toward the Mistress. Memory of their realm and the sensuous trials there disappeared. She could see the eager smile on Bruce's face, and, laughing, she sprinted across the sands.

They rushed into one another's arms, and Gillian's body immediately melted into the contours of Bruce's strong embrace. His mouth was at her ear, his voice a feral purr.

"I have missed you so much."

Gillian showered his neck and face with kisses. Her heart raced with the exhilaration of being one with the man she loved. They were together, and she was exactly where she wanted to be. All the worries she'd ever known were worlds away. She cupped Bruce's face and contemplated on the love in his shining eyes.

"How I love you. Oh, how I love you."

Bruce drew her down onto her knees and his scorching lips covered her trembling mouth. She felt his hale heartbeat against her breasts, and with her hands she loosened his trousers. His cock was hard and urgent, and as he laid her down into the warm sand, she held to him fiercely. Parting her legs, he drove into her. He thrust greedily, his large hot cock filling her perfectly. Bruce's hips rocked swiftly, filling Gillian with ravishing sensation. She felt his last, ardent thrust, and heard him cry softly as he climaxed. In its wake Gillian's pleasure reached its zenith.

"Oh, yes!" she gasped, reveling in the intense waves. "Yes!"

Bruce captured her wrists and pressed them to either side of her head. He watched, smiling, as the pleasure coursed through her. His face glowed with pride and tenderness.

"I love you, my little slave," he whispered. "In this world and the next. No matter what may come."

Gillian looked at him through heavy lids. This was the man who had aroused her most intimate passions, who had delivered her to the fruition of her wildest fantasies. The love she felt for him was more poignant than even the pleasures they brought one another; stronger than any force that dared attempt to separate them. She lifted her face and kissed his lips, relishing their salty taste. His strength sated her entirely.

Bruce kissed her mouth again. The eternal sea roared and the reassuring golden rays of full morning light drenched their flesh. This is heaven, Gillian thought, and she closed her eyes and clutched loving to this man; her true angel and only Master.